WORK IN PROGRESS

Also by Dan Brotzel
Hotel du Jack and other stories
The Wolf in the Woods
(both published by Sandstone Press)

Also by Martin Jenkins
A New Science of Navigation
(published by Soul Bay Press)

Also by Alex Woolf
Chronosphere
Aldo Moon
Dread Eagle
Assassin's Code
(all published by Salariya)
Soul Shadows
(published by Curious Fox)

For the first time!
The full story behind Channel 4's extraordinary
Bleeding Typewriters documentary . . .

WORK IN PROGRESS

The untold story of the Crawley Writers' Group

Compiled by Peter, writer

Edited by Dan Brotzel, Martin Jenkins
and Alex Woolf

unbound

This edition first published in 2021

Unbound
Level 1, Devonshire House,
One Mayfair Place, London W1J 8AJ

www.unbound.com

Text design by Ellipsis, Glasgow

A CIP record for this book is available from the British Library

ISBN 978-1-78352-962-9 (trade pbk)
ISBN 978-1-78352-963-6 (ebook)

Printed and bound in Great Britain by Clays Ltd, Elcograf S.p.A.

For Virinia, and all members – past, present and future – of the Conway Writers' Group

With special thanks to patrons of this book

Brad Feld
David Jenkins
Clarrie Wallis
Emile and Anita Woolf

Contents

Editors' note to the first edition ix

1. Little paper fingers 1

2. Story-struck! 61

3. Sacré bleu! 95

4. A faint greenish tinge 163

5. Crossover potential 233

6. Heading out for the stars 291

7. Transcript of *Bleeding Typewriters* documentary, first broadcast on Channel 4, 23.03.18 317

Postface (Do not read) 355

Appendix 1: From Encyclopaedia Progrockia 357

Appendix 2: Where are they now? 361

About the editors 371

Acknowledgements 373

Supporters 375

EDITORS' NOTE TO THE FIRST EDITION

Like many TV viewers, we were pleasantly appalled by *Bleeding Typewriters*, Channel 4's notorious fly-on-the-wall documentary about the Crawley Writers' Group. Here was a story that seemed to have it all – if, by all, you mean sex, drugs, violence, a vicious cosplay stalker, a prog rock reunion and an alien mothership invasion.

As members of a (comparatively rather staid) writers' group ourselves, we wanted to know more about this extraordinary collection of authors. Documentaries have a tendency to bring out exaggerated behaviour in people, so we were keen to uncover the real characters and trace the unguarded evolution of the group, right back to its beginnings as a twinkle in Julia Greengage's eye.

The emails gathered here, then, present a true and unvarnished account of a developing dynamic – forming, storming, norming, performing and even mourning. As editors, we saw our job as merely to facilitate the free flow of the unfolding story; to that end, we have excised material that was repetitive or merely functional, tidied up a few inconsistencies and inaccuracies, but otherwise left things as they were originally written. We conclude, of course, with a transcript of *Bleeding Typewriters* itself.

To our minds, the narrative this correspondence unveils is every bit as extraordinary as the documentary itself – exploding sheep's heads, fascinator attacks, Twiglet sex and all.

D.B., M.J., A.W.

1.

LITTLE PAPER FINGERS

From: **JuliaGeeGee@gmail.com**

To: Crawley Writers' Group

Sent: 01.12.16, 10:32

Subject: **Testing testing un deux trois!**

From: **JuliaGeeGee@gmail.com**

To: Crawley Writers' Group

Sent: 01.12.16, 10:37

Subject: **Welcome, writers of Crawley!**

My dear writers

What a fantastic response to my little notice in the library!

I'll be honest, I was a tad trepidatious before I put the idea of a writing group out there, but I just thrive on creativity and so the thought of a little community of like-minded literary searchers was irresistible to me.

Just imagine my delight when I returned to my little poster a few days later to see that all the little paper fingers with my email address on had been torn off! (The graffito about 'arty-farty slags' I could have done without, but still.)

So if you're getting this email, welcome to the group and I hope the writing is flying! I propose we meet every two or three weeks, rotating around different homes or other venues (pubs can work, but in my experience all that boozy bustle can be a tad unconducive). We'll be reading bits of our work, exchanging constructive feedback – and generally sharing the pains and pleasures of this excruciating yet exhilarating endeavour we call Literature!

I propose that we meet at my place for our first gathering – it's No 1 The Larches, the big one at the start of that private road opposite the golf course with the newly – and very dearly – asphalted carriage drive (don't ask). Shall we say two weeks from now, on the 15th? Say 7.45 for 8? Do let me know if you can come.

I thought it might be nice if we all briefly e-introduced ourselves beforehand, so we know a bit about each other before we meet? I'm Julia Greengage, 49 (though my dear hubby insists I don't look it), and I've been an actress for about 25 years (*Bad Girls*, *The Bill*, 'difficult fibroids patient' in *Holby*, etc.). My husband is big in HR at the airport, and we moved here because the commute from Richmond was sapping his spirit.

In between gigs in 'the biz of show', I moonlight as a paralegal, but my secret self has been plotting the big novel for over a decade. I've finally got an idea I can work with and a few draft chapters, and am looking forward to putting it out there!! Nothing ventured and all that! I guess style-wise I'm a mainstream fiction type, with a love of big emotions and gut-wrenching twists, somewhere between David Nicholls and Jodi Picoult. Well, one can but dream!

Anyway, enough about me. Do drop the group a line to let us know if you can come and tell us a little bit about yourselves.

Until Thursday, dear writers!
Julia

From: **aliceknowles@mewriter.com**
To: Crawley Writers' Group
Sent: 01.12.16, 18:02
Subject: **Re: Welcome, writers of Crawley!**

Hello Julia, hello everyone. I'm really looking forward to meeting you all and getting acquainted with your work. Julia, you wanted us to say a little about ourselves. OK, well I'm Alice and I'm 42, and between 9 and 5 on weekdays I'm a payroll clerk at Sussex College, but at every other time, and in every other sense, I am a WRITER. That is how I define myself.

In my writing life, I am currently in the planning stages of a novel about a young woman from Three Bridges who goes on holiday to Greece. I've been developing it for a while now, and blogging about the process on my blog AliceKnowlesWriter.com – which you're all welcome to check out. Here's a quick flavour:

> Planning should never be formulaic or routine. It's a process of revelation. It's about revealing the full potential of the story you want to tell. At its best, planning is a journey of self-discovery where all roads are open and there are no cul-de-sacs or one-way streets. When I think about planning, I don't think of lists or diagrams or flowcharts, I think of a flower with petals unfolding...

That comes from my post 'How to plan'. I've also written articles on how to write, how to write about writing, how to write about planning, and the danger of planning becoming a displacement activity for writing. Julia, as you're in the early stages of your novel, you may find some of this quite useful?

So anyway, that's me. Look forward to seeing you all on the 15th.

Alice

From: **keith_sadwicke@techsolutions.co.uk**

To: Crawley Writers' Group

Sent: 02.12.16, 02:02

Subject: **Fâh-teë sLags (aka 'Greetings all!' in Xęn"dährin)**

Hey Julia. The name's Keith Sadwicke. 29 years of age, IT consultant and Chief Moderating Golem of Helm's Deep, a Tolkien fanfic forum, where I go by the name of Wormtongue. Am currently in the midst of writing Vol 7 of my *Dragons of Xęn"räh* saga – *Ice Realm of the Otherlings*. Looking forward to sharing my latest chapter with you. It's roughly 4,873 words, so should be OK to read the whole thing.

All you need to know for background is that the Hallia of Elberon (the forest world) are hoping to team up with the Otherlings of Greensky (the ice world) to bring down the evil Idris and his Cohorts of Myce. But little do they know that the Ilf (a kind of troll-dragon hybrid) of Kelltia (the fire world) is on their trail, eager to do Idris's bidding.

The story picks up on an ice lake on Greensky. The voluptuous Bink Hallia is in conversation with Odos the Otherling, who's decided to offer her a cohort of his best warriors if she'll sleep with him. That's how the chapter starts.

For those who'd like a bit more background, I can send you the full 10,000-word synopsis, which covers the entire saga to date. Warning: the synopsis does contain some Xęn"dährin, the main language I invented for my world. There is a glossary available, but for that you'll have to pay, or else buy Vols 1–3 (available as ebooks from Amazon Media), which contain the glossary in their backmatter.

Cool. That's about it for now. Look forward to introducing you all to the world of *Xȩn"räh*.

K

From: **MPranesh@gmail.com**

To: Crawley Writers' Group

Sent: 02.12.16, 07:12

Subject: **Re: Re: Welcome, writers of Crawley!**

Hi Julia

I'll definitely be there.

Mavinder

From: **armory-wargrove.jonathan@nhs_dental-estimates.gov.uk**

To: Crawley Writers' Group

Sent: 06.12.16, 23:43

Subject: **Re: Re: Re: Welcome, writers of Crawley!**

Hi Julia,

Jon here. Yes, I can make Thursday.

A bit about myself, as requested:

I'm the wrong side of 60 – just! I'd call myself a Seeker and have, I think, learned a thing or two in my time.

I've always been a bit of a rebel. At school myself and a few other reprobates formed a prog rock band and went on to a soupçon of success after we left. The King of Elfland's Daughter was the name of our band, if anyone recalls. Couple of albums, touring – happy days (or should I say 'daze'!).

When the band unravelled I hit the hippy trail and then, back in Albion, got involved in the alternative scene: astrology, reiki, ley lines, you name it. I lived for two years in a tepee in Wales and spent a lot of the '90s laying down ambient beats in chillout rooms at 'raves'.

Anyway, long story short: health and other problems caused an abrupt return to 'reality'. I'm now working at the Dental Estimates Board (the big office block in Caversham Road) as a Senior Assessor. I've been there 15 years now.

I began writing about two years ago, the first stuff I've done since penning lyrics back in the day. I write short stories about animals; think *Wind in the Willows* or *Watership Down* and you're on the right track. They are hopefully entertaining stories which will appeal to young and old alike but they also have a message for 'those with eyes to see'.

These dark days allegory is sadly necessary – thankfully, those who promote tyranny lack the ability to read with the Inner Eye of Imagination! Think about State links to literary critics for example.

Anyway, that's me. I'm looking forward to meeting the group – I'll bring a bottle of plonk!

All the best.

Jon

Jon Armory-Wargrove
Senior Assessor

This message is sent for and on behalf of the Dental Estimates Board, an NHS Service Provider. It may contain confidential information. If you are not the intended recipient please inform the sender that you have received the message in error before deleting it. Please do not disclose, copy or distribute information in the email or take any action in reliance on its contents: to do so is strictly prohibited and may be unlawful. Thank you for your cooperation.

From: **keith_sadwicke@techsolutions.co.uk**

To: Crawley Writers' Group

Sent: 08.12.16, 02:56

Subject: **Re: Re: Re: Re: Welcome, writers of Crawley!**

Hey Jon

Can't say I've heard of your band (sorry), but just googled you. Cool cover art for your third LP – can't read the gothic font, so don't know what it's called. Was the art inspired by Tolkien by any chance? It reminds me of Arwen the elf princess on her white charger riding through the forest in Fellowship.

Keith

From: **MPranesh@gmail.com**

To: Crawley Writers' Group

Sent: 08.12.16, 09:23

Subject: **Re: Re: Re: Re: Re: Welcome, writers of Crawley!**

Hi all

Looking forward to it.

May be a few minutes late, but will def be there.

Mavinder

From: **peterpeterpeterpeter@gmail.com**

To: Crawley Writers' Group

Sent: 08.12.16, 12:12

Subject: **<no subject>**

The scene: a Post Office (this Post Office), one Saturday (this Saturday). A long queue of restless customers, each laden with Christmas parcels. And only two windows open. (Or rather: two windows, both open.)

At one window, there's a man who's just been served but won't go away. He asks: 'Was the postal order definitely for £15.75?' People in the queue tut, the woman behind the counter rolls her eyes. 'Yes!' she says. She has obviously been asked this question several times already.

The man looks, if not unkempt, then uncared for. He wears taped-up pebble glasses, a tatty anorak, a thick off-cream cardigan that is regulation charity shop. The swirls of his dirty-white beard converge oddly around his mouth. You look at him through the prism of preconception and think: 'disability benefit, bit mad, bet he doesn't have to work for a living'.

Still he hovers. By now, other people are being served. 'I just want to confirm this and then I'll be on my way,' he says stubbornly over the shoulders of the new customers. 'Was it definitely £15.75?' The tuts and groans of the queue grow louder; people start to mutter. He persists: 'Can I please just see the paper with £15.75 on it again?' Now people are shouting out: 'YES IT WAS!' 'She's told you 100 times already!' 'Someone shove a receipt up his arse!!!'

At last he shuffles off.

The next man in the queue says to the counter, 'Ten first-class stamps... And can I please just confirm that the last customer's postal order was definitely £15.75?' The queue guffaws appreciatively. The new customer is pleased with his joke too, so pleased that he repeats it five more times.

As I leave, the queue is now almost out of the door. And now I see that the postal order man has only shuffled off as far as the end of the queue.

He is waiting in line again. Just to check.

To ask the awkward question. To stand behind my truth. To withstand the barbs of outraged middlebrow taste. To re-present the present. To say what must be said (even – or especially – if it has already been said). **To articulate my anxiety. And then just get in line... and do it all over again.** This is how I see the job of Peter, writer (my real job I mean; my actual job is consulting with owner-managed small- to medium-sized enterprises on health & safety risk assessment).

And then just get in line… and do it all over again.
And then just get in line… and do it all over again.
And then just get in line… and do it all over again.
And then just get in line… and do it all over again.
See you all on the 15th.

Peter, writer

PS I note there has been an offer to bring wine – can I take ownership of the snack requirement? Does everyone like Twiglets? Or something more traditional like Monster Munch? If you can just state your preferences on the attached questionnaire, I will action.

From: **blueyblu@blueyonder.com**

To: Crawley Writers' Group

Sent: 10.12.16, 17:15

Subject: **Hello I guess**

Blue here guys my real name is Priscilla but everyone calls me Blue. I'll be along on Thursday don't worry if I seem v quiet as I have difficulty in social situations until I relax which I'm sure will be soon. I have always been a writer ever since I was little – I love poetry write poetry read poetry. Favourites are Baudelaire Rimbaud mad old poets and more recent Adrienne Rich Anne Sexton Sylvia esp. Sylvia.

My poetry is very intense and tells it like it is about me and my emotions and the world how the world is. It is like looking to see into myself and be honest and let it out so I use free verse which means no rhymes and academic bs. Just raw feels.

More about me – this is copy/pasted from my tumblr page 'A Void' (warning: some nsfw):

My name is Blue. I am Poet, Artist, Phoenix! Loves: solitude, misty graveyards. Hates: hate.

Pronouns: she/her. Body positive. Two cats: Siouxsie and Robert (the Lovecats!).

As Nietzsche said 'Beware that, when fighting monsters, you yourself do not become a monster… for when you gaze long into the abyss, the abyss gazes also into you.' This is so true – look into my void!

PS I forgot to add I work in the Heart charity shop in the town centre. You may have seen me there.

From: **armory-wargrove.jonathan@nhs_dental-estimates.gov.uk**

To: Crawley Writers' Group

Sent: 11.12.16, 23:11

Subject: **Re: Re: Re: Re: Re: Re: Welcome, writers of Crawley!**

Hi Keith,

Yeah, the font is a bit hard to read; the title is *Glimmers of the Crystal Mind*. I wouldn't say it was Tolkien specifically that inspired the cover though we were all big fans. The band's name is taken from a Lord Dunsany novel – a bit of a lost classic. Worth a try if you haven't read it.

Maybe send me your synopsis if you have a moment.

See you Thursday!

Jon

Jon Armory-Wargrove
Senior Assessor

This message is sent for and on behalf of the Dental Estimates Board, an NHS Service Provider. It may contain confidential information. If you are not the intended recipient please inform the sender that you have received the message in error before deleting it. Please do not disclose, copy or distribute information in the email or take any action in reliance on its contents: to do so is strictly prohibited and may be unlawful. Thank you for your cooperation.

From: **aliceknowles@mewriter.com**

To: Crawley Writers' Group

Sent: 16.12.16, 09:08

Subject: **About last night**

Hello everyone.

I just wanted to say, it was great to meet you all last night. Sad that Mavinder couldn't make it. I hope to meet her next time. I was blown away by the standard of work. It's really inspired me.

Peter, I can't pretend that I understood every part of your 'performance', or even any part of it, but it had its own unique quality.

Keith, your story is amazing, both in complexity and length. I don't know how you can write so much! I think one or two of us struggled at times to follow every detail – there are just so many characters and locations! Also, I got a little distracted towards the end when Jon started tapping his feet and looking at his watch.

Sorry I didn't manage to bring anything of my own. As I explained, I'm still in the planning stages of my novel, and I want to be absolutely sure of its conceptual soundness before I start committing it to words.

Alice

From: **JuliaGeeGee@gmail.com**

To: Crawley Writers' Group

Sent: 17.12.16, 09:53

Subject: **Re: About last night**

My dear dear (dear!) fellow writers

Wow, wow and thrice wow!

Firstly, I just want to apologise for not following up sooner after our wonderful first meet. It was actually my birthday yesterday, and hubby surprised me by taking the day off and whisking me to town for cream tea at the Ritz followed by a whizz round the new Caravaggio exhibition at the Royal Academy, and then tickets to see *The Book of Mormon*. Outrageous! (But so clever and so funny.)

It was a wonderful day and a lovely surprise – but all the more so as I was all aglow from the first meeting of the Crawley Writers' Group! And what a meeting it was. We sang, we soared, we *expressed* ourselves, we *created* anew. Things emerged which, I firmly believe, could not have been uncovered alone. Truly the sum of our writing voices is greater than its individual parts, and it was *so* inspirational just to be rubbing shoulders with so much artistic passion and innovation, and all of it shared so freely. Thank you, writers!!

@Alice – wonderful to hear about your project in more detail. I think it's so clever and unusual how you've written the acknowledgements page and the afterword to your book without the bit in between yet! I so look forward to sharing in your planning process and perhaps even seeing some of your actual writing! (When you're ready of course.)

@Keith – Wow again! I was totally blown away by the passion and the intensity of your reading. It had never occurred to me before that the icy elf ones would have such different voices from the fiery troll-like ones (or again the pixie-like sky beings – forgive me, I've never been very good with fantasy nomenclature, but I'm sure I shall learn them all in time). The different voices and accents you gave us – not to mention your expert pronunciation of the invented language, complete with your helpful opening remarks on its syntactic principles and basic inflectional forms – all brought it wonderfully to life for me. I don't think you should worry about reading for longer than the others – you're at a different stage to many of us composition-wise, and these things all even out in the wash eventually.

@Blue – I wanted to weep at the delicate delineations of pain and sorrow you sketched for us with your exquisite poems. Your image of the kitten with the razor blade in its mouth and the baby sparrow it eviscerates will continue to haunt me. (And how clever – and powerful – of you to make that the chorus of your epic anti-limerick!) Your writing has an incredible *lived* quality, as if we were being given a unique ringside seat on a mental breakdown. Do your parents live nearby by the way? You know, I'm often around in the day if you ever fancy a cuppa and a chat – just drop me an email.

@Peter – Extraordinary. Listening to your work I marvelled anew at the diversity of everyone's voices and the courage it takes to stand behind one's unique vision – especially yours! It took me quite a while to realise you were reciting to us the trail of the emails we've been exchanging... only backwards! And then to segue into reading the labels from the various lotions and potions you found in my bathroom! So *innovative*. Have you read any David Nicholls by the way? He can be quite experimental, can't he?

@Jon – Your apocalyptic vision of a new right-wing world order made me shudder with rueful recognition (retrospectively, at least, as I'd not been clever enough to grasp it all on first hearing) but also very soppy at the same time, as you'd cleverly reimagined the key characters/conspirators as lovely ickle beavers and otters. Shades of *Animal Farm*, perhaps? More power to your polemical and yet endearing elbow!

@Mavinder – See what you're missing! We're so sorry you couldn't make it and we'd so love to see you next time.

Talking of which, we're now heading into the Christmas madness, so how about a meet in middish Jan – say Friday 20th? Very (very!) happy to host again, unless someone else would like to? Please drop the group a line to let us know you can come and if you'd like to host.

Until then – have a cool yule(!) and see you on the other side.

Julia xx

PS Sorry – I forgot to mention that we have another new member – Tom! I've added him to the group and he's kindly offered to pen a few words of introduction in due course. Welcome and see you at the next meet @Tom!

From: **MPranesh@gmail.com**

To: Crawley Writers' Group

Sent: 17.12.16, 16:44

Subject: **Re: Re: About last night**

Hi Julia and all

Yep – really sorry. Couldn't make it in the end because, well, reasons basically. I'll definitely be there next time though.

Mavinder

From: **tom@tomcat.com**

To: Crawley Writers' Group

Sent: 19.12.16, 22:56

Subject: **And this is me**

Hola group

Tom Hilden here. Brooding TEFL bureaucrat, novelist manqué, lover not fighter.

I'm 52 but age is just a number. I've had a few minor successes, writing wise – finalist in the Wivenhoe Flash Fiction Festival comp 2012, two medical horror stories in Aching Aorta magazine (RIP alas), honourable mention in the South-south-east London Playwriters Circle Awards (Veteran Newcomer category) etc. etc. Awards are a game of course. But they give you a reason to try and finish things. It's all grist to the mill.

Like most of us, by the sounds, I write therefore I am. It's about trying to say something so well it's been said once and for all, then failing, then trying to fail better next time. Sort of. Intolerably ill-put, of course. But still.

Looking forward to seeing you all at the next group.

T

From: **keith_sadwicke@techsolutions.co.uk**

To: Crawley Writers' Group

Sent: 21.12.16, 02:56

Subject: **Cool sesh**

Hey all. Keith here. Ace meeting the other night.

@Jon, I was well impressed with your world-building. Beavers and otters that talk (and drink and fight). What's not to like? It has graphic novel all over it. Others read stuff into it about right-wing populism, Farage, Trump, etc. But for me it was just a cool yarn. And your voice when you read is like Saruman from LotR, all deep and meaningful. I could have listened to you all night. Do you go to the London Comic and Fantasy Convention ever? I could get you in cheap, if you ever want to. They have publishers, agents and stuff, it's a good place for contacts.

@All, I've decided to take a leaf out of Pete's book and go a bit meta. I'm giving each of you short (I know, not like me ☺) reviews in the character of Odos the Otherling. It's in Xęn"dährin, which I'm sure you'll all soon be speaking like Greensky natives.*

Jon: Cøöł

Julia: Lųv-lęë

Pete: WêëęRd

Alice: BlôcHđ

Blue: Slậ-shyä RīsTs

Until next time then, folks, may you all grow like gronions with your heads in the earth (traditional Elberon farewell).

Keith

*Alternatively, you can purchase the full 50,000-word dictionary for just £4.99 from my website, xendahrin.com.

From: **peterpeterpeterpeter@gmail.com**

To: Crawley Writers' Group

Sent: 29.12.16, 12:12

Subject: **<no subject>**

Thank you for hosting, Julia, and sorry about 'Christmas', everyone. Julia, you certainly have all the amenities and social skills to host the group effectively, just thought it might be useful to share some points of feedback and suggestions for future groups. And thank you for the Shloer – it's amazing how often people never think to cater for non-alcoholics!

- The living room is a good space for the group, though a more compact arrangement of the chairs might have paid dividends, acoustically speaking.
- The rabbit cage, while obviously an attraction to some, might cause a bit of a distraction to readers and listeners over time? Especially when the animal does that deep-basso wheel-thrumming motion.

- Re: reading times, again. Should we perhaps think about a way of ensuring that people receive roughly the same amount of group attention? Could perhaps we agree on a rough maximum wordcount for people to read out? What do you think @Keith?

- Perhaps also we should establish a ground rule about the type of contribution the writer is planning to make. Some people wanted to read material, while others apparently wanted to use their apportioned slot to discuss a writing issue such as 'planning my planning', or again to get feedback on synopsis and structure rather than finished work. Are these all legitimate uses of the group, do people think? If so, perhaps in the latter two cases people could table their intentions beforehand and provide material in advance, so that unreasonable demands for spontaneous insight aren't sprung on the rest of the group?

- Very happy to host next time if that suits everyone. Perhaps it might be useful to set up a hosting rota (for those who feel happy to host) so that no one writer enjoys too much 'home advantage'?

I hope these thoughts are useful and I welcome other people's feedback on my feedback. They are offered in the spirit of building on what was a good start to our new initiative.

See you all on the 20th.

Peter, writer

From: **aliceknowles@mewriter.com**

To: Crawley Writers' Group

Sent: 30.12.16, 12:46

Subject: **The start of a beginning... (part 1)**

Dear WRITERS

It feels so uplifting to be part of this little clique, this cabal of Crawley creatives. It has done such wonders for my confidence. Because I must confess there are times in the dark watches of the night, or when staring at the desolate void of an empty Word document, when I begin to harbour doubts about whether I really am a WRITER, whether I have what it takes, as it were, to WRITE.

'What nonsense!' I hear you all chorus. 'Of course you are a WRITER, Alice.' Well, bless you all for saying so! And of course you are right. For I am part of this group, the Crawley Writers' Group, and what more proof do I need?

Peter, thank you for your helpful 'points of feedback'. Point 4 was, I think possibly, a reference to me. It's true that I used my allotted time to 'discuss a writing issue' as opposed to read out my work, and I assumed that was a 'legitimate use of the group', to use your terminology. Certainly no one raised any objections at the time. We are all at different stages with our projects. Some of us are at the 'putting words down on paper' stage. I still happen to be at the planning and conceptualisation stage. But these are all different stages of what I call WRITING. I am WRITING just as much as anyone else in the group, even if I'm not actually 'writing' in the physical sense. Or not yet, for I have some exciting news...

I am, I'm sure you'll all be delighted to hear, toying/flirting/trifling with the possibility of an opening Sentence. A huge step, I realise, taking something that's been gestating within me for so long, something that feels so vast, so raw and so vibrant with potential, and committing it to actual words. What this means is that I may, just may, have something for when we next meet.

Wish me luck.
Alice

From: **tom@tomcat.com**
To: Crawley Writers' Group
Sent: 01.01.17, 19:56
Subject: **Re: The start of a beginning... (part 1)**

Alice – I haven't met you yet but I can see already you are a dreadful tease. The suspense is terrible – I do hope it will last! After all, is the text not at its most delightfully suggestive when it shows a flash of meaning/cleavage? All of which is to say that – as you continue to make us beg for more – you have already the makings of a great writer...

Happy new year all! See you on the 20th at Pete's.
T

From: **peterpeterpeterpeter@gmail.com**

To: Crawley Writers' Group

Sent: 02.01.17, 12:12

Subject: **<no subject>**

@Alice: I do not question the legitimacy of your efforts. But I think that generic writerly 'chit-chat' and deep structural review probably work best with some advance notice. Cognitively, this sort of work requires a different process to that of reacting in the moment to a writer reading their work.

Re your book's first sentence, I wonder if it would be useful – as is done in some therapeutic contexts – if you 'contracted' with the group to definitely have it ready for next time? Sometimes resolution is the enemy of follow-through.

@Keith, @Tom: It's Peter please. Never Pete!

@all: Happy New Year. I do hope your writing resolutions do not set you up to fail.

Please can you all let me know what snacks/beverages you'll be bringing so I can make up any deficiencies? And I trust no one has any objection to my videoing the session?

Peter, writer

From: **tom@tomcat.com**
To: Crawley Writers' Group
Sent: 03.01.17, 19:56
Subject: **Re: Re: The start of a beginning... (part 1)**

Come to think of it, Alice, the only person who's more of a tease than you in the whole group is @Mavinder!

T

From: **JuliaGeeGee@gmail.com**
To: Crawley Writers' Group
Sent: 07.01.17, 09:02
Subject: **Happy New Year!**

A very Happy New Year to my wonderful new, insanely artistic friends and comrades of the Crawley Writers' Group!!!

Apologies for the radio silence – we whizzed off to the Bahamas for a few days over the New Year, chasing the winter sun and all that. But I trust you all had a truly merry festive season and are now strapped back into the cockpit of creativity, all primed for a productive and inspiring 2017!

My resolution for this year is 'Finish that perishing first draft!' There, I've said it! And you can all hold me to it! But seriously, it's wonderful to enter the new year knowing that we already have the group in place, and with it a whole framework of support and motivation that gives me the best chance of actually delivering on my word. Really looking forward to the next one!

@Peter – You raised a couple of interesting points in your email. My feeling is that all of us are writers writing, one way or another, and each of us should feel free to use their time in the group as they see best, so long as it's writing-focused, of course! So if someone wants to discuss a problem with motivation, say, or try and thrash out a plotting/structure issue, then let's all muck in and help out! (You all did just that for me, of course, with our discussion about the scene in my book where the glamorous extra proves to be so good at acting a hospital patient with a slipped disc that she turns the director's head and gets offered a co-starring role on the spot. And very helpful you all were too!) What do other people think?

Re videoing the group, I appreciate that you probably have a sincere artistic motivation for doing this, Peter, but I'm just wondering if it's perhaps a bit early in the day for such an approach? As an actress I'm used to having the cameras trained on me, of course, but the group is a safe space where people can allow themselves to be vulnerable, secure in the knowledge that the words and thoughts they air will be treated respectfully and need go no further. I'm wondering whether the presence of a video camera might threaten that sense of a safe space a tad? Do you think it might make some people feel self-conscious or inhibit what they feel able to say, especially at this delicate, early stage of the group's evolution? Perhaps it's something we could consider again further down the line, once the group is more firmly established and we've all really got to know each other? But please, it's all about what the group wants/feels – what do other people think???

See you all on the 20th – stick me down to bring the red wine, Peter! (Hubby has just ordered in another case of this lovely Malbec from his wine club…)

Julia xx

From: **blueyblu@blueyonder.com**
To: Crawley Writers' Group
Sent: 08.01.17, 15:15
Subject: **Video worry**

I'm stressing a bit over this video thing Julia put it well it's about a safe space and everyone made me feel so at home (btw thanks for the kind words about the kitten image Julia the kitten is me of course).

So please please PLEASE no video because I don't think I could come. Sorry to freak over this but it would be REALLY difficult for me.

Anyway I hope everyone is writing away. I have been so creative since the meeting, the words are literally pouring out.

Blue x

From: **armory-wargrove.jonathan@nhs_dental-estimates.gov.uk**
To: Crawley Writers' Group
Sent: 15.01.17, 01:14
Subject: **Next meeting/video question**

@Pete: I can only echo what Julia and Blue have already said about the video idea. I've got pretty strong views on this; we live under enough surveillance as it is from the Powers That Be without adding to it.

Anyway, good first meet I thought. I don't mind at all if Alice or anyone else wants to discuss plans or problems with their writing – let the discussion flow!

I'm not sure people quite 'got' my allegory. It's not a matter of right or left in politics any more – I like to think we can transcend that and see the Truth for what it is. I won't spell it out now but try and think beyond the mainstream media blinkers!

Looking forward to the next meeting – I'll bring a couple of bottles of real ale.

Jon

PS @Keith: got the synopsis, ta. I misread 10,000 words as 1,000 – it's certainly a tome in its own right! Unfortunately we have just started a quarterly audit here at the DEB so I may not be able to get started on it for a while. Yes to the fantasy convention – never been but it might be a hoot.

This message is sent for and on behalf of the Dental Estimates Board, an NHS Service Provider. It may contain confidential information. If you are not the intended recipient please inform the sender that you have received the message in error before deleting it. Please do not disclose, copy or distribute information in the email or take any action in reliance on its contents: to do so is strictly prohibited and may be unlawful. Thank you for your cooperation.

From: **keith_sadwicke@techsolutions.co.uk**

To: Crawley Writers' Group

Sent: 15.01.17, 02:17

Subject: **Keith is back!**

Xęn"gol-yah, my friends. Just emerged blinking from my writing den after an insanely intense few weeks working on Chapter XXXIX: Ride of the Elberon in which Bink Hallia and her army lift the siege of Thïrït Sâním. It has a cast of literally millions and is going to rival the famous Battle of Helm's Deep in *LotR* for sheer scale and epicness. The first draft of Vol 7 is now, I reckon, about 80% complete. Just another 30k words to go and I can put this baby to bed, so still on course for my own self-imposed deadline of end of March. Cool!

Kudos, Pete, for giving the group format so much thought. Agree with you that in an ideal world everyone in the group should get roughly the same sort of time, though don't much like this maximum wordcount concept as I think it discriminates against writers of popular prose who inevitably write more (in the sense of words) than your poets and your experimentalists. I mean what if Jon, for the sake of argument, was a paragraph over the wordcount on one of his fantastic animal stories? Would he seriously have to just stop before he reached the end?

So what about this as a suggestion: what if Julia asks at the start of each sesh how much time each person needs, then we take it from there? I reckon that Alice, to take a random example, won't need as much time as, say, Jon or me, to get through her stuff. Just a thought.

As for your video idea, Pete, that's really interesting. I'd be happy to sell you the video/audio rights to my work for a sum to be negotiated. Email me separately so we can discuss further.

Keith

From: **aliceknowles@mewriter.com**

To: Crawley Writers' Group

Sent: 15.01.17, 17:01

Subject: **Such wise words!**

Julia, welcome back from your holiday, and thank you for your wise and thoughtful words. 'All of us are writers writing, one way or another.' So wise. So full of understanding. I hope you don't mind, but I have written them out on a little chalk board and placed them over my desk to act as my guide and inspiration, my muse in times of doubt.

With regard to Peter's video idea, I've given this a lot of thought, and I've concluded that (sorry, Peter!) I don't think it's a good idea. We are, in the end, WRITERS, and WRITERS are creatures of the word, not the image. Words are the soil from which we grow, and the waters through which we swim, and to introduce video would, I fear, pollute that soil and/or muddy those waters, depending on which metaphor you prefer. I like both of them, and that (ha ha!) tends to be my problem!

Tom, forgive me but I'm a little confused. I certainly didn't intend to be a tease or anything with my suggestion that I might have my opening Sentence ready to read out. Whatever you meant by that comment, I'm not sure. Anyway, I look forward to meeting you and seeing everyone else next week.

Alice x

From: **aliceknowles@mewriter.com**

To: Crawley Writers' Group

Sent: 15.01.17, 17:11

Subject: **<no subject>**

Keith, I'm sorry but your constant references to your prolific output sound to me a lot like, forgive me, a kind of literary turkey-cocking. You don't seem to appreciate that to WRITERS like myself, who labour over every word, every semicolon, and who often find, after hours of toil at their desk, that they have deleted more than they have written, it's not pleasant to have to listen to someone boast of having 'just another 30k words to go', as if words were something you could pour from a tap rather than be painfully extracted from the poetic core of one's being, which is how it feels for me.

Furthermore, the idea that I might not need as much time as you or Jon during the meeting, simply because I don't produce as many words, undermines the egalitarian principles upon which our little group is based. We are all WRITERS, as Julia says, and we should all be allocated equal time, regardless of what kind of WRITER we are. I feel sure Julia will back me up on this.

Alice

From: **MPranesh@gmail.com**

To: Crawley Writers' Group

Sent: 18.01.17, 16:02

Subject: **Video/Next meet**

Hi all

Not really fussed re video question but happy to go with flow.

See you all next time
Mavinder

From: **keith_sadwicke@techsolutions.co.uk**

To: Crawley Writers' Group

Sent: 19.01.17, 02:56

Subject: **Dønb"ite-mïe-hèdöff!**

Täy"ki-tęEz-eê, Alice, as the Greenskians often say. I wasn't boasting or turkey-cocking or whatever, just reporting on my progress. I thought you'd be happy for me. I mean I get that you're in a different place with your stuff right now, and that's cool. Let's just live and let live, yeah?

As for this whole debate about time allocation, I don't want to make a big deal out of it. If Julia wants to give us all equal time, that's cool – I'm just against equality of wordcount, that's all, as I think it discriminates against the kind of fast-paced, commercial fiction I specialise in. I've been listening to *The Silmarillion* on audio recently, and I've noticed that when I stick it on 1.5x speed or even 2x speed, I can still follow the story, and this has given me an idea I'd like to try out on you guys. I'm going to start speed-reading my book to you. I'm already quite a fast reader, but I reckon, with practice, I could get up to around 260 wpm – that's 2x average reading speed, so you'd end up getting twice as much of my book in the same time allocation. That's pretty good value, don't you reckon? And what's more, for you guys, because you're my friends, it's all absolutely free!*

Keith

* Of course I can't offer the whole book on these terms, not even to you special people. I'll be reading an abridged version for the group. If you want the full, unexpurgated audio version, an edition will be available later this year for just £15.99. Keep checking my website xendahrin.com for the latest news on that and all other *Xęn"räh*-related matters.

From: **tom@tomcat.com**

To: Crawley Writers' Group

Sent: 19.01.17, 21:53

Subject: **An eye for an eye will only make the whole world blind**

Guys guys!

We all want to do the group. We all want to support each other. We're all still finding our place, finding our voice, feeling a little vulnerable perhaps. So let's all be gentle with each other. And let's not get hung up on these petty logistical points before we've even really started.

So let's just agree on a few ground rules so we can move on to the good stuff:

- no video for now
- everyone has c30 mins each, to use in any writerly way/ read at any speed they choose
- any disagreements over contentious issues to be decided by group vote
- Monster Munch to be included at all meets*

But beyond the above, and most of all – let's celebrate our differences! You don't get harmony when everyone's singing the same note, after all...

You're welcome,

Tom

* That one's a deal-breaker...

From: **JuliaGeeGee@gmail.com**

To: Crawley Writers' Group

Sent: 20.01.17, 08:01

Subject: **Nice one, Tom**

Well said, Tom!

See you all tonight at Peter's!

Julia x

From: **MPranesh@gmail.com**

To: Crawley Writers' Group

Sent: 21.01.17, 14:23

Subject: **Sorry sorry**

Hi all

I am so sorry to have missed the group again. I was on my way out the door but something came up.

I am really keen to attend – life has a habit of getting in the way at the mo. I even had a poem to read, or the start of one.

This is what I was going to read:

Warrior Queen, you are Nobody's Prey
You live your Dream, you live for the Day
You have the Wolf inside you, and also the Bear
Crushing all who Defy you, all who Dare.

Blown by the Gale and burned by the Fire
Onward you sail, something something Desire/never Tire.

I'll try and finish it and bring it next time, promise!

Mavinder

PS I do exist really! Despite what some people think...

PPS I'm in awe of you guys!

From: **aliceknowles@mewriter.com**
To: Crawley Writers' Group
Sent: 22.01.17, 11:03
Subject: **Lovely evening!**

Dear all
I so enjoyed our WRITING group on Friday. I thought it went very well, didn't you? It's only our second meeting, yet I already feel so at ease with everyone. But first, some apologies:

1. Peter, I'm sorry I didn't manage to complete the questionnaire you handed round as we came in. I'm afraid I got rather stressed by all those multiple choices you posed, and perhaps I don't feel entirely comfortable about pigeon-holing myself as a particular kind of WRITER, at least not at this early stage in my career. I was also possibly a little ill at ease in the room you showed us into – your 'specularium' I

think you called it, which sounded to me, I'm sorry, but quite medical and unpleasant. The room itself was fine, if a little long and narrow, but the way you arranged us all at one end, with the rows of seats facing us with shop mannequins sitting on them, made me feel like a performer in front of an audience, and I've never liked audiences – even, or especially, ones made up of dead-eyed shop mannequins.

2. Tom, I'm sorry for squealing like that when you put your hand on my arm! I know you were just doing it to emphasise a point you were making. I suppose I got a fright, that's all. I come from a decidedly non-huggy family, which may have something to do with it. Even Tiggy, my cat, sometimes startles me when she rubs against my leg. Anyway, I'm sorry for my weird over-reaction. It didn't help that our seats were so close together. I realise Peter wanted us to be compact, but there wasn't a huge amount of space to move one's arms and gesture, was there? In fact, thinking about it, perhaps you didn't mean to touch me at all. Now I'm just very confused.

3. Jon, I'm sorry if I appeared to snap at you at one point. I wasn't angry or anything, I just thought you were being a little hard on our host, that's all. Peter didn't video us in the end, did he? And, as he explained, his decision to 'hold a mirror' up to us while we read out our work was a purely artistic one. Something about 're-presenting the present' I think – I didn't really understand it, but that doesn't mean it wasn't valid.

We're all trying to find our way as WRITERS, after all, and we need to be more understanding of each other. And I have to say, your suggestion that there was a secret camera or microphone inside the actual mirrors struck me as just a tiny bit paranoid.

4. Everyone. I know I said I might actually have something to read this time, and I'm really sorry to let you all down. I did actually create an opening sentence that wasn't entirely horrible, and I was planning to read it to you. But then, as I was leaving for the group, I suddenly realised that the adverb wasn't quite working, so I changed it, and unfortunately that ended up wrecking everything. Which also explains why I was late. I'm so sorry. I think possibly a fundamental rethink may be required.

5. Mavinder, sorry you couldn't make it. I was so looking forward to meeting you. Perhaps next time? Loved the poem, by the way. And please don't feel in awe of us. We're really very normal. Most of us!

See you all at the next meeting, at Jon's I believe.

Happy WRITING everyone.

Alice

From: **peterpeterpeterpeter@gmail.com**

To: Crawley Writers' Group

Sent: 24.01.17, 12:12

Subject: **Who took my corkscrew?**

People were not to be upset by my live writing experiment. I'm very interested in metafictive discourse as you know, and I wanted to 'write down' the experience of 'writing down' my experience as it happened. To do this during a writers' group added an extra layer of narrative recursion which pleased me greatly. What is it like to experience someone experiencing you? And, of course, what is it like to experience the experiencing of that experience?

Obviously the only way I could do this was to 'mirror' – dictating my thoughts live to a piece of voice recognition software, which of course also meant recording my observations of people's reactions to me recording my observations about them being recorded. This might have been a bit frustrating at times (e.g. when I said things like, 'Tom sits down and scratches his behind, then tries to surreptitiously remove a piece of crusted mucus from his nose, and wipe it on my cushion... Now Tom looks at me with great hostility for a very brief moment, then recovers himself and smiles very sweetly in a way which he hopes will cover up his earlier expression of hostility... Now Tom looks for a moment as if he's going to hit me, then sits back, raises his wine glass with an ironic "Cheers" and gives me a two-fingered gesture which he hopes will be interpreted as the ironic gesture of a good sport…' etc. etc.) But I trust that the seriousness of the artistic purpose was at least clear.

Obviously it might have allayed some of the possible friction which ensued if I'd told you what I was doing beforehand, but then of course the authenticity of the experiment would have been entirely undermined.

Peter, writer

PS If you took my corkscrew, please can you return it? It's about the only thing I have left from the convent.

From: **tom@tomcat.com**

To: aliceknowles@mewriter.com

Sent: 25.01.17 17:09

Subject: **Re: Lovely evening**

Hi @Alice

Hope you don't mind me emailing you off-list, as it were, but I so enjoyed Thursday and especially your sharing of the exquisite unfolding process of the creative act. I so identified with what you were saying! – I remember a period back in the mid-nineties when I had so many ideas, my mind was literally fizzing with tropes and themes that I literally didn't/couldn't start.

I wondered if it might be useful to meet up and discuss the sublime agonies of the writing journey some time? Perhaps we could sit down at our typewriters and, as it were, bleed together? Discipline makes the magic happen, after all, and I'm sure we have much to teach each other on that score. There's a new gastropub over towards Tilgate Park that looks worth a try – perhaps Friday night? Or we could do a coffee at mine one morning over the weekend? (I'm in one of the 'swanky' new flats in the redeveloped convent complex off Old Horsham Road.)

See you soon
Tom

From: **armory-wargrove.jonathan@nhs_dental-estimates.gov.uk**
To: Crawley Writers' Group
Sent: 25.01.17, 01:14
Subject: **No idea where your bloody corkscrew is!**

Good meeting for the most part (I'll get to the downside soon). I thought the 30-minute slots worked well, and my headache from all those infinite reflections of mannequins in mirrors everywhere died down after the first quarter of an hour.

Keith, I didn't think it was possible to read that fast! I really thought you were going to choke on your dry roasted at one point and I was preparing to do the Heimlich manoeuvre! Maybe a bit slower next time, mate?

Alice, the 29-minute preamble to The Sentence was obviously heartfelt and your description of your struggle with the intractable nature of language to truly express what you mean etc. was very moving. It was a crying shame you couldn't bring yourself to actually read The Sentence out when it came to it, though I guess your silence, broken only by a sob, spoke volumes. I feel for you, I really do.

What I really didn't need was the constant background commentary from the man in the head mic. Sorry, Pete, but I don't think I'm being oversensitive when I say you were bloody rude. (It might also be noted that my so-called surveillance paranoia has turned out to be rather well-founded.) I don't mind being called 'an old hippy' and I'd be the first to agree I have a slight paunch (it's an age thing) but the stage-whispered description of me as 'Jon, a superannuated rebel, hoisting a *prodigious* beer belly over his Hawkwind belt buckle' went too far. I think an apology to me and the rest of the group is called for.

Anyway, let's look forward to the next group and put a lid on the meta-whatsit nonsense.

Jon

Jon Armory-Wargrove
Senior Assessor

This message is sent for and on behalf of the Dental Estimates Board, an NHS Service Provider. It may contain confidential information. If you are not

the intended recipient please inform the sender that you have received the message in error before deleting it. Please do not disclose, copy or distribute information in the email or take any action in reliance on its contents: to do so is strictly prohibited and may be unlawful. Thank you for your cooperation.

From: **JuliaGeeGee@gmail.com**

To: Crawley Writers' Group

Sent: 26.01.17, 22:01

Subject: **Another wonderful meet!**

Hi all

Sorry for not weighing in sooner – these Pilates retreats really take it out of one!

But anyway, another wonderful meet! We are really starting to cook creatively, and with extra virgin no less!!

I can only echo all the *positive* comments that others have said so far.

@Blue – Your poems were once again exquisite, such a delicate finessing of the grief of thwarted love, I thought. And the tears of 'blood' you dripped on to your pure white T-shirt as you read. So original! (At least I hope it wasn't real blood!!)

@Keith – Extraordinary! Again! And so fast! By the way, is it wrong that I have developed a bit of a crush for the dark dwarf-lord one???

@Alice – You go girl! It's the journey, not the arrival that counts!

@Peter – You continue to challenge us in the most unexpected ways. @restofus – It's not always easy when one can seem to be the butt of an artist's experimentation, I know, but it's surely incumbent upon a group like ours, I feel, to support the sincerity and the diversity of our fellow writers' visions (especially in these globally troubled times... whoops – bit political!). So more power to your metafictive elbow, I say, Peter! (And 17 types of snack to choose from! You have set the comestibles bar very high, I fear...)

Thanks all for your comments about my novel in progress, *The Casting Couch*. The points about narrative glue and creating 'clearings in the story forest' (love that phrase @Tom! – and of course your own story about the cyclist who doesn't know he's dead) were especially useful, and I hope to have something a bit more polished for you next time.

What a shame that Mavinder couldn't make it again. @Mavinder, I know it's hard to fit everything in with a busy schedule but we do so hope to meet you at the next one.

Happy writing, one and all!

Julia xx

From: **peterpeterpeterpeter@gmail.com**

To: Crawley Writers' Group

Sent: 27.01.17, 12:00

Subject: **Still no sign of the corkscrew**

Hi Jon

I can only apologise.

I think what I actually dictated was 'Mötorhead', not Hawkwind! Thanks for the correction, which I am happy to incorporate in my write-up.

See you at the next one

Peter, writer

PS I note that Julia's charming round-up of the last group had some positive feedback for everyone's work but yours, Jon. I do hope the obvious conclusion to draw here is not the correct one.

From: **tom@tomcat.com**

To: JuliaGeeGee@gmail.com

Sent: 29.01.17, 21:53

Subject: **The stories we share...**

Hi Julia

Hope you don't mind me emailing you off-list, as it were, but was just wondering if you'd be interested in hooking up to talk through the narrative forest idea in some more detail?

I've had a few more thoughts about your delightful piece since too, and would be delighted to share. Alone we can only do so much, after all; but together we can do SO MUCH!

As I'm Director of Studies at the Academy now, I have fewer teaching hours and my schedule's pretty flexible – I could maybe pop round yours late one morning next week – say Tuesday or Wednesday?

Happy writing!

Tom

From: **aliceknowles@mewriter.com**

To: tom@tomcat.com

Sent: 04.02.17, 11:34

Subject: **Re: Re: Lovely evening**

Hi @Tom

Thank you for your kind and thoughtful message. Your offer to meet is tempting. However, I'm not sure how you would find time for me in your busy schedule what with being 'Director of Studies at the Academy' and meeting up with Julia, too. 'Alone we can only do so much, after all, but together we can do SO MUCH!' Perhaps if togetherness is what you're after, you could meet with the two of us at the same time? Kill two birds with one stone as it were.

NB. You are not the only one who emails people 'off-list'!

See you at the next meeting.

Alice

From: **keith_sadwicke@techsolutions.co.uk**

To: Crawley Writers' Group

Sent: 05.02.17, 02:56

Subject: **Fëno"mēnàllif-åst**

Thank you all for your kind words about my speed-reading. In private I have reached even higher speeds (approaching 3x average velocity), although I'm not sure you're ready for that yet. Maybe in a few weeks.

Although I am probably the most successful writer in this group in purely commercial terms (I'm talking copies sold as well as *Xȩn"räh*-related merch), I am fully willing to admit I may not be the most talented author. That accolade has to go to Jon, whose story at the last meet about the badger with bovine tuberculosis who offers to share his burrow with a family of homeless rabbits had me in floods. I haven't blubbed so much since watching Sam carry Frodo up Mount Doom in *The Return of the King*. I wish I could generate one tenth of the emotion in a thousand words that Jon manages in six (having said that, the stats don't lie – 87 downloads of Vol 5 in the last 11 months – maybe I'm being too modest!).

@Julia, I know what you mean about Bór"ntöøsh-õrt, the 'dark dwarf-lord one' – he's quite buff, isn't he? Or, as the Otherling females say, *Ph"oøwaârfänsēe-im*.

@everyone, If you feel like leaving a review on Amazon (5 stars only, please) it will help boost the book in their algorithms. As an extra incentive, if you buy it through my website, I can offer you a 5% discount on your purchase.

The good news is I am feeling frighteningly prolific right now. The muse is flowing with the speed of a golden snidget on steroids. If I'm going to ride this mighty wave of creative effluence to its fullest potential, I'll need to disappear into my den for the next few weeks. My target is to spawn 65,000 publishable words by the end of the month, which would be a PB. Wish me luck!

Sadly this means I won't be able to attend a February meeting of the group. Can I suggest that we skip this month and have the next meet at my place on March 13? Agreed? Cool!

Keith

From: **blueyblu@blueyonder.com**
To: Crawley Writers' Group
Sent: 08.02.17, 13:47
Subject: **Sorry about the prawns**

Sorry should've written sooner but a lot of volunteers were off at the charity shop with this seasonal bug so all hands to the pump. Nice of you to pop in Tom, sorry we couldn't speak properly I was rushed off my feet I hope you understand – did you find something for your aunt in the end?

Anyway I just wanted to say how much I enjoyed our last meeting, I can't believe I already feel so at ease with you all.

First off, to Peter, sorry for freaking when you brought out the Thai prawns, I have a thing about seafood, one of my phobic things, I have to cross the road when I pass the fishmonger on the high street, honestly it's that bad. Your writing is very clever and probably a lot goes over my head but your collage in the bathroom made up of shopping lists, transcribed travel bulletins and marginal comments found in library books was totally mad – in a good way!

and Tom your story was very clever and funny too – the scene with the policeman obsessed with bicycles was brilliant, how do you think up your wild ideas?

and Alice, dear Alice, I feel for you, I really do. We are all here for you and willing you to finish that sentence. Finishing a sentence is not a problem for you, Keith, the words just tumble out of you like the words tumble out of me, except with more elves. I am slightly lost because of the huge backstory but somehow that doesn't seem to matter!

Jon, loved the badger thing, really I did, but I think you are overreacting to Peter, he is just trying to do something new and I think we all ought to support each other. I found his commentary in the background strangely soothing, like listening to the radio when you are falling asleep.

Last but not least, our lovely Julia – *The Casting Couch* was like you, glamorous and poised, and the story of a young girl cursed by enormous wealth, talent and beauty really made me think how lucky I really am. And thank you for your kind comments on my thing. It wasn't actually a tear of blood btw – my new piercing had scabbed over and it seeped a little as I was reading – happy coincidence!

luv

Blue

From: **armory-wargrove.jonathan@nhs_dental-estimates.gov.uk**
To: Crawley Writers' Group
Sent: 09.02.17, 01:14
Subject: **An apology and an explanation**

Hi guys,

OK, OK, perhaps I overreacted to Pete's 'experiment'. If I can explain a little. I am involved with the Disclosure Now! group which is lobbying for the government to open its files on the UFO phenomenon – I know, real tinfoil hat stuff! But it is a FACT that 'certain agencies' have been monitoring our group and like-minded researchers. *That* is the reason I am nervous about being recorded in any form. I won't say any more on this now but if anyone is interested in the UFO phenomenon please let me know.

Anyway, let's move on. I'm sorry for any offence I may have *inadvertently* caused.

Jon

PS @Keith – sorry, still haven't had a chance to read through your synopsis as still under the cosh of the quarterly audit but will get round to it asap. When's the fantasy con?

J

Jon Armory-Wargrove
Senior Assessor

This message is sent for and on behalf of the Dental Estimates Board, an NHS Service Provider. It may contain confidential information. If you are not the intended recipient please inform the sender that you have received the message in error before deleting it. Please do not disclose, copy or distribute information in the email or take any action in reliance on its contents: to do so is strictly prohibited and may be unlawful. Thank you for your cooperation.

From: **aliceknowles@mewriter.com**

To: Crawley Writers' Group

Sent: 11.02.17, 11:34

Subject: **Sentenced!**

Dear friends and fellow WRITERS

Thank you all so much for your kind and heartfelt support regarding my struggles with The Sentence. It's funny how that word has two meanings, because sometimes it feels like a sentence, this burden of expectation I am obliged to carry around with me. It's almost like being in a prison cell with a great heavy iron ball and chain attached to my ankle.

I know, I know, the pressure isn't coming from any of you, it's coming from me. I keep telling myself, it's only a sentence, Alice, and not even a very complicated one. Just a set of words containing subject, predicate, main clause and a single subordinate clause.

And the latest draft of The Sentence is not bad – really! It reads well, it's balanced, rhythmic. It sets up the story, hopefully arouses some curiosity in the reader and makes them want to read on. In short, it does everything an opening sentence ought to do. It ticks all the boxes.

The trouble is, it's wrong. Deeply and fundamentally wrong. Because it's not true to myself or to the novel I want to write. It's a creative-writing-class opening sentence. And although it might be perfectly OK for any other novel, it's not OK for *my* novel.

It makes me want to cry because I have spent a ridiculous, absurd number of hours honing and crafting the wretched thing, and I will never get that time back. I keep thinking there must be something I can salvage from the wreckage. Perhaps one of the commas. Must I really junk the whole thing?

So this is where you find me, my friends, vacillating between yet another edit and a wholesale delete. Which will it be?

And now Tiggy's mewing outside my door. She wants feeding. And I need another coffee. Displacement activities – sometimes I really love them! Speak to you all soon.

Alice x

From: **peterpeterpeterpeter@gmail.com**

To: Crawley Writers' Group

Sent: 12.02.17, 12:12

Subject: Re: **An apology and an explanation**

@Jon: Of course they are watching us. What only matters is the quality of our *watching back*.

Peter, writer

From: **JuliaGeeGee@gmail.com**

To: Crawley Writers' Group

Sent: 12.02.17, 19:22

Subject: **Better together | Just a thought, Alice...**

Hi all

Loving all this creative conflab! And wonderful to see how we are slowly but surely moving beyond friction into... fiction!!

See what I did there?! OK, suit yourselves. But seriously, I've seen this process happen so often in theatre ensembles, when the initial tensions and misunderstandings as people find their place in the group start to give way to true creative collaboration and a desire to help each other shine. Brilliant!

Now in that spirit and please ignore this if you prefer, Alice, but dare I suggest a thought... I don't know if it's just me, or what others think – but personally I'd be really intrigued by a story which begins:

Oh, now Tiggy's mewing outside my door. She wants feeding. And I need another coffee.

Julia x

From: **keith_sadwicke@techsolutions.co.uk**

To: armory-wargrove.jonathan@nhs_dental-estimates.gov.uk

Sent: 14.02.17, 03:47

Subject: **Cool**

Hey Jon

It's totally OK that you haven't read my synopsis yet. I get that you're busy. As the Otherlings say, dœn"wòrrêee-båhtet, which basically means 'no problem'.

Btw, I totally relate to your fears about government cover-ups about UFOs. I've read about Area 52 and all that. It's scary that you're being monitored. I'm guessing you must be onto something. Personally, I reckon it would be totally cool to meet an alien. In the fantasy genre, humans rub along just fine with other intelligent species, be they dragons or elves, so why not with aliens?

Speaking of fantasy, the London Comic and Fantasy Convention is on 26–28 May at the ExCel Centre. I've decided to buy myself a stand this year, so I can flog some merch and raise awareness of *Xȩ̣n"räh*. I'll buy you a ticket, if you don't mind wearing a Blarf the Bellow T-shirt and directing people my way. Blarf, by the way, is the orange-faced scourge of Mount Kàttërwãll from Vol 3. He can kill an elf at 60 paces just by yelling at it. By the time we go, you'll have read the synopsis for sure, so you'll know enough about Blarf and the world of *Xȩ̣n"räh* in general to field a few questions.

Cheers mate.

Keith

2.

STORY-STRUCK!

From: **peterpeterpeterpeter@gmail.com**
To: Crawley Writers' Group
Sent: 14.02.17, 12:12
Subject: **Your one-word challenge**

Hi all

Please can you each send me a single word, which I will use to shape and inform my next creation.

Regards

Peter, writer

From: **MPranesh@gmail.com**
To: Crawley Writers' Group
Sent: 14.02.17, 12:15
Subject: **Re: Your one-word challenge**

Can someone please help m

From: **peterpeterpeterpeter@gmail.com**

To: Crawley Writers' Group

Sent: 14.02.17, 13:13

Subject: **<no subject>**

Thanks, Mavinder!

I meant just a single word – the instruction is there quite clearly in my email – but I appreciate your prompt response. Are you OK if I just take 'help' for my purposes?

Anyone else ready with their word?

Peter, writer

From: **tom@tomcat.com**

To: keith_sadwicke@techsolutions.co.uk

Sent: 16.02.17, 19:42

Subject: **Fancy a pint of goblin's fingernail or 3 some time?**

Hi Keith

Hope all's well.

Just wondered if you fancied meeting up for an ale some time to discuss the writing game? I'd love to pick your brains about world-building and wordcount discipline...

All the best

Tom

From: **tom@tomcat.com**

To: armory-wargrove.jonathan@nhs_dental-estimates.gov.uk

Sent: 17.02.17, 19:44

Subject: **Fancy a Jagermeister or 5 some time?**

Hi Jon

How you doing? Still sticking it to the man?

Wondered if you fancied catching up for a bevvy or two (and/or a smoke...;)) some time, to discuss matters literary and political?

Very interested to know more about this research you've been looking into (about them looking at us etc.).

Maybe one night this week or next in The Crown?

Tom

From: **JuliaGeeGee@gmail.com**

To: Crawley Writers' Group

Sent: 18.02.17, 14:12

Subject: **Re: Re: Your one-word challenge**

Hi all and many thanks for the challenge @Peter!

My word for you is...

Onwards!

Btw, did we confirm the next meet? I think Keith suggested his on March 13, because he has set himself a personal target of 65,000 words to get done in February (eek!), and a few people were going to double-check diaries? (I have to say not meeting in Feb would work well for me too, as we were hoping to do a bit of minimalist seafront-villa shopping on Menorca – will be nice to have somewhere to retreat from the British winters!) Is that all still OK with everyone? And you especially, Keith?

Do hope so! Very keen to see the place where the giant elf-lordy ones were first conceived!

Julia xx

From: **tom@tomcat.com**

To: Crawley Writers' Group

Sent: 19.02.17, 16:47

Subject: Re: Re: Re: Your one-word challenge

Hi all

Perhaps my word for Peter's interesting challenge should be 'sorry' or 'guilty' or 'sheepish'.

The impression has got about recently – and I can quite see why now – that I am some sort of amatory predator, bent on setting up clandestine liaisons with all the female members of the group, spurred on by a dark romantic masterplan to string them all along at the same time.

I'm very sorry to have given that impression. And I'm very glad to have this opportunity – in an email to the whole group – to clear up the misapprehension.

Let me be clear: I love writing. It's all I really think or feel about. But it is a bitter, solitary business at times, when all you've got to hold out for is the hope of making the shortlist of *The Anglesey Herald's* Tall Tales Competition (my grandmother was Welsh, by the way, so I am eligible; this year's theme: 'The valleys of the heart').

Writing is lonely and, frankly, so am I. I crave companionship and collaboration and the sharing of ideas, and since my muse Marianne departed (another misunderstanding there, alas, though I admit that the photos did seem incriminating), I have been alone – with myself, my disappointments, my aching unrequited literary dreams.

Until, that is, this group came along. At last I found a space to connect and share with like-minded souls who care about writing as much as I do. I was overjoyed, I still am. But in my haste to deepen and cement these new connections, I see now I came on a bit strong.

Meeting once a month wasn't enough for me, and so I started putting out feelers to catch up with people on an individual basis between meets. I began with those where I felt the closest literary connection in terms of thematic and stylistic aspiration; they happened to be female. But – as the lads in the group can testify – I have also reached out to them in the hopes of a meet to tide me over till the next group too.

So: apologies to one and all if my passions appeared misplaced. But what I can make no apology for, of course, is my passion for writing.

And so, finally, Peter, to rise to your challenge. My word for you is...

Story-struck!

See you all soon – March 13th works for me.
Tom

From: **MPranesh@gmail.com**
To: Crawley Writers' Group
Sent: 20.02.17, 03:03
Subject: **Re: Re: Re: Re: Your one-word challenge**

trapped

From: **peterpeterpeterpeter@gmail.com**

To: Crawley Writers' Group

Sent: 23.02.17, 12:12

Subject: **<no subject>**

Hi writers

Thanks to all those who have volunteered a word. Please can I get everyone else's word by the end of the week, as I have a strict window for completing this project, which cannot be allowed to overrun for reasons that are obvious to me.

@Julia: Thank you for 'onwards'. Very you. I will take the liberty of excising the exclamation mark.

@Tom: Ditto yours re '!' Yours is not really a word either as such, of course, and not much of a neologism either, but my brief is to work with what I'm given – to harmonise the unknown – so I'll do my best with it.

@Mavinder: Please no more words! I appreciate your enthusiasm but instructions are important too. I've started with 'help' now, so I'll have to stick to that one.

See you all on March 13, 2017.

Peter, writer

From: **JuliaGeeGee@gmail.com**

To: Crawley Writers' Group

Sent: 24.02.17, 14:17

Subject: **Re: Re: Re: Re: Re: Your one-word challenge**

@Mavinder – Are you all right, darling, or was that just another suggestion for Peter? Sorry for my foolishness if the latter but I just thought I'd double-check. It'd be SO nice to see you at the next group!

Julia x

From: **keith_sadwicke@techsolutions.co.uk**

To: Crawley Writers' Group

Sent: 26.02.17, 02:41

Subject: **Re: Re: Re: Re: Re: Re: Your one-word challenge**

Hi Peter

Here's my word:

Buym"ybööksthèyresœgreâtyouwón'tregrȩtit (traditional Xȩn"dährin greeting)

Or if that's a bit long for you, here's another which I've always loved the sound of: *monetise*

Julia and everyone: yeah, fine to meet at mine on Monday 13th. You can meet Aragorn my pug and see my writing den, or Rivendell, as I call it, with the orc skull in pride of place above my desk.

@Tom, yeah, cool. Let's have an ale sometime. Maybe Jon could join us?

Keith

From: **aliceknowles@mewriter.com**

To: Crawley Writers' Group

Sent: 26.02.17, 18:01

Subject: **Hopeless dreams**

Dear Peter

What an interesting request! I have thought long and hard about what word I should offer you – time I should have been spending on my Sentence, but I can't blame you for that! My first impulse was to submit the word WRITER – just like that, all in capitals. But then I thought that would have been too obvious a choice. So I carried on pondering until another word suddenly popped into my head, a word I've always loved as much for its sound as its meaning, and that word is...

oeuvre

It's beautiful, isn't it? Very difficult for an English person to pronounce properly with that v followed immediately by the rolled r, but always worth an attempt! It means 'body of work', and for me ever to accumulate such a thing is probably just a foolish dream. I should set my sights lower. I should aim to write just one book (or even finish my perishing Sentence) before I shuffle off this mortal coil. And yet I can't help clinging to this wild fantasy that one day there will exist in a library somewhere a row of leather-bound books on a shelf, all with my name printed in gold leaf on the spine, and a librarian will say to a customer, yes indeed, madam, we're lucky enough to possess the complete oeuvre of Alice Knowles.

A girl can dream!

See you all on the 13th.
Alice

From: **aliceknowles@mewriter.com**
To: Crawley Writers' Group
Sent: 26.02.17, 18:13
Subject: **Re: Just a thought, Alice...**

Julia

It was so thoughtful of you to suggest that opening to me. Thank you! And you're right, it is quite intriguing as the beginning of a story. Cats are so straightforward in their desires, aren't they? Sometimes I wish I were a cat! However, it pains me to say this one won't work for my purposes. The Sentence must, I feel, involve a salad – a salad with olives. And possibly a waiter. But no cat, sadly. See you on the 13th.

Alice x

From: **armory-wargrove.jonathan@nhs_dental-estimates.gov.uk**
To: Crawley Writers' Group
Sent: 26.02.17, 23:22
Subject: **Word up!**

Hi everybody,

For the next meeting a word @Pete:
how about 'tosser' (as in someone who tosses or throws something)

Working hard on a new piece and looking forward to the next meeting!

cheers
Jon

Jon Armory-Wargrove
Senior Assessor

This message is sent for and on behalf of the Dental Estimates Board, an NHS Service Provider. It may contain confidential information. If you are not

the intended recipient please inform the sender that you have received the message in error before deleting it. Please do not disclose, copy or distribute information in the email or take any action in reliance on its contents: to do so is strictly prohibited and may be unlawful. Thank you for your cooperation.

From: **blueyblu@blueyonder.com**

To: Crawley Writers' Group

Sent: 28.02.17, 16:12

Subject: **GLOOM**...

...is my word for you, Peter.

The reason is I'm in a very anxious place at the moment but the thought of the next meeting is keeping me going. I normally have a safe space to go – creative visualisation, not real – it's like a sunny country scene with a babbling brook and weeping willows but last time I went there it was GLOOMY and there was a black swan just floating, a dead black swan. It freaked me out but I am turning it into a poem it is just pouring out. So just to warn everyone about my next piece – it is really deep, soul-searching and harrowing.

luv

Blue

From: **armory-wargrove.jonathan@nhs_dental-estimates.gov.uk**

To: tom@tomcat.com

Sent: 28.02.17, 22:32

Subject: **Drinks**

Hi Tom,

Yes, drinks at The Crown could be a goer. Sorry not to say so sooner, but I'm free pretty much any evening over the next couple of weeks.

You strike me as someone who isn't easily taken in by the 'liberal' consensus so I think a political discussion would be interesting.

catch you soon

Jon

PS How do you feel about Pete? He really burns my butt tbh.

Jon Armory-Wargrove
Senior Assessor

This message is sent for and on behalf of the Dental Estimates Board, an NHS Service Provider. It may contain confidential information. If you are not the intended recipient please inform the sender that you have received the message in error before deleting it. Please do not disclose, copy or distribute information in the email or take any action in reliance on its contents: to do so is strictly prohibited and may be unlawful. Thank you for your cooperation.

From: **armory-wargrove.jonathan@nhs_dental-estimates.gov.uk**

To: keith_sadwicke@techsolutions.co.uk

Sent: 01.03.17, 14:38

Subject: **Comic and Fantasy Convention etc.**

Hi Keith,

You're on for the Comic and Fantasy Convention! It would do me good to get out and broaden my horizons a bit. You never know, I might meet an editor I can pitch my stories to!

I'll give you the money for the ticket – I don't mind wearing the T-shirt at all!

Tom's asked again about that beer at The Crown next week; maybe we could go together?

cheers

Jon

Jon Armory-Wargrove
Senior Assessor

This message is sent for and on behalf of the Dental Estimates Board, an NHS Service Provider. It may contain confidential information. If you are not the intended recipient please inform the sender that you have received the message in error before deleting it. Please do not disclose, copy or distribute information in the email or take any action in reliance on its contents: to do so is strictly prohibited and may be unlawful. Thank you for your cooperation.

From: **aliceknowles@mewriter.com**

To: Crawley Writers' Group

Sent: 05.03.17, 11:03

Subject: **The Sentence. I have it. Here it is.**

Friends. All of you. Listen. Something is happening. It started this morning, early, as I was waking from a silent, empty dream. I felt this freedom, unbelievable freedom, and trembling, as if day was finally breaking after a six-month Arctic winter night. I saw ice crystals cracking in the amber dawn, and felt the chill bonds of my stifled heart start to melt. Words, now thawed, tumbled freely through my blood. My voice, numbed with fear for so long, had returned. The Sentence, that frozen echo of countless abortive efforts, The Sentence that has lain inert and dead within me all these weeks, is *alive*. I felt it stir and then, just now, I caught it as it rushed through my hands like snowmelt. The Sentence. I've written it down for you. For each of you. For all of you. Here it is

From: **peterpeterpeterpeter@gmail.com**

To: Crawley Writers' Group

Sent: 05.03.17, 12:12

Subject: **<no subject>**

Alice

OK WHERE IS IT?

Peter, writer

From: **keith_sadwicke@techsolutions.co.uk**

To: armory-wargrove.jonathan@nhs–dental-estimates.gov.uk

Sent: 07.03.17, 04:56

Subject: **Cool man Armoury War-Graves**

Hey Jon

Nice seeing you last night at The Crown. Strange that Tom didn't turn up, isn't it, considering he was the organiser. Abducted by aliens d'you reckon? Or maybe by that mad ex of his, Marianne? That text he sent was very confusing.

Anyways, great to gossip as ever. Your inside knowledge about CIA/GCHQ eavesdropping on our lives is a real mindf**k. The stuff released by Wikileaks isn't even half the story, if what you say is right. Can they really spy on us through our devices?? I'm starting to get jittery just thinking about some of the internet searches I've done recently (all for research, obv!).

See you at the next group night.

Keith

From: **armory-wargrove.jonathan@nhs-dental-estimates.gov.uk**

To: keith_sadwicke@techsolutions.co.uk

Sent: 08.03.17, 17:35

Subject: **Top night out!**

Hi Keith,

Yep, a very agreeable night, glad you enjoyed it too.

Shame Tom was a no show – I thought I saw him in the wine bar on West Street on my way home but can't be sure. It was singles night so I doubt he was there with his ex!

Whatever. We had a good time. It's nice to meet someone with an open mind who is willing to listen – just hope I didn't go on too much!

Wikileaks is a smokescreen, believe me. I had a pretty high profile in the UFO research community before I realised how deep it all went so my 'cover' is blown, so to speak. I don't wish to be melodramatic but carrying on with my investigations means putting my head above the parapet every single day.

If *you* are going to get into this I'd seriously advise you to be very wary, not just about your online searches but even who you talk to. Word to the wise.

I should get a chance to start reading your synopsis tonight – tomorrow at the latest.

See you at the meeting. More beer soon?

Jon

Jon Armory-Wargrove
Senior Assessor

This message is sent for and on behalf of the Dental Estimates Board, an NHS Service Provider. It may contain confidential information. If you are not the intended recipient please inform the sender that you have received the message in error before deleting it. Please do not disclose, copy or distribute information in the email or take any action in reliance on its contents: to do so is strictly prohibited and may be unlawful. Thank you for your cooperation.

From: **tom@tomcat.com**

To: armory-wargrove.jonathan@nhs–dental-estimates.gov.uk; keith_sadwicke@techsolutions.co.uk

Sent: 09.03.17, 10:11

Subject: **Sorry about the other night**

Hi lads

Just wanted to say sorry that I didn't make it to our drink in

The Crown. I'd been really looking forward to it – and especially to hearing your thoughts on the extraordinary (extraordinarily irritating) phenomenon that is Peter, writer. Is he an alien perhaps, Jon? Or a goblin in disguise, Keith? I think the nation deserves an answer.

Anyway, as red-blooded men you'll appreciate my excuse. I've been having a bit of a flirty chatty thing with Jerry, one of the staff at West Green Library – just shooting the breeze across the shelves, wondering if she'd ever let that bun down, that sort of thing. So on Tuesday I was in there just before closing doing a bit of research on Victorian astrology (for a new novella thing I'm attempting) when I noticed Jerry seemed rather upset about something. Turns out there are redundancies in the offing... Well, a problem shared and all that, so I chivalrously lent a shoulder, and before you knew it we were sharing a bottle of Pinot Grigio over at Cava Cava in West Street...

So sorry I missed you both, but let's just say that I fancy the whole clichéd librarian fantasy thing won't even begin to do justice to the reality... Will pop in there again tomorrow to see if Jerry is able to stamp my ticket, so to speak.

See you at group (unless I'm, ah, booked up again...)

Tom

From: **JuliaGeeGee@gmail.com**
To: Crawley Writers' Group
Sent: 12.03.17, 13:19
Subject: **Viva La Sentence!**

Hi Alice

So glad The Sentence is coming along!

Will you be performing it tomorrow night? Vv exciting!!

Julia x

From: **MPranesh@gmail.com**
To: Crawley Writers' Group
Sent: 14.03.17, 03:57
Subject: **Sorry I didn't make it**

Sorry everyone. I wish I could have made it but my life's been a real shitstorm lately. I can't go into details but just so you know, things are better now. I've made some decisions. Here is my manifesto:

I will not be dominated by fear.
I will not live forever in the shadows.
I will face up to my obsessions.
I WILL definitely make the next meeting.

Mavinder

From: **JuliaGeeGee@gmail.com**

To: Crawley Writers' Group

Sent: 15.03.17, 14:34

Subject: **Such, such joys!! xx**

Hi all

Wowsers! What an absolutely stonking night!

Peter doing poetry! Jon singing! Alice revealing the main verb of her Sentence! Blue's dead rodent impression! The extraordinary Hobbit-themed decor of Keith's wonderfully intimate pied-a-terre!

Once again I'm in awe of you all. What a joy to create together!

Julia x

PS Sorry for brevity – I've got a meeting in town with an agent who wants to talk through my synopsis!!

PPS Go Mavinder! I do so love a good manifesto! We are all rooting for you, darling!

From: **peterpeterpeterpeter@gmail.com**

To: Crawley Writers' Group

Sent: 16.03.17, 12:12

Subject: **<no subject>**

Hello everyone

Thank you, Keith, for hosting the group. I will bring some antibacterial hand gel next time.

Many of you asked for a copy of the poem I composed and read, based on the words you supplied me. Here it is…

Julia, our mother
Chirping in her nest
'Onwards'! Her cry
'Let's all do our best!'
Monetise! say the cash-till eyes
Of Keith, the wordcount-whore
Of fame and cash and readers' clicks
Our kid bruvva just wants more
Never been seen, our aunt Mavinder
She's the one that got away
Just need my help, mum's secret wish,
So you'll come home to us one day??
Grandpa Jon, he's been round the block
He's done some shit, he's seen some things
With an eye in the sky and a soul wrapped in foil
He shoots at windmills with alien wings.

(**Tosser**)

All is **gloom** and doom in blue Blue's world

In the teenage bedroom of her heart

Like Alice's **oeuvre**, this sister's soul

Is a creation that's yet to start

What does mum see in stepfather Tom

The **story-struck** Jack the lad

There's many a peruse behind his apercus

But he'll never be our dad!!!

Dying to write, writing to breathe

Peter, writer, runt of the hive

Sibling, grandpa, mother, lover

I hate you all. (You keep me alive)

And that is all from me at this time

Peter, writer

From: **aliceknowles@mewriter.com**

To: Crawley Writers' Group

Sent: 18.03.17, 09:45

Subject: **EMBARRASSED!**

Fellow WRITERS.

Great to see everyone at the group. Thanks for hosting, Keith. I'm impressed at how you can work in that crowded, dim space and also with music playing. I have to have complete silence and an empty desk in order to create.

Julia, exciting news about your agent wanting to discuss your synopsis! Do please let us know how it goes.

Sorry, by the way, everyone, for the long radio silence following *that* email. I almost didn't make it to the group, though I'm glad I did in the end. You're all such a support. As I said on the night, I realise the email must have seemed very strange, what with all the build-up and then no end product. It was so embarrassing. You see I had it, The Sentence, in all its glory, burning before my eyes in letters ten feet high, and it was glorious to behold. But stupid me! I didn't write it down. Instead I wrote that stupid email, all that childish, sentimental stuff about ice crystals cracking in the amber dawn, and I was going to end with, you know, the thing itself. But by the time I'd composed the email, the bloody Sentence had of course entirely vanished from my mind. I know. So stupid. Anyway, I was devastated. And in my panic and despair, I hit 'send', and the email went off without The Sentence.

I was mortified. I wanted to crawl under a rock and disappear for a year, maybe two. But as you all saw, I did the brave thing and went along to the group. I even revealed the main verb of The Sentence – the only part of it I managed to salvage after several hours of meditation. Which is ironic of course, since the verb happened to be *salvage*. Now all I need to do is to remember the rest of it...

Love you all

Alice

From: **keith_sadwicke@techsolutions.co.uk**
To: Crawley Writers' Group
Sent: 19.03.17, 02:09
Subject: **Cool night**

Hey all

What a cool night at mine, and cheers for making it all the way out to Maidenbower. Mavinder, sad for you you couldn't be there. Next time, yo? As for the rest of you, now you've seen the alchemist's lair, the dream factory where I first invented legendary characters like Idris, Odos, Bink Hallia and the Ilf. Even I get a little shiver sometimes when I think of all the amazing thoughts I've had, the lightyears I've travelled and the lives I've inhabited in that little space. And as a bonus you got to meet Aragorn my pug. Ain't he the sweetest? Pete, I'm sorry about him rubbing his groin on your leg while you were reading out your poem. I know Jon laughed, and he shouldn't have, but you've got to admit it was kind of funny. As the Otherlings say, your poem was *th'edögsbôlóx*, which is maybe the point Aragorn was trying to make.

Keith

From: **blueyblu@blueyonder.com**
To: Crawley Writers' Group
Sent: 19.03.17, 10:48
Subject: **OMG my bad**

Dear all, it was a good night and I loved Keith's place – all that stuff! It's a bit like my flat tho' I've got more skulls!!

BUT what I really want to do is explain about my thing...

When Alice announced her WORD I was so happy for her I just let rip when it was my turn, improvising a poem based on her WORD – only I thought she said SANDWICH not SALVAGE – no wonder everyone looked so confused!

My head was in a bit of a strange place that night, I was a bit spaced. Personal stuff. I really hope I haven't upset anyone, especially you, lovely Alice!!

Blue xx

PS I still think the image of a rat sandwich is good tho'!!!

PPS my skulls aren't real I hasten to add lol

From: **armory-wargrove.jonathan@nhs_dental-estimates.gov.uk**

To: Crawley Writers' Group

Sent: 19.03.17, 11:42

Subject: **Good meeting!**

Hi folks,

I have to agree it was a very enjoyable meeting. Keith's gaff certainly was something – very compact.

The 'artefacts' everywhere made Keith's world come to life – it's amazing what you can do with papier mache, balsa wood and a dab of acrylic paint. Btw Keith, sorry again for squashing your Wyvern King's Hammer of Smiting, but I toppled over your dog which was making a beeline for Pete's leg. Ha ha!

Don't worry, Blue – your poem was a blast and you certainly weren't the only one a bit spaced out! I'm ashamed to say I'd shared a 'jazzman's Woodbine' and a few pints of real ale before the meeting. I'd met up with Richard, the bassist from my old band. Hadn't seen him for 12 years, longer maybe. Hence the singing – some of our old songs. Probably slightly slurred but the old voice still good, I hope!

Long story short, the whole band is meeting up for the first time in decades (except for Jason, RIP*)!

all the best

Jon

* See Appendix, page 357

This message is sent for and on behalf of the Dental Estimates Board, an NHS Service Provider. It may contain confidential information. If you are not the intended recipient please inform the sender that you have received the message in error before deleting it. Please do not disclose, copy or distribute information in the email or take any action in reliance on its contents: to do so is strictly prohibited and may be unlawful. Thank you for your cooperation.

From: **tom@tomcat.com**

To: JuliaGeeGee@gmail.com

Sent: 21.03.17, 20:21

Subject: **Well done – and good luck!**

Hi Julia

Wonderful to hear that you've got some interest from an agent! Your story has the makings of a real page-turner to me and you thoroughly deserve to see your name in print! We all HATE you and wish you were dead!!! (Joking.)

It's a real rush, isn't it, the first time something you've created, that's very personal to you, gets the attention of the 'real world' – and a real agent no less!

I've had a few skirmishes with publishers and agents and editors in my time, of course – my first comic novella, *Eyes Front! (And Back!)*, about a Victorian school for time travellers, got lots of interest from a local publisher. In the end the only reason we didn't go ahead were the upfront printing fees, which I just couldn't afford at the time.

If all goes well you might get some press interest too. Around the time of my Wivenhoe Flash Fiction Festival success, the local papers were constantly on my back, and I learned a few strategies for turning all the attention to best advantage.

Anyway, I'm rambling now so I'll stop. All I really meant to say was well done, and that I'd be delighted to lend an ear or a spot of hopefully wise counsel if you're ever in need of a second opinion, publishing wise.

All the best

Tom

From: **peterpeterpeterpeter@gmail.com**

To: Crawley Writers' Group

Sent: 23.03.17, 12:12

Subject: **<no subject>**

Julia

Just a note to say congratulations on securing the interest of an agent. Judging from other people's emails, this seems to be the appropriate sentiment to evince at this point.

I do wonder, though, whether publication is quite in the spirit of what we are trying to achieve here? My understanding was that the group is a forum for creative expression rather than a focus group for commercial exploitation? But I could be wrong. Or at least others may so think.

Best regards

Peter, writer

PS Please can we think about scheduling the next group quite rapidly now, please? According to my spreadsheet the average elapsed time between meets has been increasing at a rate of over 7% for two months now. I only mention this because I imagine this development might be anxious-making for some.

From: **aliceknowles@mewriter.com**
To: Crawley Writers' Group
Sent: 25.03.17, 09:39
Subject: **We're on tenters!!**

Hello everyone

Julia, do drop us a line and let us know how your meeting went with the agent. We're all on tenterhooks here...

I must take issue with Peter when he says that the group should be about creative expression, not commercial publication. Can't it be about both? Publication, for me, would be an absolute dream come true. Just the thought of strangers

I've never met reading my prose gives me the shivers. (For me, success these days is putting down a subclause – even if most of it subsequently gets deleted!) I'm sure even you, Peter, in your avant garde ivory specularium, must secretly relish the idea of reaching a wider audience.

One other silly little thing, but it's been sort of on my mind. Blue, I was in the high street yesterday taking Tiggy to the vet when I saw you. I would have stopped to say hello, only you seemed to be in a very deep and quite heated conversation with someone – a girl or boy, I couldn't really be sure – who I didn't know. Anyway, I lost my nerve and didn't say anything. I hope you don't think I was being rude.

See you all at the next meeting.

Alice

From: **keith_sadwicke@techsolutions.co.uk**

To: Crawley Writers' Group

Sent: 26.03.16, 02:08

Subject: **Nice work if you can get it**

Hi all

Congrats, Julia. Cool that you're meeting with an agent, though I don't personally have much time for them. I approached two or three in the early part of my career, because everyone told me I had to, but to be honest I found them a bit up their own åâršęž, as the Greenskians are wont to say, and I just thought, you know what, why am I crawling to these people? I can do this myself. I know my fans, because I used to be a fan myself. I know what makes them tick and what ticks their boxes. Why should I hand over 15% of my earnings to some upper-middle-class woman – they're almost always women – who knows about as much about what young fantasy fans are reading these days as my pug, and whose only asset is that she's got the editor at Doubleday on speed-dial?? I don't need agents, and I don't need publishers either. As far as I can see, they're a dying breed, part of an outdated model of publishing that's had its day. Having said all that, let us know how it went.

Keith

3.

SACRÉ BLEU!

From: **JuliaGeeGee@gmail.com**

To: Crawley Writers' Group

Sent: 27.03.17, 16:56

Subject: **Back from the Big Smoke**

Hi all

Thank you @Alice, @Keith, @Peter and @Tom for your kind words about my meeting with the agent.

I'm sorry not to have had a chance to fill you all in sooner about how it went – I've been away filming for the next series of *Midsomer Murders*! Very exciting – I can't give too much away except that my character – who has seven or eight speaking lines – is notorious in the village as a black-widow cougar type who may or may not have a reason to wish ill on Sir Martin, the retired industrial chemist. But enough! I've said too much already! You'll all just to have to tune in to find out what happens next... (Does anyone know what a milf is by the way? I was too shy to ask...)

Before that, of course, I had my coffee with the agent, Jill, in the Big Smoke. Absolutely delightful she is too – turns out we've even used the same people for our spa/sauna extension, how funny is that??

Anyway, it was very much a working meeting. To be honest, I wouldn't have even dared send my writing to Jill if it wasn't for Ilyana, our mutual ashtanga yoga friend – but Jill says she's very interested in the story and the chapters I've done so far and thinks the story has lots of potential. What the market loves at the moment, she said, is 'quality commercial fiction' – a strong storyline, strong women characters, and a juicy issue that the reading-group crowd can really get their teeth into.

'What's my issue, then?' I asked, mystified. 'Oh, that whole thing about whether success is about talent or just about looks and who you know,' said Jill. I was intrigued and secretly vv chuffed – I hadn't even realised I'd got any meaty issues in my story at all! (But of course now that I know that this angle plays well, I'll need to make more of it in the rest of the draft.)

So there you are. After a brief but fascinating discussion of the various merits of anti-ageing potions, and a daring digression into the pros and cons of 'the cosmetic option', we went our separate ways. Not a deal of course, or anything like that, but certainly very encouraging and plenty of inspiration to feed into my writing.

So thanks again, one and all, for all your kind words. I wouldn't have got this far without all of you – and I fervently wish all your writing dreams come true. @Tom – I'm forwarding the email you sent me on 21.03.17, which I'm sure you meant to send to the rest of the group anyway? It'd certainly be fascinating to talk publishing some time – as you'll all see below, Tom has kindly offered to share the benefits of his experiences with the rest of us. Perhaps we could spend some time talking about this as a group next time?

Lots of love to you all – and happy writing!!

Julia

PS How about a meet on April 1? (Not a joke!!) Or is that too short notice? I can host if no one else can??

From: tom@tomcat.com
To: Crawley Writers' Group
Sent: 27.03.17, 17:01
Subject: **Let's do mine**

Hi Julia, Hi all

Thanks very much for forwarding my email to the rest of the group, Julia – yes, that was my original intention of course. Fat-finger syndrome got the better of me again, no doubt. And well done again! It sounds like a very promising meeting. Fingers crossed! (If I can cross such fat ones, that is!)

I'm very happy to host the next group at my place on 1.4.17 – map and deets to follow. It's one of the flats converted from the old convent. It's called 'The Penthouse' but don't let this rather grandiose name deceive you, it's really a very modest contemporary live:work:space loft thing. Anyway, we'll be lovely and smug and it'll be a pleasure to have you all.

And now I shall return to editing my own opus, always reminding myself that the road to hell is paved with adverbs...

See you soonly!

Tom

From: **aliceknowles@mewriter.com**
To: Crawley Writers' Group
Sent: 02.04.17, 11:03
Subject: **Feeling positive**

A really positive meeting last night, wasn't it? I feel, as so often after our meetings, that I have been given the strength and courage to slay my writing demons and really crack on with my novel. I am drinking from a well of creativity at the moment, and the more I drink the more there seems to be! I feel so invigorated. Thank you, everyone. I hope this time that I can hold onto all this positive energy and not let it slip through my fingers as the familiar voices of self-doubt start creeping in.

Tom, your 'Penthouse' is quite something. Apologies for arriving early – whenever I go somewhere new I'm always nervous and allow too much time, assuming I will get lost. I suppose it did give you a chance to show me around – I love that you've kept the charm of the old Victorian architecture while carving out a space that meets your domestic and creative needs. The 'art' posters in your bedroom were not really to my taste, though I acknowledge the courage and imagination that must have gone into creating them, both for photographer and model. Funny to think the place used to be a convent!

Julia, thanks for bringing us all up to speed on your exciting news – both on the acting and writing fronts. I honestly had no idea what a milf is. Thank you, Keith, for enlightening us at the meeting! It's interesting what your agent said (re WRITING) about the need for a 'juicy issue' for the reading-group community. It makes me wonder what the 'juicy issue' in my book is. Perhaps it's about how to hold onto the child within as we mature into grown-ups. I can imagine that sparking some interesting debates in reading groups – *if* the book ever gets written of course...

Alice

From: **peterpeterpeterpeter@gmail.com**

To: Crawley Writers' Group

Sent: 02.04.17, 12:12

Subject: **<no subject>**

@Tom – I hereby acknowledge your efforts in hosting the most recent group. I felt that the hygiene standards were adequate and, while not extensive in range, the choice of snacks achieved at least the minimum quality threshold.

@Julia – I express appropriate sentiments at the news of your successful meeting with the agent. I hope that you are not asked to trade on your sexuality to achieve your literary ends, as you seem to have to do in your acting.

@all – Many of you have expressed surprise at my apparently very conventional/conventual offering – a short story, you will recall (and here I recap for Mavinder's benefit), relating the experiences of a girl raised by nuns who must learn to master her feelings of mortal panic at the hands of carers who see pain only as a gift to offer up to God.

Allergies, phobias and neuroses – while very real to the girl – are either ignored by the nuns, or else seen as an occasion to earn God's grace – in which case the greater the pain, the greater the spiritual gain. So great is the girl's anguish that, by the end of the story, she is moved to attempt her own crucifixion as a plea for help to the medical and mental health authorities.

As she is at last led away for sectioning, momentarily relieved that she has been rescued from her infernal agony, the story ends with a close-up on the ward's head psychiatrist. As we learn that he has a face like a screaming skull (Golgotha) and has for unspecified reasons earned himself the nickname 'Herod', we realise that the girl may only have swapped one hell for another.

So far, so conventional. Except perhaps that the girl is me, and the convent in question is now Tom's live:work:space.

And that is all from me at this time.

Peter, writer

From: **keith_sadwicke@techsolutions.co.uk**
To: Crawley Writers' Group
Sent: 06.04.17, 02:56
Subject: **Great sesh**

Löñgtįmėńøspęêk – traditional greeting of the notoriously taciturn Forest People of Elberon.

I am so fired up since our last meeting, working really hard on the third draft of Vol 7. Still can't decide whether Idris's Cohorts of Myce should be burned in the Kaldron of Fyre or drowned in the Great Soop of Ministron. The good news is I'm still on course to complete the final draft by the end of

July, so you'll all be able to buy it in August – mates' rates of course.

Quick note to Jon: I've now bought myself a stand at Comic Fantasy Con for the full three days, so we're all set for 26–28 May, yeah? No need to do any prep, but if you can just learn yourself a smattering of Xęn"dährin that would really help when we're trying to sweet-talk the fans and the curious. Just a few basics like: *Hello*, *Thank you*, and *Buy the full set for a 5% discount because these books will change your life*. That sort of thing. By the way, sorry for bamboozling you with the lingo when we met up that night at The Crown. I wasn't aware you didn't know a single word at that point. But no doubt you've boned up a bit since then.

I thought the group the other night was brill. Cool pad, Tom. Shame I never got to see the posters in the bedroom that Alice mentioned. You should have given all of us a tour, mate, don't keep that sort of thing to yourself. Liked your story btw, Tom, about the bloke back from university who gets seduced by his girlfriend's mum, Mrs Roberts. Speaking of cougars, Julia, I can't say I've ever watched *Midsomer Murders*, but obviously I will now. Let us know when the show is going out.

Blue, I'm still feeling kind of sad thinking about your poem about the crumbling old bench by the river where the old man with cancer sits for the final time before drowning himself. And the way you wrote it from the point of view of the bench. That was pretty cool.

OK, gotta go. *Xẹn"gol-yah*, my friends.

Keith

From: **MPranesh@gmail.com**

To: Crawley Writers' Group

Sent: 06.04.17, 03:01

Subject: **I was going to come but...**

When I was on the bus I suddenly realised I'd forgotten to write down Tom's address. I was still sure I'd find it though because I've been past the old convent dozens of times, but it turned out that was the Old Conventionals rugby club. So I was completely in the wrong part of town and to top it all my phone died and I couldn't even call you. So far my manifesto pledges aren't working out very well! Sorry to all and next time I'll staple the address to my head.

Mavinder

From: **peterpeterpeterpeter@gmail.com**

To: Crawley Writers' Group

Sent: 07.04.17, 12:12

Subject: **<no subject>**

Dear Peter

I must express some surprise at the reaction of your Writers' Group.

There you were, pouring out your heart and soul, expressing your innermost fears and pains, and no one seems bothered enough even to acknowledge your testimony.

I thought you told me they were your friends? I thought you said you had managed at last to forge some sort of connection with these people?

It's enough to make you want to return to your solitary ways, isn't it? It's tempting just to give up, isn't it, chuck it all in? But remember we said we wouldn't go back to that place, no matter what.

Yours

pETER

From: **JuliaGeeGee@gmail.com**

To: Crawley Writers' Group

Sent: 07.04.17, 17:12

Subject: **We're here for you, darling!**

Hi Peter

I'm sorry not to have replied to your email sooner. After the last meet, hubby surprised me with a gift of a week's intensive plot and structure workshopping at the Arvon Foundation! So wonderful just to immerse oneself totally in the joys and challenges of *storytelling*, without having to worry about briefing the tradespeople for a whole week!

And then, after that, I was straight back to filming on *MM* – it seems my character has caused a bit of a stir, and she may end up as a bit of a potential love interest for DCI John Barnaby! (I have a feeling what you might say to this, Peter – will come back to this later.)

But first off I wanted to say that we *do* feel your pain, Peter. We all do, and we all care about you. If I understand you correctly, the story you read was actually a thinly disguised biographical account of your younger years? In which case I can only echo what I'm sure everyone else must be feeling – complete sympathy for the agonies you went through, darling. Please know that we are there for you and support all your literary endeavours, especially if they are helping you to process some of this terrible pain you must have experienced. If the others haven't mentioned it yet, I think it's only a reaction of collective shock, a feeling of inadequacy in not knowing quite how to respond to what you have shared with us. You have experienced horrors that the rest of us can only guess at, my dear, and we are still struggling to find ways to express our sympathy and support.

(Although I was a teensy bit peeved, I must admit – and just in the spirit of full disclosure, which is of course very much your thing – at your remark about me using sex to further my acting career. I know your way is to provoke and to challenge, but I must say that this sort of comment isn't really fair or accurate. I am an *actor*, I interpret the roles that are put in front of me. Of course, physically, you need to look vaguely the part, but there is a whole world of technique and craft that goes into every performance, whether you're playing the dowdy vicar's wife (a role I also auditioned for, incidentally, and which originally had about 30 more speaking lines) or my 'local mature sex goddess' role (screenwriter's words, not mine of course).)

Anyway ignore me – just wanted to get that off my chest. The main thing, dear Peter, is that you know we are here for you. *You are our friend*, and we want to help and support you any which way we can.

Do drop us all a line soon and let us know how you're doing.

Julia xx

From: **aliceknowles@mewriter.com**
To: Crawley Writers' Group
Sent: 07.04.17, 18:03
Subject: **Brave**

Peter

It was incredibly brave of you to return to the scene of your awful childhood, and even more so to read out your story in that place. School desks and chairs may have been replaced by leather armchairs and recliners. Scuffed parquet may have disappeared beneath oak-effect laminate flooring. And the blackboard may now be a flatscreen TV. Yet I am sure none of that diminished the trauma of sitting there in that room, and all the horrid memories that must have stirred.

I am full of admiration for you, Peter. And, despite the distress it must have caused you, I do see something very positive in all this: it proves that you are a true WRITER, able to transubstantiate your pain into art. The nuns saw your agony as a gift to offer up to God. Well, they may have been right in a sense – except that this 'gift' in its new form is a story, and it is our good fortune that we were able to listen to it and be moved, in my case to tears, by its emotional and artistic truth and what it says about your indefatigable spirit.

Whatever you were, Peter, you are a WRITER now, as are we all. And with our pens we will slay the demons that stain our memories by doing the one thing only a WRITER can: putting those memories down in words.

Alice

From: **keith_sadwicke@techsolutions.co.uk**

To: Crawley Writers' Group

Sent: 08.04.17, 02:56

Subject: **Just asking**

Were you a girl then, Pete? Sorry, mate, I don't want to pry or anything, I'm just really interested to know if you had an operation or something?

Cheers

K

From: **blueyblu@blueyonder.com**

To: Crawley Writers' Group

Sent: 08.04.17, 17:08

Subject: **pAin**

Hi guys,

Oh poor, dear Peter! I never knew you carried such pain and so sorry we didn't connect and empathise especially me who knows the burden of inner turmoil and how difficult it can be to open up. You always seem so in control but that can mask an abyss of anxiety. If you want to talk I'm here for you.

@everyone else: let's not blame ourselves but share our feelings and respect each other's triggers.

Peace
Blue

PS I loved your photos, Tom! I wandered in to your bedroom by mistake, looking for the loo. Pretty full on but black and white is very artistic isn't it. The one over the bed reminded me of when I used to do yoga I could get my feet behind my neck as well. Not while doing that though!

From: **armory-wargrove.jonathan@nhs_dental-estimates.gov.uk**
To: Crawley Writers' Group
Sent: 10.04.17, 23:16
Subject: **Badger reset (ffs)**

Yo,

Firstly, a point on my contribution. A strong character is not necessarily a Bad Thing. Karnak the badger is a powerful and WISE leader, not a Kim Jong Un type figure as everyone seemed to assume. He has to make tough decisions: without him the simple field mice would be lost to the New Weasel

Order. It's in Plato ffs, the philosopher king. I'm touching on the Eternal Gnosis here – liberal blinkers off, please!

Slight misinterpretation of my story aside, it was a good session, though Pete has retrospectively put a downer on it. Sorry to be unsympathetic, Pete, but delivering your story in a slow, barely audible monotone conveyed nothing more than a slightly pissed-off indifference. You seemed bored, and frankly so was I. I'm guessing that you'd looked into Tom's pad having been a convent or whatever (though not for 50 years I think) and wrote the story in advance as one of your usual meta-fictional exercises. Let's face it, you've got form for this sort of thing.

@Blue: I hear what you're saying but we are not a therapy group; we all have issues but can people just SAY WHAT THEY MEAN!

Jon

PS Keith, got your 57 pages (!) of 'briefing notes' for the Comic Fantasy Con thing. I'll try and read through them but the Audit is dragging on due to alleged 'irregularities in accounting procedures'. A quick meeting in the pub might be easier and more convivial!

J

Jon Armory-Wargrove
Senior Assessor

This message is sent for and on behalf of the Dental Estimates Board, an NHS Service Provider. It may contain confidential information. If you are not

the intended recipient please inform the sender that you have received the message in error before deleting it. Please do not disclose, copy or distribute information in the email or take any action in reliance on its contents: to do so is strictly prohibited and may be unlawful. Thank you for your cooperation.

From: **peterpeterpeterpeter@gmail.com**

To: Crawley Writers' Group

Sent: 12.04.17, 12:12

Subject: **<no subject>**

Retrospective downer

Great sesh, me old mates.

Sweet-talk the fans.

Cool pad, Tom.

Speaking of cougars, Julia

The old man with cancer

The fans and the curious (5% discount)

The old man with cancer was pretty cool.

Chuck it all in? We're here for you. Darling

No need to worry about briefing the tradespeople!

We do feel your pain, darling

We all do, darling (5% off) (cancer is cool)

Thinly disguised mature sex goddess

(not my words, darling)

Terrible pain, darling.

Collective shock, a feeling of inadequacy (Pilates! the pool!)

An abyss of anxiety beneath your mask of self-control
(But let's not beat ourselves up) (cheap cancer for the fans)

Just wanted to get that off my chest.

Your incredibly brave flat-screen TV
Oak-effect laminate flooring transubstantiates pain into art
None of the trauma diminished, I'm sure (*darling*)

You are our friend (I am an *actor*)
Badger reset: liberal blinkers off, please!

With our Pilates and our real ale (and our erotic prints)
We will slay the demons that stain our memories.
Were you a bird then, mate? (I don't want to pry) (I am an actor)
We all have issues, *mate*

You seemed bored, and frankly so was I.
Eternal gnosis ffs! I was only looking for the loo.
We feel your pain. (Though I was a teensy bit peeved)
Cancer is 5% off.

OK, gotta go.

Peter, writer

Please note: to be the intended recipient of this message is prohibited.

From: **tom@tomcat.com**

To: blueyblu@blueyonder.com

Sent: 12.04.17, 21:56

Subject: **Hey you**

Hey Bluesy Blue

Just wanted to drop you a line to say how much I enjoyed our chat. It was lovely to have you round again. And I'm so pleased you really get my pics! People think they're just cheap erotica, but really it takes incredible artistry and vision to get the naked form to so resemble an aubergine.

It was so moving to hear you reading some more of your poetry. I can still hear those lines now, just as you read them, your lovely voice struggling not to break:

And so I enter the tunnel of your despair
You gouge out my eyes, you burn my hair

I have honestly never ever thought of a carwash in that way!! You have such a unique vision – there's more creativity in your jet-black accent nail than in a thousand Taylor Swifts or Jeanette Wintersons!

Might stop by the shop tomorrow. Maybe we could go for a hummus-and-pepper pitta over at the Veggie-Might Café? (And how funny that that's both our favourite place to eat!)

Keep writing, keep feeling, Bluebird – you have a gift for us all. Remember that when you create, it's your job to have mind-blowing, irresponsible, condomless sex with whatever idea it is you're writing about!!

Tomcat x

From: **peterpeterpeterpeter@gmail.com**

To: Crawley Writers' Group

Sent: 13.04.17, 12:12

Subject: **<no subject>**

Please can we confirm the date and venue of the next meet-up?

According to my spreadsheet, and on the balance of suitability (Jon and Blue being our only other options), we are probably due a visit to Alice's residence next. But she is of course welcome to betray our expectations.

Peter, writer.

From: **aliceknowles@mewriter.com**

To: Crawley Writers' Group

Sent: 15.04.17, 11:03

Subject: **Heavenly Host**

Shall I host? Of course I shall host! For who would dare betray the expectations of Peter's spreadsheet? Not I! But in all seriousness, I'd be proud to. I propose we meet this coming Thursday, 20 April. I hope everyone can make it because this might possibly be the most writerly thing I've ever done. I can already see it spawning a series of blog posts: how to host the perfect writers' group.

As you can see, I'm excited. I'm also nervous. It has to be right, you see. It has to be perfect. As host, I shall have to 'chair' the meeting, as that seems to be the tradition that's developed. That means deciding who reads first, and for how long, and then sort of leading the discussion that follows. Oh, the power! There will have to be rules. If it's to be perfect, you'll all have to play your part.

So, the rules...

1. Please don't make too much noise when you come in. This applies especially to you, Tom, with your rather loud, hail-fellow-well-met bonhomie. Tiggy has a nervous disposition (as do I) and she's not used to visitors (nor am I, as you can probably tell!).

2. This one's specifically for Peter. Please would you mind not doing that thing with your eyes as you inspect my house? I know you don't mean to, and I'm probably misinterpreting, but, as another member of the group once confided to me, it does rather leave one with the sense of being judged.

btw: my front room is *small*. Barely enough room to swing a... *hideous* expression, but you know what I mean. Anyway, just a warning: we may have to bunch up a little.

3. What can 3 be? There has to be a 3. Ah yes. Be respectful. Of each other I mean. Let's listen with open minds and hearts, knowing first-hand the blood, sweat and tears* that have gone into the crafting of our work, not to mention the courage it takes to bare our souls to each other.

* except maybe Keith who seems to find this WRITING lark enviably easy.

Finally: Snacks. tbh this is the part that makes me most nervous of all. I tell you now I'm not going to do a Julia, providing trays of mini crostini topped with crab, lime and chilli, nor will I try to emulate Peter's pickled ewe's milk cheese and ugli fruit confection, nor Tom's liqueur-laced coconut macaroons (delicious but certainly not aphrodisiac – sorry, Tom!). Like Keith, I shall be offering a selection of shop-bought crisps and nuts (though possibly not Cheesy Wotsits). I hope no one's disappointed. My main fear is that if I add to the stress I'm already feeling by trying to compete with my predecessors on the snack front, it may just bring on my psoriasis.

Alice

Venture Inn
Comfort at a VERY Low price
BOOKING CONFIRMATION
Reference No. 174839650

Booking details
Booking Date: 15/4/2017
Booker Name: Mr Keith Sadwicke
Booker Contact: +44 7*** *****133
Booker Email: keith_sadwicke@techsolutions.co.uk

Stay details
Hotel: Venture Inn, 24 Swines Lane, Soho, W1L 5SQ
Room Type: Double
Check in: 26/5/2017
Check out: 28/5/2017
Guest names: Mr Keith Sadwicke, Mr Jon Armory-Wargrave

Price breakdown
Room fee: £19

Admin fee: £2.50

Total price paid: £21.50

Terms and Conditions:
Please note we practise a strict check-in and check-out policy
Only people named as guests are allowed to check in
No visitors allowed in rooms
No pets or livestock of any kind
Bookings are non-refundable with no exemptions
We reserve the right to search guest's luggage on check out in case of any pilferage of hotel property (especially kettles)
Room service – we do not provide room service
We reserve the right to eject guests who make undue nocturnal noise or if they engage in activities deemed by the management to offend accepted standards of morality and decency
We reserve the right to impose a surcharge on guests for any or all of the following:
- breakages of hotel property
- leaving hard to remove stains or bodily fluids on hotel furnishings
- leaving uncomplimentary reviews on Tripadvisor or other review sites

We hope you enjoy your stay!

From: **keith_sadwicke@techsolutions.co.uk**

To: armory-wargrove.jonathan@nhs–dental-estimates.gov.uk

Sent: 16.04.17, 02:57

Subject: **Fun in the Big Smoke**

Jon mate, I've booked us into a very pleasant little hostelrie for our trip to Comic Fantasy Con at the end of May. I've forwarded you the booking confirmation so you should have all the details. And don't worry by the way, it's all on me. Call it a thank you for helping me out at the fair. I suppose I could have gone for somewhere a bit more convenient for the ExCel Centre but I've heard the nightlife's a bit dead around there, and I thought if we're going to do London we might as well go where the action is, like in the middle of Soho where the hottest actresses and models hang out. Maybe we could try out a few clubs while we're there. As Odos the Otherling was once heard to say during a visit to the red-light district on Sleezia 3: *chëk-owt-dôze-lâydę̄ze*!

Oh yeah, one thing I should probably mention: to get the best deal, I had to book us a double room. Trust that's OK?

Keith

From: **armory-wargrove.jonathan@nhs–dental-estimates.gov.uk**
To: keith_sadwicke@techsolutions.co.uk
Sent: 17.04.17, 08:12
Subject: **Room issue...**

Keith,

Frankly, I'm not sure a double room is a good idea. I'm no stranger to rough-and-ready sleeping from my days in the band and dj-ing. An overcrowded yurt in a sodden field outside Burton Coggles holds no terrors for me. I'm thinking more of you – I suffer from sleep paralysis (with occasional atonic seizures) which can involve a fair bit of shouting and kicking as I come out of it.

I know time is short but can we PLEASE rebook. If it's money I am more than happy to stump up.

Jon

Jon Armory-Wargrove
Senior Assessor

PS I'm having nothing to do with 'women of easy virtue', not after the incident in Swansea. I'll tell you about it over a pint sometime.

This message is sent for and on behalf of the Dental Estimates Board, an NHS Service Provider. It may contain confidential information. If you are not the intended recipient please inform the sender that you have received the message in error before deleting it. Please do not disclose, copy or distribute information in the email or take any action in reliance on its contents: to do so is strictly prohibited and may be unlawful. Thank you for your cooperation.

From: **blueyblu@blueyonder.com**

To: tom@tomcat.com

Sent: 18.04.17, 19:54

Subject: **Re: Hey you**

Hi Tomcat (feel really self-conscious typing that!)

Thank you so much for your kind words about my humble efforts at poesy – it really is hard for me to keep it together when I read! Didn't think you'd like it, you seem so together but I guess beneath that calm exterior there are hidden deeps! The language of despair is universal don't you think?

A bite to eat could be nice. Funny I've never bumped into you in Veggie-Might before – I practically live there! Can't do tomorrow but I'm in the shop the day after if you want to pop in – about 12.30ish?

You've probably picked up on my 'trigger' topics but could you please also avoid talking about:

- global warming (really stressed about this at the moment)
- plastic wrapping, especially cling film
- cotton wool
- Eamonn Holmes
- bridges

Also, can you tell me if you are going to make any form of bodily contact.

Blue x

From: **keith_sadwicke@techsolutions.co.uk**

To: armory-wargrove.jonathan@nhs–dental-estimates.gov.uk

Sent: 19.04.17, 02:57

Subject: **Re: Room issue…**

Jon

No worries, mate. I totally get the sleep paralysis and the atomic seizures (which sound quite nasty!). You probably remember the incident in Vol 4 (if you've read that far) when Vänwiįn Kūl from Dormis fell asleep for twenty solar cycles, then killed the drongid who woke him. The drongid's family took their revenge, so it was R.I.P. Vänwiįn Kūl.

But it's all fine. The bloke at the Venture Inn was really accommodating when I called him. He says they can't actually change the booking at this late stage, or refund the deposit, but if we ask for him when we get there, his name is Malc, he says he'll sort us out. He has this extra room at the back, which he rents out to a local masseuse, but he reckons it'll be free for most of the night, so you could sleep there for, he says, a 'nominal fee'.

I hear what you're saying about women of easy virtue. I know you like the classier style of lady, as do I. And I'm sure you attract them with that grizzled Harrison Ford charm of yours. Not that I'm saying you're really old or anything. I'm talking Harrison Ford circa *Blade Runner*, or maybe, to be more realistic, circa that last Indiana Jones movie, *Kingdom of the Crystal Skull*, when he was still in his mid-sixties.

Cheers
K

From: **aliceknowles@mewriter.com**
To: Crawley Writers' Group
Sent: 22.04.17, 11:03
Subject: **Really, truly sorry**

All I can do is apologise. Apologise to all of you, and also to myself. I've let myself down. I had such hopes. I wanted it to be perfect. I wanted it to be the best writing group ever. That was my only reason for introducing the workshop element at the start of the evening. I thought it might be an ice-breaker, a way of releasing the creative juices. In my idealistic way, I thought something collaborative might help deepen the creative bond between us, forge a group identity that could be bigger than all of us.

That was why I decided to offer up those random words, and hand around the pencils and paper. I thought why not see if we can come up with the start of a little story – something we might even continue, maybe, in groups to come. It certainly wasn't to make up for my own 'creative barrenness', Peter. Or about stealing ideas, Keith. Or about 'favouring the natural-born extemporisers', Tom. And Jon, I had no idea you never used that brand of pencil 'on principle'. Neither did I realise that 'canal' was one of your trigger words, Blue. I promise it was randomly selected from the dictionary. And Julia, I know you didn't really have to take that 'super urgent' call from your agent and were only looking for an excuse to leave the room. It was sweet of you to try and spare my feelings, but I knew then, when even you, dear sweet Julia, abandoned me, that the game was up. The experiment had failed. It seems the only person I didn't upset was Mavinder, and only because she wasn't there.

So please can we all try and forget the first part of the evening ever happened. We're all WRITERS, aren't we? We know how to edit out the bad stuff. Select, Delete. There, it's gone. The rest of it was OK, wasn't it? Despite my occasional bouts of tears. And Blue's popping. And Tom's sneezing fit – I'm sorry, my dear, you should have warned me you were allergic to cat fur.

I sit here in nervous anticipation of your individual and collective judgement. Please don't be too harsh (Peter…?!).

Your Alice

From: **JuliaGeeGee@gmail.com**
To: Crawley Writers' Group
Sent: 22.04.17, 12:32
Subject: **Don't be silly, darling!**

Dearest darling Alice

Whatever possessed you to feel you needed to issue an apology for the evening you hosted so admirably the other night?

I'm so sorry to see you've been in distress about this, and doubly sorry I haven't had a chance to reply sooner. (We were in Stratford for a preview of the new *Tempest*: a wonderfully innovative staging with the island recast as a sort of *Big Brother*-style reality-show house! Too clever! And yet somehow tremendously affecting at the same time. Russell Brand as Ariel is *inspired* casting, and of course dear Sir Michael's Prospero is absolutely everything one dared dream of from the great man. Do you know he's the only actor I've ever written a fan letter to? He *roared* when I told him!)

But I digress. It was a wonderful evening, very much in the spirit of our group, with all its lively creative crossing of swords and dazzling – and dazzlingly brave – performances. I must apologise about the start – I missed the initial instruction and thought people were just warming up before they recited – it's the sort of thing we actors often do. So I stepped out for the call (and yes *of course* it was a real call, silly! Turns out I may have a publisher!!).

The night was certainly intimate – I'm not sure how we'd have all quite fitted in if Blue hadn't volunteered to sit on Tom's knee – but then again, I thought that just brought us all closer together in creative collaboration, both metaphorically and physically. The sneezing was certainly intense, but worse things happen at sea. (Though some, like sea spray, are quite similar. Only joking, Tom!)

As always, I was deeply moved by Blue's poetry. @Blue darling, I thought your ode to a dying daddy-long-legs was Plath-like in its intensity, accentuated if anything by the constant popping sounds coming from your person. @Tom, I marvelled anew at your inventiveness – I love the idea of a short story that turns out to be narrated by a cat! @Keith, your world-building fluency continues to beggar belief – and with the arrival of the new double-headed giant ones, I do really start to fear for the future of the giggly little hairy ones! I do wonder if even the cool time-travelling renegade outlaw one with the name that sounds like Keef can save them now? *So* exciting.

@Peter – your 30 minutes of 'silence' was extraordinary! Not silence, I mean – and how ironic that, now I come to think of it – but of saying the word 'silence' over and over again for exactly 1,800 seconds. It was a sort of extraordinary sculpture made up of words and of time, and I found myself experiencing an extraordinary range of emotions as the time ticked by. (I think the presence of the digital countdown timer was an enormous boost to the experience, actually, both to performer and audience alike.) Extraordinary!

@Jon – again I was both delighted and delightfully thought-provoked by your tale of the pigeon gang who carried out their nefarious deeds in accordance with atonal grunts from a mysterious stoat figure, grunts which only they could hear. Much to reflect on! And @Alice – I loved the adverb! It's absolutely perfect. Divinely, felinely, effortlessly so! Adverbially speaking, it's just right!

Many of you were kind enough to comment on my revised – slightly raunchier – first chapter of my novel. Glad no one thought the casting-couch scene was too barbaric or OTT – especially as the director does offer to get the tabasco stain out in a later chapter. Mind you, it's quite innocent really, compared to some of the things you hear these days!

See you all at the next one, darlings – whose turn is it next?!

Julia

PS Happy Shakespeare's birthday for tomorrow, one and all!! May your writing be truly bardic!!

From: **tom@tomcat.com**

To: Crawley Writers' Group

Sent: 22.04.17, 15:16

Subject: **Great night**

Alice

Just wanted to echo Julia's words – it was a top night with some great writing. All in all, another classic group.

Apologies to all for the sneezing – the welts are coming down at last too. And many thanks to Blue for agreeing to be my lap cat. I didn't mind if she didn't…;> (I always think that women and cats should do as they please, and men and dogs had better just get used to the idea…)

Re hosting, I'm thinking the only pads we haven't been to yet are Jon's and Blue's?

See you all soon

Tom x

PS @Pete – it'd be great if you could send around a transcript of your piece – really powerful stuff.

From: **keith_sadwicke@techsolutions.co.uk**

To: Crawley Writers' Group

Sent: 22.04.17, 15:56

Subject: **No need to apologise**

Hey Alice, don't stress about it. I had a great time.

Re your workshop idea, I just have to be a teeny bit careful with the old brand, that's all. See, I normally filter my raw text through a number of grammar and spellcheck apps before pushing the publish button on any new volume. If some unedited Sadwicke prose got out there, it could allow a little too much daylight in on the magic, let the fans see behind the wizard's curtain at how the sausages get made, if you know what I mean! Besides, it was hard to produce my best work with Blue beside me sounding like a flipping popcorn maker on high heat.

@Julia, thanks for the praise. However deserved (I leave that to others to judge), it never gets tiring to hear. By the way, the cool time-travelling hero you mentioned is actually named Káœhâëriff, though you're right it does sound a bit like Keef when spoken.

Keith

From: **peterpeterpeterpeter@gmail.com**

To: Crawley Writers' Group

Sent: 22.04.17, 16:12

Subject: **<no subject>**

Hello everyone

It has come to my attention that Alice experienced distress at the thought that her group was not a success. I think Alice's concerns are partially misplaced – the heating was only a couple of degrees too high, snacks were more adequate than one had been led to believe, the session ran broadly to time, no laws of the land were broken, and no health complications appear to have arisen from Tom's insalubrious mucous explosions.

Some of you have requested a transcript of my work. Please see it below my signature. I was not able to read out the full piece because of various interruptions – Blue popping, Keith fidgeting, Jon's ringtone, repeated sneezings from Tom, and the applause which broke in rather too early. All these interruptions have been marked as struck-through text, together with my best effort to recreate and account for each. In this way, my fellow writers can profitably compare the pristine and performance versions of the work, which incidentally I have chosen to call *seconds*. (The word I repeated was not *silence* but *second*, Julia. This Freudian lapsus on your part constitutes an additional element of interest to the oeuvre to my mind, even as it casts doubt on the sincerity of the reactions you delineated in your last email.)

And that – text of *seconds* notwithstanding – is all from me at this time.

Peter, writer.

'seconds'

secon~~d second second second second second second second~~ *[initial group fidgeting and throat-clearing]* d second *[Blue popping]* second~~ second sec~~ *[Keith fidgeting]* ond second second second second second second second second second second second second second second *[Blue popping]* second *[Blue popping]* second *[Blue popping]* second second ~~second seco~~ *[sneeze #1 – Tom]* nd second second second second second second second second *[Blue popping]* second second second second second second second second second second second second *[Blue popping]* second second second second second second second *[Blue popping]* second second second second *[Blue popping]* second *[Blue popping]* second *[Blue popping]* second second second second second second second second second second second second *[Blue popping]* second

second second second second second second second second second second *[Blue popping]* second seco~~nd second second second second second~~ ~~secon~~ *[sudden odd squawking sound from Julia, quickly stifled]* d second *[Blue popping]* second *[Blue popping]* second second second second second second second second second second second second second *[Blue popping]* second second second second second second second second second second second second second second second *[Blue popping]* second second second second second second second ~~second second second second second second second second second second~~

~~second second~~ *[sneeze #2 – Tom]* second s~~econd second second second second second second second second second second second second second second secon~~ *[infuriating Led Zeppelin ringtone – Jon]* d second second second second second second second second second *[Blue popping]* second *[Blue popping]* second second second second second second second second second s~~econd seco~~nd *[and again! – as if deliberately]* second

second second second second second second second
second second second second second second second
second second second second second second second
second second second second second *[Blue popping]*
second *[Blue popping]* second *[Blue popping]* second second
[Blue popping] second second second *[Blue popping]* second
second second second second second second second
second second second second second second second
second second second second second second second
second second second second second second second
second second second second second second second
second *[Blue popping]* second *[Blue popping]* second second
second second second second second second second
second second second second second second second
second second second second second second second
second second second second second second second
second second second second second second second
second second second second second second second
second second second second second second second
second second second second *[Blue popping]* second
second second second second second second second
second second second second second *[Blue popping]*
second second second *[Blue popping]* second *[Blue popping]*
second second second *[Blue popping]* second second
second second second second second second second
second second second second second second second
second second second second second second second

second *[Blue popping]* second second *[Blue popping]* second *[Blue popping]* second *[Blue popping]* second secon~~d second sec~~ *[low whisperings from Tom to Blue on lap – something about alfalfa??]* ond *[Blue popping]* second *[Blue popping]* second second *[Blue popping]* second second *[Blue popping]* second *[Blue popping]* second *[Blue popping]* second *[Blue popping]* second second *[Blue popping]* second second second *[Blue popping]* second second second second second second second second second second second second second second second *[Blue popping]* second *[Blue popping]* second second second second *[Blue popping]* second second second *[Blue popping]* second

second second second second second second second second second second second second second second second second second second second *[Blue popping] [Blue popping] [Blue popping] [Blue popping]* secon~~d second second second second second second second second second second second second second second second second second second~~ *[Blue popping]* ~~second second~~ second ~~second second second second second second second second second second second second second second second second second second second~~ *[Blue popping]* ~~second second second second second second second~~ *[Blue popping]* ~~second second second second second second second second second~~ *[Blue popping]* ~~second second~~ second *[Blue popping]* second second ~~second second second second second second second second second second second second second second second second second second second second~~ *[Blue popping]* ~~second second second second second second second~~ *[Blue popping]* ~~second second second second second second~~

~~second second second second second second second second second sec~~ *[sneezes #3–#6 – Tom]* ond second second second second second second second second second second second *[Blue popping]* second *[Blue popping]* second second *[Blue popping]* *[Blue popping]* second *[Blue popping]* *[Blue popping]* *[Blue popping]* second second second second *[Blue popping]* *[Blue popping]* second sec~~ond second~~

~~second second second second second second second~~
~~second second second second second second second~~
~~second second second second second second second~~
~~second second second second second second second~~
~~second second second~~ *[Blue popping]* ~~second second~~
~~second second~~ *[Blue popping] [Blue popping]* ~~second second~~
~~second second second second second second second~~
~~second second second second second second second~~
~~second second second second second second second~~
~~second second second second second second second~~
~~second second second second second second second~~
~~second second second second second second second~~
~~second second second second second second~~ *[Blue*
popping] ~~second second second second second second~~
~~second second second second second second second~~
~~second second second second second second second~~
~~second second second second second second second~~
~~second second second second second second second~~
~~second second second~~ *[Blue popping] [Blue popping]* ~~second~~
~~second second second second second second second~~
~~second second second second second second second~~
~~second second second second second second second~~
~~second second second second second second second~~
~~second~~ *[Blue popping] [Blue popping]* ~~second second second~~
~~second second second second second second second~~
~~second second second second second second second~~
~~second second second second second second second~~

~~second second second second second second second second second second second second second~~ *[Blue popping]* ~~second second second second second second~~ *[Blue popping] [Blue popping]* ~~second second~~ *[Blue popping]* ~~second second~~ *[Blue popping] [Blue popping] [Blue popping] [Blue popping]* ~~second second~~ *[Blue popping] [Blue popping] [closing section drowned out by spontaneous and prolonged – albeit premature – applause from entire group; more sneezes from Tom]*

From: **tom@tomcat.com**
To: Crawley Writers' Group
Sent: 22.04.17, 20:45
Subject: **Thanks, Peter**

Thanks, Peter – I'll go through this properly as soon as I get a sec!

Tom

From: **tom@tomcat.com**
To: blueyblu@blueyonder.com
Sent: 23.04.17, 07:16
Subject: **Wow**

Hey Bluey Blu

Wow.

I've never not done that before. I mean I've not done that loads of times – I'm not doing it now in fact. But I've not done it with you. Not like that.

Dare I hope that we might not do that again some time? Just you and me – not doing it?

(I didn't mean any of this, but then you made it so easy…)

T-Cat x
PS I love alfalfa now!

From: **MPranesh@gmail.com**

To: Crawley Writers' Group

Sent: 23.04.17, 13:46

Subject: **Sorry**

I found it this time. (The outside of your house is lovely btw, Alice.)

I had my finger on the doorbell but I just couldn't press it.

I really wanted to, but I was in a weird mood and I didn't want you all to see me like that.

Also I still haven't finished the poem.

Anyway it sounds like it went well – I don't think you should worry, Alice.

My Lord and my s

From: **tom@tomcat.com**

To: blueyblu@blueyonder.com

Sent: 24.04.17, 03:57

Subject: **Only me...**

Hey Bluesy BluBlue

Only me again!

Just wondering how you're diddling and how the shop went

today? (I popped in yesterday but forgot it was your afternoon off.)

Did you manage to finish that piece for three voices about the doner kebab dentata? So dark and original and strangely lovely! Like other things (other peeps) I could mention...

Anyhooz, it'd be lovely to hear from you some time, just to know how you're doing. Sometimes I think that even cowards can endure tough stuff; but only the really brave can endure suspense!!

Maybe a bite down Veggie-Might one afternoon?

T-Cat xx

From: **blueyblu@blueyonder.com**
To: Crawley Writers' Group
Sent: 24.04.17, 18:44
Subject: **Fab night, Alice!**

Hi

O Alice! it was a lovely evening and thank you Julia for your kind words about my poem like all my others it came from the heart. If we can't cry for the suffering of a simple daddy-long-legs we won't be able to cry for ourselves – when the poor thing literally goes down the plughole it is about our own inevitable death... But will we be flushed towards the light (maybe through the overflow pipe) or enter the purgatory of the sewers??? We do not know.

Also I feel I am ready to host the next meeting! I wouldn't have believed that possible a few short weeks ago thank you, thank you all.

luv

Blue

From: **armory-wargrove.jonathan@nhs_dental-estimates.gov.uk**
To: Crawley Writers' Group
Sent: 24.04.17, 23:15
Subject: **Good one**

Hi all,

I enjoyed the last meeting as well, Alice!

I was a bit out of sorts at first – stuff at work mainly – but good company and a few bottles of Old Peculiar soon put paid to the glooms! And Peter's contribution gave us all a chance to have a nap!

Sorry about the pencil hoo-haa – it may sound crazy but the graphite in pencils can conduct certain rays which are beamed at us. I'll say no more but do google it!

Jon

Jon Armory-Wargrove
Senior Assessor

This message is sent for and on behalf of the Dental Estimates Board, an NHS Service Provider. It may contain confidential information. If you are not the intended recipient please inform the sender that you have received the message in error before deleting it. Please do not disclose, copy or distribute information in the email or take any action in reliance on its contents: to do so is strictly prohibited and may be unlawful. Thank you for your cooperation.

From: **blueyblu@blueyonder.com**

To: tom@tomcat.com

Sent: 25.04.17, 03:46

Subject: **Oh Tommy Tom-cat!**

Hi Tom-cat,

I'm all of a dither and it's all your fault, you naughty puss!

Despite the guidelines I set out at our meeting at the café it all went out the window when you asked me to sit on your lap in the group!

As you know I have issues with physical contact but I just went for it!! It just felt right. And with lots of bubble wrap (never leave home without it!), seven blankets, three cushions, Alice's duvet, a sheaf of padded manila envelopes and that pink bath mat with the little suckers, it was all very cosy and comfortable (despite the mobile in your pocket).

Joining the writers' group has been SOOO good for me – I feel I am a chrysalis that may yet become a butterfly. As long as it's not a daddy-long-legs!

So yes, I'd love to meet up again! I'm at the shop all the rest of this week so do drop by.

Blue x

From: **tom@tomcat.com**
To: Crawley Writers' Group
Sent: 04.05.17, 09:11
Subject: **See you chez Blue!**

Hi all

As you all know, Blue has kindly agreed to host the next meeting of our esteemed group, on the 18th of this month.

This is quite a big deal for her, as I'm sure you can all appreciate, so let's all muck in and make it as positive an experience for her as possible, OK? Blue has kindly allowed me to help out with a few details and arrangements, to which end:

@Peter – can you be on non-alcoholic beverages? Blue is very fond of the white-grape variety of Shloer, but I must ask that no one actually say the word out loud as she thinks it might be the cause of her hives.

@Alice – would you mind bringing some plates and glasses? Blue has never invited more than a single person into her home before, so she's understandably a bit short on cutlery and crockery etc.

@Julia – would you mind being wine monitor? Some of that Burgundy we had last time at yours would do just fine. (I'm sketchy on the details, but I think it was a Morey St-Denis Clos de la Roche Grand Cru from 2014, was it?)

@Jon and @Keith – I know you guys can be relied on for beers, wet wipes, folding chairs etc.

@all – do please bear in mind that this is a really important milestone for Blue, so let's be as supportive and respectful of her and her space as we can. So please do not attempt to turn on any electric lights (there will be plenty of candles, natch), make sure you go to the loo before you arrive (these internal compost units are still a bit of a work in progress, in my view). And please, please, no one mention Eamonn Holmes.

Thanks for all your help, everyone! I always think that if everyone is moving forward together, then success can only take care of itself. It's going to be a great, great night and we can't wait to have you all over!!

Tom

From: **peterpeterpeterpeter@gmail.com**

To: Crawley Writers' Group

Sent: 04.05.17, 12:12

Subject: **<no subject>**

Dear Tom (and Blue) (or 'Dear Blue (and Tom)')

Thank you for agreeing to host the next writers' group.

It was strictly Jon's turn to host, of course, according to my spreadsheet which tabulated the initial intentions we had formulated as a group (and which I circulated to unanimous if silent approval on 06.01.17), but you are to be congratulated for issuing the invitation before a reminder needed to be sent. Indeed, I put the elapsed time between the conclusion of our last meeting and the invitation issued for the next at 32.63 hours – our second-promptest meeting-to-invite interval since the group's inception (second only to my meeting-to-invite interval achieved on 23.02.17).

I will as requested organise and administer non-alcoholic beverages. (In the absence of white-grape Shloer, an increasingly common occurrence if the – admittedly anecdotal – evidence of my recent shopping expeditions for the group can be extrapolated from, I am operating on the assumption that the group will pre-authorise me to make an executive decision about alternative flavours. White grape and elderflower is my default back-up at this point; I remain gustatorily unconvinced by the new no-added-sugar, mango & passionfruit variant.) (Incidentally, do not be alarmed if the packaging seems different: I read in the *Journal of International Business-to-Consumer Marketing* that Shloer carried out a major rebrand in 2015 to highlight the playful, sociable essence of its brand DNA, and to better codify its consumer promise as a premium alcohol-free alternative. The introduction of a demotic handwritten font and brighter, bolder grape-led iconography were the key modifications here. (Whereas my previous bottles were from my personal supply; they were bought in bulk in 2014 and pre-date the rebrand.))

As an additional gesture of support, I will in my official capacity visit Blue's residence in the week preceding the group meeting, in order to carry out a full health & safety and personal hygiene check. I will gladly provide this service at cost, including full documentation and certification for Blue to display afterwards (if so awarded). Please supply your geopositional details, Blue, and I will confirm the appointment time before close of business tomorrow.

Finally, you may recall that the dimensional challenges of Alice's flat made necessary certain physical proximities among group 'members', some of whom chose to manipulate this unfortunate constraint for their own psycho-erotic gratifications. I do hope that there will not be a repeat of this oppressive teenage-style tactility. They know, they of whom I speak.

And that is all at this time.
Peter, writer.

From: **tom@tomcat.com**
To: Crawley Writers' Group
Sent: 05.05.17, 11:41
Subject: **Re: See you chez Blue!**

Hi @Peter

Thanks very much for sorting soft drinks.

I don't think we'll need to take you up on the inspection offer – though Blue is very appreciative of the gesture. I'm pretty confident that her personal hygiene needs are all sorted too.

I don't really know what your last bit meant, Peter. It was a bit of a squeeze at Alice's, so we all had to scooch up and as you know Blue remained safe and protected and untriggered at all times. Which reminds me – Blue's living room is actually rather smaller than Alice's, so we were wondering if one or two people could maybe Skype from the kitchen? Or even from the pub on the corner? Or you could just dial in from your place and not actually come at all, Peter??? Sounds like you'd be an ideal candidate to try out this new semi-remote interaction style – could be really artistically interesting/innovative. And, as I always think, sometimes we can see things more clearly when we move further away from them. Closeness has nothing to do with physical distance, after all.

Anyway, thanks again and let us know what you think.
Tom

From: **peterpeterpeterpeter@gmail.com**
To: tom@tomcat.com
Sent: 06.05.17, 12:12
Subject: **<no subject>**

Dear Tom

I will join by Skype on this occasion, from a location as yet to be determined.

This development aligns well with my present preoccupations.

Please forward me all appropriate joining instructions.

Peter, writer.

From: **tom@tomcat.com**

To: blueyblu@blueyonder.com

Sent: 12.05.17, 16:16

Subject: **Sacré Blue! (everything has changed)**

Hey Bluey Blu

Blue is the colour and poetry is your game! Blue, you've got me singing the blues! (In a good way, obvs.)

Everything has changed and yet I have never been more myself. Without you, life itself were a mistake.

The curve of your eyes does the tour of my heart. Not even the rain has such small hands as yours! You have the mind of a mermaid – shall I dare swim in its depths??!!

Not all that wander are lost, and yet now I find that I am found. If I had a flower for every time I thought of you... there'd be no more bald patches in the shared gardens of my block of contemporary loft-style flats off Old Horsham Road!

So... shall we meet at midnight tonight... in the forest of my dreams? Or failing that, how about dinner in The Cardamom Kitchen in Langley Green? I'm told they do lovely vegetable sambars, rasams and kootus, which are of course three common stew-like dishes typical of southern Indian cuisine, a style less seen in British restaurants but distinguished by its drier dishes, loose-textured curries and griddle-cooked snacks. But of course you know all this!

Pick you at up 7? I sometimes feel there is nothing more artistic than to, uh, *like someone vv much*.

A ce soir?

Tommy Tomcat

PS Note to Blue: please, *please*, just go on being constantly, consistently, continually, adorably, *you*. True Blue *you*.

PPS

And that is all from me at this time.

Tom, lover

From: **blueyblu@blueyonder.com**
To: Crawley Writers' Group
Sent: 12.05.17, 20:04
Subject: **Ce soir**

The beavers of despair have felled the trees
From the forest of murk
And dammed the river of my life and love,
Turning my heart into a fetid pool in which
The discarded bicycle frame of joy

Has been thrown...

O! Tommy Tom-cat, this is the opening verse of my new poem, pages and pages of it are pouring out! You've helped me tear up the rule book! I feel LIBERATED!!!!

And thank you for your lovely email.
Oui, ce soir, my ikkle-likkle tigger!

your loving Bluey-Blue
xxxxxxxxxxxx

PS would you be able to give me a lift to the big Asda to get stuff for the next meeting?

From: **tom@tomcat.com**
To: blueyblu@blueyonder.com
Sent: 12.05.17, 20:12
Subject: **Re: Ce soir**

Err, did you mean to email that to everyone?

Not that I care – I want to tell the world! – but I thought you wanted to keep things under wraps for now??

Tomcat xx

From: **peterpeterpeterpeter@gmail.com**
To: Crawley Writers' Group
Sent: 13.05.17, 12:12
Subject: **<no subject>**

Dear all

It is clear to me from recent email correspondence – and despite the very legitimate concerns voiced in my email of 12:12 on 04.05.17 – that certain members of the group have obstinately proceeded in their blindly lustful quest to confuse the concepts of artistic and sexual intercourse.

Aside from being subjected to the distasteful spectacle of other people's pet names and mawkish romantic doggerel – the online equivalent of being forced to watch teenagers snogging on the bus – this sort of behaviour threatens to undermine the very nature of the group which we have all worked so hard to establish and nurture: a forum facilitating the free flow of engaged, constructive feedback between cordially attached – but not, one had assumed, carnally involved – writers. A creative workshop rather than a fetid knocking-shop.

If this gruesomely lubricious tendency goes unchecked, I can see already how future groups will play out:

> 'What did you think of my poem, darling?'
> 'I loved it, darling. I love your legs and your breasts too.'
> 'Thanks, darling. Yours too. And your short story.'

'Thanks! Shall I see you in bed later for an exchange of bodily fluids?'

'Ooh yes please.'

I look to other group members to add their own condemnation of this disturbing development to mine, and to the parties themselves to provide an undertaking that this highly regrettable liaison will cease forthwith.

Finally, in case these libidinous shenanigans have given others any ideas of a similarly debased nature, let me state plainly and for the record that I am not available to be considered as fuck-buddy or sex object material by anybody at this time.

Peter, writer.

From: **armory-wargrove.jonathan@nhs_dental-estimates.gov.uk**

To: keith_sadwicke@techsolutions.co.uk

Sent: 13.05.17, 18:56

Subject: **Blimey. Did you see that email?**

Strewth. Looks like Tom has finally got his claws into one of our ladies. I'm guessing that Blue will give as good as she gets though.

Pete's being a typical dick about it, of course. We should bring an industrial drum of lube and sack of sex toys to the next meeting and totally freak him out!

J

From: **aliceknowles@mewriter.com**

To: Crawley Writers' Group

Sent: 13.05.17, 20:03

Subject: **Re: Re: Re: Ce soir**

Sacré bleu, Blue!

I'm so happy for you. And for you, too, Tom. Our little WRITING group has spawned a story – a real-life romantic story!

It may not have been quite what we had in mind or what we intended when we started out, but perhaps we shouldn't be surprised, because we are WRITERS after all. We live life so intensely, and between us we generate so much creative heat, it's inevitable sparks will sometimes fly when we meet, and for at least two of our number those sparks appear to have been amorous ones.

As a WRITER, I am, of course, sensitive to these undercurrents, and I did sense loneliness in both of you when we first met. Blue expressed this movingly in her poetry, while Tom did so in his badgering of one or two of the group's female members to meet up. He may not have been successful at first, but credit to him he kept trying and I'm so happy that he eventually got lucky with Blue.

You both deserve this happiness, and I hope you enjoy it for as long or as short as it lasts. Will it be a quick, passionate short story, or the start of a multigenerational epic romance? I for one am avid to know what happens next.

Alice

4.

A FAINT GREENISH TINGE

From: **tom@tomcat.com**

To: blueyblu@blueyonder.com; cc: Crawley Writers' Group

Sent: 16.05.17, 03:43

Subject: **Re: Re: Re: Re: Ce soir**

Hey Bluesy Blue

Have we got everything we need for the group on Thursday? How are you feeling about it all? Are you still thinking of debuting your Carwash of Oblivion sequence?? (You must, you totally must.) Do you think everyone will respect your vegan ground rules?

So many questions, sorry. Just one more, and it's the only one that is piercing me to my core: Are we *OK*? I only ask, because I haven't heard from you since our Asda trip, and I can't help wondering if you're disappointed in me because of the way I reacted when that email you wrote about us (that glorious, heart-stopping email) found its way to the whole group.

At first I thought you'd sent it to everyone by mistake, and I was worried that you'd feel exposed. But when you didn't reply when I asked you that – and when you didn't say anything about it in the aisles of Asda – it got me thinking that maybe you were showing me that you didn't care who knows. In which case you might have found my response to be cowardly and craven.

Forgive me. I failed the test. Let me try again.

I WANT YOU! I WANT THE WORLD TO KNOW! I'll put it on a T-shirt! I'll stand outside Peter's house and march up and down wearing a sandwich board that says: Tom HEART Blue!!!

I don't care who knows! And that's why I'm cc-ing everyone! Enjoy this, people! Enjoy our love!!!! We're out and we're proud! We want to be together! And we want to write together!

I love you, Blue!

Tom

xxxxxxxxxxxxxxxxxxxxxxxxxxxxxxxxxxxxxxxxxxxxxxxxxxxxxx
xxxxxxxxxxxxxxxxxxxxxxxxxxxxxx

PS Just realised we never got any wasabi peas. Shall I pop to that new Tesco Metro and see if I can get some??

From: **blueyblu@blueyonder.com**

To: tom@tomcat.com

Sent: 16.05.17, 03:43

Subject: **OMG OMG OMG!**

I'm so, so sorry Tom I didn't mention the email I sent it by mistake but I just couldn't talk about it I felt so exposed and it's too soon, too soon, I feel naked and vulnerable and it's all out in the open and I'm sorry and the cats are slinking around looking at me in a funny way and we forgot the wasabi peas and it was so lovely just going round the supermarket together like a normal couple and that's why I couldn't mention it I didn't want to break the spell.

I'm sorry my wonderful Tomcat I'm sorry.

I'll understand if you never want to see me again and OMG the next meeting is here shall I cancel or what?

Blue xxxxxxxxx

From: **JuliaGeeGee@gmail.com**

To: Crawley Writers' Group

Sent: 17.05.17, 21:26

Subject: **I'm back!!**

Hello, young writers and lovers, whoever you are!

Apologies for radio silence – just back from a bungee yoga course in Croatia – a lovely spot, set in a ducal manor on a tiny car-free island about an hour's ferry ride from beautiful and sad – beautifully sad – Dubrovnik. Such an energising and transformative form of bodywork! Not at all what it sounds like and actually really quite profound and grounding, not to say a tad tantric… (In fact on the last night I think I reconnected with my inner pubic skydancer, but that's a story for when I see you all. Hubby didn't mind, let's just put it that way…)

Anyway it's wonderful to be back to the keyboard – I tap away hour after hour, trying to ignore the texts and calls and emails (and bouquets, strewth!) from the dread agent, breathing down my neck with her reckless talk of foreign rights and options and three-book deals. Must learn to manage my expectations – it's all pie in the sky and the thing isn't even written yet. Many a slip etc. etc.…

Wonderful, too, to hear about your budding romance, Blue and Tom! This group is growing all sorts of connections – ideas are forming, inspirations are nurtured, friendships are blooming, and the work pours forth from us all, each in the way and to the extent that suits him or her best – a seven-novel saga here, an animal fable there, a live conceptual experiment on this side, a gloriously apposite adverb on that side! Darling Peter is of course right to seek to protect the integrity and founding spirit of the group, but I'm sure that dear Tom and Blue will be able to show him in no time that their special friendship will serve only to strengthen our creative ties, not undermine them (you will, won't you, dears?).

So looking forward to seeing you all tomorrow – and so exciting to visit a new place, Blue!

Your friend in words

Julia xx

PS What do you all think of Delphine Delacroix as a pen-name? Too French?

From: **tom@tomcat.com**

To: blueyblu@blueyonder.com

Sent: 18.05.17, 23:59

Subject: **'Our' 'first' group...**

So tonight! That was intense. And scary. And kind of amazing. And weird (Peter). And hilarious (Jon). And adorable (you).

Can you believe our emails crossed like that? I'm so sorry that I doubted you – I should have trusted my first instinct that you would have wanted to keep things private. And then I went and blurted everything out to everyone again, like the crass oaf that I am.

It felt so strange, that first half of the group. I was so desperate to touch you, but I just didn't know how you wanted to play things. And your cats were really giving me evils. (I started sneezing again too!) And then none of the others seemed to know how to behave around us either. Alice and Julia were sweet if non-committal, Peter made a couple of his usual comments about 'creative incest' by Skype that I trust you didn't notice. And then Jon and Keith seemed to have their own private joke going on the whole night – something about doing the Stray Cat Strut? (A real-ale reference, I'm guessing.)

But the evening turned – and he shouldn't have, he really shouldn't have, but God it was funny – when Jon muted Peter as he was reading his piece: 'A tour of my fridge in 27 minutes' or something. There was just this footage of various kinds of yogurt, a heel of Edam, a bowl of lychees, and what looked like a sheep's brain attached to a Marigold filled with jelly (or slime?). I was actually quite curious to know what story Peter was weaving about all these objects, but Jon looked so tickled (and slightly fierce) that I didn't have the heart to challenge him (and nor did anyone else really, despite a few half-hearted attempts from the ladies).

And anyway it was round about then that nothing mattered any more because your hand brushed mine and I grasped your perfect little pinkie and for the rest of the group we were together, one. I thrilled to be in contact with you, and everyone else was cool. And so we clung on together as Jon did his thing about the fox whose lies are uncovered by the penetrating gaze of the porcupine (I'd thought from the previous story that the fox was GCHQ but I'm not so sure now; the porcupine is definitely Julian Assange (unless he's Tom Cruise? or David Icke? or is Icke the vole?)). Julia read more from her *Casting Couch* book (the heroine wins the audition despite being unable to find a working parking meter in Islington, then having no change, and then having to endure the rudeness of a cashier in Sainsbury's – phew! Talk about staring into the abyss!). And Keith went batshit crazy, single-handedly acting out the crazed leaders of the seven different factions that make up his latest intergalactic war – thank God he brought the hats, is all I can say, though you've got to admire his energy.

And then, I was going to read… and I thought of you, and of how you tower above me in light and art and beauty and mystery… and I felt that words just wouldn't do. I felt moved to prostrate myself symbolically, to lay my soul open to your soul, with just God (and, well, the rest of the group) as my witness. With the available space, however, laying myself at your feet also meant laying myself at the feet of Julia, Alice, Keith, Jon… and, briefly, a cat.

There was a moment, I'll admit, where I felt a tad silly. But then you smiled down at me, one of your infinite eternal sad smiles, and I knew all would be well. And then *you* read the opening lines of 'Vortex Cortex' ('See how she dies/in the doom-pools of his eyes…'). And we were all awestruck, as the first audience of *The Rite of Spring* must have been. It was extraordinary. Your words were exhilarating in their artful intensity. And as a gesture of helpless veneration, I may briefly have licked one of your Miss Fluffy Cozy Catkins slipper socks. So use me! I mean sue me! (And use me too if you'd like!!)

And then, when everyone else had left, and we finally got the place straight (you washing, me drying, in symphonic silence), you turned to me and said, 'You've got a Twiglet in your ear.'

And I had, indeed I had. I slipped out into the night, and I sucked on that Twiglet all the way home, and I thought of you.

Sleep well, my lovely.

Tomcat xxx

From: **JuliaGeeGee@gmail.com**
To: Crawley Writers' Group
Sent: 19.05.17, 11:48
Subject: **Another corker!**

Hello everyone!

Just wanted to drop you all a note to say what a wonderful group, as always. I so enjoyed everyone's contributions!

Jon – your 'forest of rumours' is getting more sinister by the week! I wouldn't trust that porcupine as far as I can throw him! Btw, is anyone else nursing a bit of a pash for the dark brooding badger? Powerful stuff.

Keith – that wasn't a reading, darling, that was a performance! What mesmerising characters and accents and lightning costume changes! You've been hiding your light under a bushel, darling – have you never thought of panto? Or hospital radio perhaps?

Blue – another heartbreaking jewel of a poem. My heart bleeds, darling! But please tell me – did the lady-narrator adrift on the lake of the blood of her pierced heart make it home safely in the end?? I'm on tenterhooks!

Tom – Wow! Kinetic sculpture, was it, darling? And why not?!

Peter – a wonderfully evocative video tour. We lost a little bit of sound at one point – is there any chance you could send us all a transcript?

Alice – I loved your talk on 'Writing about getting ready to write something on the subject of getting ready to start writing (about writing!)'! So witty and wise, and yet some hidden depths there too. Do keep almost writing, darling!!

It was wonderful to see everyone on such fine form – especially as my agent has mentioned that she's very interested in our little group. I was telling her about you all – about what a wonderful support you've been to me, and how we all egg each other on creatively – and she said it'd be a wonderful scene in the documentary she wants to make about me and my little book! Don't be silly, I said, we don't even have a deal on the table yet (at least not one that doesn't expect me to drop my trousers and bend over on foreign subsidiary rights), but she will insist! 'Once you go mass-market,' she says, 'your fans will hoover up all that big-star-surrounded-by-a-bunch-of-nobodies stuff!!!'

So who knows, darlings, you might all get to be on the telly soon!

Julia xx

From: **keith_sadwicke@techsolutions.co.uk**
To: Crawley Writers' Group
Sent: 20.05.17, 02:09
Subject: My acting days…

Great to see you all at Blue's last night. Everyone was on top form.

Nice of you to say I might have some acting talent, Julia. Maybe you noticed in the autobiographical section at the front of the synopsis I circulated a few months back, where I mention that I played a flying monkey in our school production of *The Wizard of Oz*. A limited part, but I gave it my best and garnered a favourable mention in my mate Merv's review in the school mag. Nothing came of it, but I must have got the smell of goosefat in my nostrils because after I left school I joined an am-dram outfit, the Latchwood Green Players. I was only getting minor parts, but one of the older thesps, a nice man called Hugo, took a shine to me. He promised to put a word in to get me some meatier roles. We hung out and he told me all about his marriage woes. He even moved in with me for a while during his divorce. Hugo was a hoarder of costumes and make-up, and I've still got a box of his stuff in my wardrobe. Then one night he got drunk and something happened, which I can't really talk about. I told him to leave and he did, the next day, and that was the last I saw of him, or the Latchwood Green Players.

But to be honest, I'm more of a words man than an actor, Julia. If I have talent, as you suggest, I shall be keeping it under my bush at least for now. Maybe once I've finished the final draft of Vol 7, I'll turn *Dragons of Xę̄n"räh* into a musical and cast myself as Odos!

But the real inspiration for my performance at Blue's was a disturbing incident that happened to me the other night. It was gone 10 o'clock and I was down in my den writing when Aragorn suddenly started going crazy. Turns out someone had smashed a hole in my front window. Amid all the broken glass I found a brick with a note tied to it. It read: 'In an age of dragons, elves and dwarfs, a world in tumult cried out for a leader. She was Bink Hallia, princess of Elberon, the forest world. With eyes the colour of leaf mould, dark hair as tangled as the roots of the spageto tree, and a will as strong as the trunk of the iron-oke, she would change the world…' It was the opening words of *Dragons of Xęn"räh*, Vol 1, Chapter 2. That was crazy enough but it was from an earlier draft, which I'd never published. Had someone been rooting around in my hard drive?

I was so panicked, I decided to go out, since I no longer felt safe in my house. For extra safety, in case the brick thrower was lurking in wait somewhere, I decided to disguise myself. So I raided Hugo's box and put on a cloak and hat, knee-length boots and a false nose. I painted a scar on my face and gave myself some purple eye shadow, and deliberately walked into a table so I'd have a realistic limp.

Then I squeezed out through the bathroom window. In my frantic state of mind, I fell into a plant pot in the garden and got covered in mud and opened up a genuine cut on my chin. As I scrambled over the back fence and ran out into the street, it started raining and my disguise became bedraggled and the paint and the blood on my face started to run. I hailed a bus, but for some reason the driver wouldn't let me on. So I hung around in the street for a bit until I felt brave enough to go back home. When I glanced in the hallway mirror I realised I looked exactly like Bêërnùckęl the Cage-Smiter turned Overlord of Blood Moon from Vol 5. And that was what gave me the idea for the performance...

Keith

From: **MPranesh@gmail.com**
To: Crawley Writers' Group
Sent: 20.05.17, 10:37
Subject: **See you next time?**

Hello everyone

Sorry once again that I didn't make it.

The longer this goes on the harder it's going to be to just walk in and meet you all. But I know I must.

I feel like I need to break the ice somehow. Or at least break something.

Anyway, hope to be at the next one. See you there if I don't see you before.

Mav Inder

From: **aliceknowles@mewriter.com**

To: Crawley Writers' Group

Sent: 20.05.17, 11:19

Subject: **A Day in the Life of a WRITER**

Thank you, Julia, for your kind words about my contribution at the recent group. I was quite proud of it myself. In fact, I thought I might give you all a sneak preview of my latest blog post. It's called 'A Day in the Life of a WRITER' (this would be a Friday, Saturday or Sunday – as I'm at work the rest of the week).

7 am: Wake Up. As I go about my morning routines, I always try to LISTEN, and OBSERVE. Everything is important to a WRITER. So I listen to the water pouring out of the tap as I run my bath. What sort of sound does it make? Try to put that sound into words. I look at my face in the mirror. What feelings does it evoke? Self-pity? Disgust? Good! I can use that!

8 am: Breakfast: I recommend Ginkgo Biloba herbal tea because it's thought to improve cognitive function, to help turn one's brain into a smooth-running WRITING machine. If I'm suffering from the mouse,* I might try orange apricot or pink rose tea to jump-start those creative synapses. In terms of food, I always start my day with eggs, either scrambled or poached, on brown toast, for a steady burn of brain energy.

9 am: Setting the Mood: It's so important to create the right kind of WRITING ambience. I try to wrap myself inside a holistic

cocoon of sights, sounds and smells carefully curated to inspire the imagination and enhance the WRITING experience. I always start with the visual. By clearing my desktop of any unnecessary clutter – used tissues, dirty mugs, phone, address books, 2-for-1 vouchers for Café Rouge, whatever – I offer my eyes a clean horizon with no possibility of distraction. Next, I work on creating a stimulating soundscape. I enjoy 'Rainy terrace', 'Boots crunching through snow' or 'Café de Paris' (the murmurs of customers and dishes clinking is perfect background for a romantic story). To complete the mood, I light an aromatic candle, such as Parisian Night or Bamboo Zen. With my mind and senses now completely primed, I'm ready to begin my roam through the world of words.

10 am: The Reviewing Stage: I wake my computer and open the document I've been working on. My first task is to review my previous day's work. This would be, in my case, the latest version of The Sentence (the opening sentence of my novel, for those new to my blog). To avoid getting too overwhelmed, I normally focus on one part of it. For example, the part that's currently obsessing me is the third word, which at the moment is 'determined'. I think about the word for a while. I say it to myself aloud and in my head. I try to imagine the character saying it. In the end, I decide, on balance, that it's probably not quite right, being a little too resolute for the character. I need to find something softer. But before that, it's time for some refreshment...

11 am: Tea Break.

11.30 am: New Writing. The hour and a half before lunch is my most fertile period. This is the part of the day devoted to New Writing. I return to the word 'determined'. I look at it in context this time. It forms part of a phrase: 'determined to salvage'. I've agreed that this is not right for the character, so I try out a few alternatives. How about, for example, 'intent on salvaging'? Again, too decisive. I'm not sure Freya's ever knowingly had an intention in her life. I consult my thesaurus. What about 'committed to salvaging'? That's slightly better – except it sounds like a politician. These are the sorts of problems I wrestle with every day, except for the days when I'm too tired. The Sentence is all about Freya's desire to salvage some olives from her salad before the waiter comes to take it away. She is prepared to sacrifice the tomato, feta and cucumber, but not the olives. She cannot exactly say why. It's important because it's a metaphor, and also key to everything that follows. But I digress.

1 pm: Lunch.

2 pm: After all the efforts of the morning, afternoons are usually a creative downtime for me. It's good to know that I've pushed on with The Sentence, that I've made real progress, and I feel OK about rewarding myself with a little social media, some Facebook, Pinterest, tumblr, Instagram, Twitter, and of course my blog. I'm religious about that. I always try to post something every day, even if it's just a few paragraphs, just to

remind my readers I'm still here. My readers are very kind, mostly. I've had so many suggestions for how to complete The Sentence. People care about Freya and her salad, and they want to know the significance of the olives. Social media and my blog take me up to around 5 or 6 o'clock, after which I'm ready to curl up with my cat Tiggy and a book, or go for a run, or maybe think about seeing a movie.

And that is a typical WRITING day, folks! Of course, they're not always so productive. Sometimes, if I'm tired, I might skip the 'New Writing' segment, but I'm religious about everything else.

* Regular readers of my blog will know that 'the mouse' is my name for WRITER's block. I gave it the name of a small, inconsequential creature to try to lessen its power over me.

Alice

From: **peterpeterpeterpeter@gmail.com**
To: Crawley Writers' Group
Sent: 20.05.17, 12:12
Subject: **<no subject>**

Dear all

It has come to my attention that my Skype performance piece was muted approximately 2 minutes and 31 seconds into its transmission.

I expected as much – which is why the narrative actually ceased after 2 minutes 42 seconds. For the record, the words you missed were: '...which is why Dutch cheese has always played a powerful role in the intimate psychogeographical cavities of all my white goods, right back to my very first mini fridge, purchased in 1984 to house my stepfather's lager.'

The rest of the film was silent. In other words, by attempting to sabotage my work, you (you know who) ended up ensuring it was viewed in the exact style and format its creator intended.

Who, I wonder, is laughing now?

Peter, writer.

From: **keith_sadwicke@techsolutions.co.uk**

To: armory-wargrove.jonathan@nhs–dental-estimates.gov.uk

Sent: 24.05.17, 02:13

Subject: **Comic Fantasy Con!**

Not long to go now, Jon. I'll see you at the station on Friday. I know you must be really familiar with *Xęn"räh* by now after all the reading you've done. I'll test you on it on the way up to London.

Keith

From: **armory-wargrove.jonathan@nhs–dental-estimates.gov.uk**

To: keith_sadwicke@techsolutions.co.uk

Sent: 24.05.17, 19:12

Subject: Re: **Comic Fantasy Con!**

Hi Keith,

Yeah, whatever.

The 'irregularities' that the audit had picked up here at the Board are causing a poisonous atmosphere and I just need to get out of it, literally. Keep it under your hat. I'm sure you won't mind if I bring some 'herbal stressbusters'.

Looking forward to seeing the costume you've made for me!

Jon

Jon Armory-Wargrove
Senior Assessor

This message is sent for and on behalf of the Dental Estimates Board, an NHS Service Provider. It may contain confidential information. If you are not the intended recipient please inform the sender that you have received the message in error before deleting it. Please do not disclose, copy or distribute information in the email or take any action in reliance on its contents: to do so is strictly prohibited and may be unlawful. Thank you for your cooperation.

From: **keith_sadwicke@techsolutions.co.uk**

To: armory-wargrove.jonathan@nhs–dental-estimates.gov.uk

Sent: 27.05.17, 10:13

Subject: **Where are you??**

Jon

Just wondering where you are, mate. I'm on the stand. We were supposed to meet at 8.30. Had to set up on my own. Luckily, there haven't been too many visitors as yet. Did you manage to get some kip last night? I heard sounds of a fight or something around 2 am. Lots of drunken swearing. Trust that wasn't you! I didn't see you at breakfast.

Listen, mate, I hope you're not sore or anything after our little altercation on the train coming up. I realise I may have got a little peeved after you admitted to not having read a single word of the *Xęn"räh* synopsis even though I sent it to you FOUR MONTHS ago. Worse still was when I discovered that you hadn't even mastered a single word of Xęn"dährin, which became painfully clear when I attempted some basic, beginner-standard banter with you.

I may have flown off the handle at that point. Didn't I say you'd need some lingo for conversing with punters on the stand? But it goes deeper than that. See, I thought I'd found a kindred spirit in you, Jon, what with your interest in all things mystical and mythical.

I'm not excusing myself. I probably did go over the top, and if so I apologise. Still, I thought we'd patched things up by the time we got to the hotel. We had a pleasant enough meal in that vegan place you found in Carnaby Street, The Great Sage or Happy Parsnip or whatever it was called. I ate all the weird shit they served up, and didn't complain too loudly when they refused to give me ketchup or a side order of fries. I thought, no, this is Jon's choice, let's not kick up a fuss. And I didn't even grumble when you declined to join me for a nightcap at Club 49 on Greek Street. I couldn't believe you were immune to the charms of those classy blondes queueing up outside, all of them looking like goddesses from the ice moon of Hyperia, compared to the painted morlocks you see outside Six Degrees on Crawley High Street on a Saturday night.

So where are you, Jon? It's well past 10 now, and the hall is filling up, though not too many coming this way as yet. It would have helped if you'd been here in your Blarf the Bellow get-up (did the wig fit by the way?) leafleting the passing traffic. Virtually my only visitor so far has been this dark-haired gnome-like female who's been pestering me for the past twenty minutes. Claims she's read all my stuff and is my number one fan. I'd be flattered if she wasn't so clearly unhinged, and if I didn't reckon she says this to every author she meets. She's actually getting on my nerves. Hurry up,

Jon – I think I may need you for pest control...

Keith

Sent from my iPhone

From: **armory-wargrove.jonathan@nhs-dental-estimates.gov.uk**

To: keith_sadwicke@techsolutions.co.uk

Sent: 27.05.17, 10:37

Subject: Re: **Where are you??**

All right, chill man. I'm actually here; I'm in the coffee shop on the level one mezzanine. Thank God they've got wifi – as you know, I don't use mobile phones because they can track you, though it's a pain lugging a laptop around. I'm trying to get my head together after last night.

Firstly, please cut me some slack. Not only have I had this post-audit shitstorm at work to cope with, but you've sent me nearly a quarter of a million words of 'briefing' and it just goes ON and ON and bloody ON. Frankly, someone ranting at you in a crowded train in Xęn"dährin is not just upsetting but suggests a certain instability on your part.

Your behaviour in The Merry Courgette wasn't much better. Constantly calling the waiter 'Manuel' was bloody rude and fyi he was actually Italian so it should have been 'Oi, Luigi'. Your constant loud complaints about 'rabbit food' were neither funny nor original; there is nourishment other than burger, fried chicken and fries, you know.

Also, did you see the prominent Adam's apples and outsize slingbacks on the 'classy blondes' you refer to???

As for the hotel, I can only assume the mice survive by eating the cockroaches. The only danger to this rich ecosystem is that they will all drown in the rising damp. The bedsheets looked like a relief map of the Alps.

At about 2 o'clock I was drunkenly trying on the Blarf costume (fits nicely btw!) when a lady of the night burst into my room with a punter. He looked like a well-known Tory MP. Anyway, there I was dressed as a fucking goblin and brandishing my Staff of Smiting, which, let's face it, looks like a giant dildo: the punter did a double-take and then decided, not unreasonably, that he was going to get more than he'd paid for and cut up rough.

A bit of a barney followed in which I got caught on the temple with his attaché case but the Staff of Smiting lived up to its name and the punter beat a hasty retreat under its mighty blows.

Turned out the lady of the night was called Mihaela and she kindly tended to my wound. She then produced a bottle of something 'from the old country' that tasted like paint stripper flavoured with cherries. We sat on the bed and drank and talked. She got maudlin and started crying about home, somewhere in the East, I forget. I comforted her and she offered me a freebie but I didn't have the heart.

We stayed up all night and went out to a caff in Dean Street early. A really nice woman, a very sad story.

Let's start afresh, no hard feelings. I'll finish my mochaccino and be down in 20 minutes or so.

Jon

Jon Armory-Wargrove
Senior Assessor

This message is sent for and on behalf of the Dental Estimates Board, an NHS Service Provider. It may contain confidential information. If you are not the intended recipient please inform the sender that you have received the message in error before deleting it. Please do not disclose, copy or distribute information in the email or take any action in reliance on its contents: to do so is strictly prohibited and may be unlawful. Thank you for your cooperation.

From: **armory-wargrove.jonathan@nhs-dental-estimates.gov.uk**

To: keith_sadwicke@techsolutions.co.uk

Sent: 27.05.17, 11:08

Subject: **Re: Re: Where are you??**

Sorry, mate, give us another 30 mins.

Just met a charming lady dressed as the Scarlet Witch. She has made the splendid suggestion that we step outside for a quick spliff.

45 mins tops.

J

Jon Armory-Wargrove
Senior Assessor

This message is sent for and on behalf of the Dental Estimates Board, an NHS Service Provider. It may contain confidential information. If you are not the intended recipient please inform the sender that you have received the message in error before deleting it. Please do not disclose, copy or distribute information in the email or take any action in reliance on its contents: to do so is strictly prohibited and may be unlawful. Thank you for your cooperation.

From: **keith_sadwicke@techsolutions.co.uk**

To: armory-wargrove.jonathan@nhs–dental-estimates.gov.uk

Sent: 27.05.17, 11:14

Subject: **Re: Re: Re: Where are you??**

All right, mate, I get that you're a bit busy right now with the Scarlet Witch, and sorry to hear about the ruckus with the Tory MP last night. Hope the head's OK. But just saying I'd appreciate a hand down here when you're ready. It's getting really busy, and people keep trying to nick stuff from my stand, assuming it's all free. I'm also kind of bursting for the loo. I'm in two minds about whether to temporarily hand over to Riva, the short dark one, as she seems really keen to take charge. Her knowledge of the *Xẹn"räh* universe is pretty staggering tbh, and she can speak Xẹn"dährin like a Greensky native, so she'd probably do a better job of selling it than you would, mate, no offence. All the same I don't know her from Adam and I'd rather you were here, at least to keep an eye on her and make sure she doesn't make off with all my merch. Hey, wait a minute, it's all kicking off here...

OK, back now. A kid dressed as a Power Ranger just tried to snatch one of my Odos the Otherling keyrings and Riva chased him away and gave him a clip round the ear for good measure. But then the kid's Iron Man dad starts screaming at her. This caught the attention of a passing Wonder Woman, who thought Iron Man was threatening a child – Riva's only about four foot tall. So Wonder Woman starts yelling at Iron Man, and he turns on her and it's all looking a bit hairy at this point, if I'm honest. I mean WW is DC and Iron Man is Marvel so they'd never meet in real life. Anyway, at the last minute this enormously fat Princess Leia shows up who turns out to be WW's girlfriend. She basically sits on Iron Man, after which he becomes a lot quieter.

I have to say I'm starting to be impressed by Riva. She's as fiercely loyal as Dögnâbbít the Tèrriä from Vol 3, who she also vaguely resembles. I'm thinking I can probably trust her to take over for ten mins while I go to the loo, and maybe grab a coffee. I'll see if I can find you on the mezzanine while I'm about it. Toodle pip.

K

Sent from my iPhone

From: **armory-wargrove.jonathan@nhs-dental-estimates.gov.uk**

To: keith_sadwicke@techsolutions.co.uk

Sent: 27.05.17, 15:37

Subject: **Re: Re: Re: Re: Where are you??**

Keith,

I'm crouched among the bins in an alley behind a Pret-a-manger, piggybacking on their wifi.

Sorry, it's all gone tits up.

Me and the Scarlet Witch nipped out onto a fire escape at the back of the conference centre for a quick toke. We got pleasantly blasted but then realised that the fire door had closed behind us and we couldn't get back in. We started walking round to the entrance but met some of the Scarlet Witch's mates on the way to the pub, so I sort of tagged along.

Few real ales, couple of tequila slammers. Noticed I was being watched. I reckon it was the MP back at the hotel tipped them off.

So I ran.

I saw their black helicopters.

It started to chuck it down and the dye in my costume began to run. I'm stained green, possibly permanently. I've got sick down my tabard. My head still hurts with the blow from the briefcase.

I think it is all clear now, so I'm coming back.

Can you have a damp cloth, hot chocolate and some paracetamol ready?

J

Jon Armory-Wargrove
Senior Assessor

This message is sent for and on behalf of the Dental Estimates Board, an NHS Service Provider. It may contain confidential information. If you are not the intended recipient please inform the sender that you have received the message in error before deleting it. Please do not disclose, copy or distribute information in the email or take any action in reliance on its contents: to do so is strictly prohibited and may be unlawful. Thank you for your cooperation.

From: **keith_sadwicke@techsolutions.co.uk**

To: armory-wargrove.jonathan@nhs–dental-estimates.gov.uk

Sent: 27.05.17, 16:49

Subject: **Re: Re: Re: Re: Re: Where are you??**

Fuck this, Jon. The halls are emptying. There's skin on your (now cold) hot chocolate. People are packing up for the day. I've waited patiently for you, mate. It pains me to say it, but you've let me down. While you've been out getting stoned with the Scarlet Witch and chased by helicopters, I've been quietly getting on with the job we were both supposedly here to do, which is selling and promoting the *Dragons of Xęn"räh*. And I've been quite successful at it. I've collected 63 new email addresses for marketing purposes. In addition, I've sold:

- 14 Odos the Otherling keyrings (10p each)
- 3 Bink Hallia mugs (£1 each)
- 104 Bór"ntöøsh-õrt beer mats (free, but good promotion)
- 71 Idris and his Cohorts of Myce wristbands (free, but ditto)
- 0 Xęn"dährin dictionaries (but lots of expressions of interest)
- 0 CDs of audio books (but, again, lots of interest)
- 1 booking for a live, private reading of Vol I (date and price to be confirmed by the customer [Riva])

I have to pay huge credit to the ever-loyal Riva Demn for a lot of today's success. She is an awesome saleswoman. You should have seen her flog the third Bink Hallia mug to this passing Harley Quinn. She had her pinned down for nearly twenty minutes before the woman finally broke. It was like a scene out of *Glengarry Glen Ross*. ABC, mate. Always Be Closing.

Jon, what can I say. You're still not here. I'm going to have to pack up. Hope I'll see you back at the hotel. I'll need Blarf back when you can, dry cleaned of course.

K

Sent from my iPhone

From: **keith_sadwicke@techsolutions.co.uk**

To: armory-wargrove.jonathan@nhs–dental-estimates.gov.uk

Sent: 28.05.17, 23:02

Subject: **Home again**

Hey Jon, mate

I'm back in Maidenbower. Aragorn cannot stop wagging his tail and licking my face. Comic Fantasy Con was great, wasn't it? I know Saturday was a bit of a wash-out as far as you were concerned, but you really made up for it big time today. And I really enjoyed last night, chez Scarlet Witch. She is one spiritual character with a well-stocked bar. Pretty too. What's not to like? And thanks for inviting me along. You both disappeared at one point, I think it was while I was in the middle of telling you about Vänwiįn Kūl of Dormis from Vol 4. Finding myself alone, I ended up crashing in a big basket full of blankets I found in her kitchen (surprisingly comfortable). Someone climbed in with me in the night. I won't tell you who I thought it was, but it turned out to be her dog.

Today, as I said, you were great on the stand. Your rumpled, easy charm and green skin really drew in the punters. Admittedly, we didn't sell anything, and I wasn't totally sure about your philosophy of giving all the merch away for free, even the CDs, but I suppose, like you say, it's all good promotion. I can't imagine what happened to Riva, though. She promised she was going to be there. It's a shame because

I was hoping to introduce you to her. I don't buy your theory that she's an alien (though I accept what you say that aliens are frequent visitors at Comic Fantasy Con because they find it easier to fit in among all the costumed humans, and the CIA tends to turn a blind eye at these events). True, Riva does look a bit weird, but she definitely seemed human to me.

Hope you got back OK, Jon. See you at the next group.

Keith

From: **armory-wargrove.jonathan@nhs–dental-estimates.gov.uk**

To: keith_sadwicke@techsolutions.co.uk

Sent: 30.05.17, 09:27

Subject: **Scarlet blow-back...**

Yo Keith,

Sorry, been meaning to drop you a line re: Comic Fantasy Con but the audit team are still sniffing around.

Saturday was a bit of a nightmare, granted, but the Jonster always bounces back and Sunday was a real blast! Mark my words, freebies will build your fan base and I gave at least two agents a bundle of goodies!

The Scarlet Witch was an absolute sweetie and very generous with the booze and blow. Sorry we disappeared during your lengthy and fascinating exposition of Vol 4 but the Witch wanted to show me her collection of action figures; it was a real eye-opener I can tell you.

I came down during the night to get a glass of water and you and the dog seemed very cosy – I just hope you don't get mange! Was Aragorn jealous?

Drink soon? We can rope Tom in as well and get the latest gossip.

Jon

PS I still have a faint greenish tinge; no one will sit next to me on the bus.

Jon Armory-Wargrove
Senior Assessor

This message is sent for and on behalf of the Dental Estimates Board, an NHS Service Provider. It may contain confidential information. If you are not the intended recipient please inform the sender that you have received the message in error before deleting it. Please do not disclose, copy or distribute information in the email or take any action in reliance on its contents: to do so is strictly prohibited and may be unlawful. Thank you for your cooperation.

From: **keith_sadwicke@techsolutions.co.uk**

To: armory-wargrove.jonathan@nhs–dental-estimates.gov.uk

Sent: 02.06.17, 02:02

Subject: **Midnight Madness**

Hey Jonster

A drink sounds good. I need it after the night I've had. Last night I only got another brick through the window! The window I'd just had reglazed! Like before, there was a note attached, which this time read:

It's all messed up! Don't you dare kill Bink. I won't let you do it.

The really freaky thing is, I haven't told anyone about the death of Bink Hallia. It was just a thought I'd had as a way of concluding Vol 7 and wrapping up the series. I hadn't written it down anywhere either. It was literally an idea in my head. Maybe I mumbled something about it to the Scarlet Witch's dog while I was sharing its bed last weekend. I wasn't really myself that night, mainly due to the effects of that cake the Witch baked for us. Having said that, I very much doubt the dog could have written the note or lobbed the brick, or even cared enough about the fate of a character in my book – even a major one like Bink – to bother. So who did it in that case?

Keith

From: **tom@tomcat.com**

To: keith_sadwicke@techsolutions.co.uk; armory-wargrove.
jonathan@nhs_dental-estimates.gov.uk

Sent: 02.06.17, 22:56

Subject: **Fancy a pint or three?**

Hola there hombres

I'd love to take you two up on your offer of an ale or two.

Keen to hear about this Scarlet Witch and what really happened at Comic Fantasy Con, you sly old dogs…

Shall we say 8 in The Crown on Tuesday? Blue's doing the late shift for that new trans-bi-curious helpline, so I'll be glad of the company.

Advance warning: please don't hate me if I go on about Blue a lot. It's a really special thing, and I just can't stop pinching myself. But you *know* her – not quite like I do, hopefully, but still – so you get why I'm so delirious right now.

T

PS Shall we keep it lads only? Obvs I wd ask Julia but I think it's her limo driver's day off.

PPS Should we ask Peter or have I gone soft in my old age?

From: **JuliaGeeGee@gmail.com**

To: Crawley Writers' Group

Sent: 06.06.17, 17:06

Subject: **Eek! Hosting issue...**

Hello one and all (she said nervously)

I'm so sorry – I know it's my turn to host next (seeing as Jon tells me he's not best placed to host just at the mo) and I know that some of us are real sticklers for respecting the roster as far as possible (and rightly so, of course)... but would you all mind if someone else hosted the next one?

It's just that the place is going to be absolute chaos for the foreseeable. Hubby's very taken with the idea of one of these kidney-shaped infinity-style pools in the garden, and I must agree we'd save a fortune on memberships in the long run if we had that to complement the new gym and workout room.

It'll take a while, and there'll be lots of dust and mess, alas, but of course you're all welcome to come for a dip once it's done! I'll still be attending all groups religiously, of course – you've all got me where I am today! (Not that appearing on *Woman's Hour* is quite all it's cracked up to be once you get behind the scenes, as with so many of these shows.) But it would be nice to have the work all done before the documentary crew get here. (Looking like early September for that one, by the way, so do keep your diaries clear!)

Thanks so much, everyone, for understanding – I promise to reward you all for your forbearance with extra-lovely canapes and bubbles next time you're here!

I'll leave it to the rest of you to decide who should pick up the hosting baton next. On paper it would be Peter, but it's obviously not for me to start dictating such things having put you all out myself!! (Though, Peter, if you could host that would make a lot of sense, as we can just keep the rest of the order and I can slot in when the work's done??)

Thank you all again for your patience and understanding – I've already drafted a special section for you all in my 'Acknowledgements'!!

Julia x

From: **keith_sadwicke@techsolutions.co.uk**

To: armory-wargrove.jonathan@nhs_dental-estimates.gov.uk

Sent: 07.06.17, 00:19

Subject: **Black and blue**

Hey Jon, mate

Bit of a 'mare at the pub tonight, wasn't it? Like being dangled over the Kaldron of Fyre while simultaneously being forced to listen to an anecdote from Monoton the Drear (Vol 5), I think you'll agree. Pete hardly says a word all evening, except to complain about the quality of the crisps and the position of our table vis a vis the hearth. (He actually used the word 'vis a vis' in speech. Is he human?) Apart from that, he mostly just sips his Appletiser and watches us like a slow-blinking toad.

Meanwhile, Tom won't stop banging on about you know who. I mean, there you are in the middle of telling us about the products you're trying out to deal with your green skin problem, and Tom interrupts with a long (and deadly dull) story about what he found in Blue's bathroom cabinet. And my story about the brick through the window is his cue to mention that 'brick' (or was it 'window'?) is one of his girlfriend's frigging trigger words. So you rightly ignore him and start talking about your troubles with the auditors at your work, and the reappearance of the black helicopters, which may or may not be connected, and he leaps in with some blether about the symbolism of black and how it's Blue's second favourite colour, which prompts Pete to open his mouth for the first time in about half an hour with some stat about how it's only the 26th most commonly used word in her poetry, and we're all sitting there shuddering at how he could possibly know something like that…

Anyways, I could see things were getting a bit tense by the end when you and Pete started squaring off over some money issue. Was he saying that you'd spent 42p less than everyone else on drinks? We were all possibly a little tired. The night got even worse when I came home just now to find a message on my fridge door from the 'Save Bink Society', threatening to smash up my laptop if I dare kill off their heroine. It gave me quite a scare, I can tell you. How the hell did they get into my house? Am I going mad? I know you told me that's what *They*, as in the deep state, want us to think. So what is this, Jon? And has it got anything to do with the black helicopters?

Keith

From: **disclosure_now47@aol.com**

To: keith_sadwicke@techsolutions.co.uk

Sent: 07.06.17, 00:45

Subject: **black hellicpotersd etc.**

Yeah keith fuckuing right bloody pete it was actually 47p I sent it him on paypal tight git. anD tom blue blue blue

yeah peolpl say i'm paranoid but I just say I jsee that bit deeper and yes, the blacvk helicopters, it was the bloke in the hotel tipped them off, it's closing in.

Bastard auditors put me on' gardening leave' due to ucking "irregularities thisi s not a conincidence. Just watch your bacvk that's al;l I can say. Gota go, i'vr had a fair

bit

your friend Jon

From: **blueyblu@blueyonder.com**

To: tom@tomcat.com

Sent: 07.06.17, 11:23

Subject: **Freak on my floor...**

Darling Tommy Tom cat,

You're a freak – just like me!

Of course you can lie on the floor and kiss my likkle tootsies!

Not in real life of course that would be ick, the no touch thing remember. That's why I wear three pairs of slipper socks! But you are a total sweetie pie.

Your TRU BLU xxxxxxxxx

PS Since the meeting the downstairs loo has been a teeny bit blocked; could my yummy scrummy pussycat come round and help???

PPS If you do come round, maybe I could rethink the no-touchy thing?!

From: **tom@tomcat.com**

To: blueyblu@blueyonder.com

Sent: 07.06.17, 16:23

Subject: **on my way**

on my way

From: **peterpeterpeterpeter@gmail.com**

To: Crawley Writers' Group

Sent: 11.06.17, 12:12

Subject: **<no subject>**

Dear group members

Please join me for our first outdoor group on Thursday, June 15, at 19:45 hours for a prompt 20:00 start.

I will provide light snacks and a selection of soft drinks (Shloer). Please bring your own vintage wines and pale ales if addiction so requires.

Please also bring a rug, deckchair, shooting stick or other suitable seating application which you know will satisfy your own comfort needs.

Alcoholic gel will be provided for all as always, but please bring your own ant-mosquito repellent (advised).

The venue is the disused lido in the middle of Goffs Park Woods.

Peter, writer

PS Please also bring a torch and a blunt weapon in case of self-defence, such as a cosh or a golf putter.

PPS The lido is the inside of my head. What does yours look like?

PPPS @keith and @Jonathan – I apologise that I have mis-calculated our relative spending from the other night in The Crown (Dry roasted). Please could you supply me at your earliest convenience with an additional 17p and 49p respectively?

From: **JuliaGeeGee@gmail.com**

To: aliceknowles@mewriter.com

Sent: 11.06.17, 16:32

Subject: **Thanks for the chat!**

Alice lovely

It was *so* nice to have a proper chat with you over a coffee after our fortuitous encounter in the high street on Saturday! (And thanks for enlightening me – I would never in a million years have guessed you can get a decent-ish cappuccino in Morrison's of all places!!)

It was *such* fun to catch up and compare notes about our little group, which as we both agreed has done so much to get the creative juices out of the jar and into the wok of actually writing!! (Well, virtually so, in your case.)

Though we were perhaps a tad too polite to say it (it's possibly a 'third-cappuccino conversation'!), I sensed that we are both a little troubled by recent developments in the group, namely 'The Couple'!! Now I'm no prude (as you'll have seen from my last appearance on *Midsomer Murders*; I was also houri #3 in a Badedas advert once!). And we all bring our eccentricities to the group, that's part of the fun. But I just wonder if the delicate balance of things could be upset if we allow these two in our midst to go on cavorting on the carpet and slobbering over each every time?? (Oh dear, darling – am I beginning to sound like Peter?!)

It's a tricky one – we both know what it's like to have to fend off Mr T-Cat's over-enthusiastic and rather indiscriminate attentions, so on one level I'm actually rather grateful to Blue for taking him in hand (and I suspect she'll prove rather more capable of running that show than her frail persona suggests). But it is getting a bit embarrassing, is it not? And – only a minor point, this, but perhaps one to consider nonetheless – how is this all going to come across in the upcoming doc about my rise to bestsellerdom? (Not that I'm a bestseller or anything! Pre-sales are only at the 7k mark, but it's a good sign apparently that people already want to talk TV rights.)

I suppose we need to find a way to blend a bit of endearing eccentricity (Peter, Blue, etc.) with a few dangerous ideas and concepts (Jon, Peter again?), but show all this against a backcloth of serious productivity and craft (you, me, Keith at a push?). Does The Couple quite fit into this mix? I suppose

– and forgive me for my crudity, but this is the reality of TV folk, darling, as I pray you'll never have to find out for yourself – I just don't want the producer to turn to me mid-morning on the first day of filming and say: 'But Julia, they're a bunch of fucking loons!'

Anyway, just a thought. Not really quite sure what can be done here, except maybe you mix things up by pretending to try and seduce Tom! That might cool things off a bit! Only joking, darling! (Though of course, I do appreciate that for an attractive single woman such as yourself, eligible males tend to be rather thin on the ground in Three Bridges, and I sense that you did maybe take a wee shine to Tom in the early days before he rather tried to spread himself too thin?)

Anyway, I do rattle on. Just thinking out loud really – and so nice to be able to share these thoughts with a fellow WRITER!!!!

Let's do coffee again soon, perhaps somewhere we can get a proper soya latte. My treat next time!

Julia xxx

From: **tom@tomcat.com**
To: blueyblu@blueyonder.com
Sent: 12.06.17, 03:54
Subject: **OMG, wow, fuck me etc.**

Hey Bluesy Blue

Two words:

Tantric marmite!

I had no idea

Tomcat (can't sleep but purring a lot) (who needs touching?)

From: **aliceknowles@mewriter.com**
To: JuliaGeeGee@gmail.com
Sent: 12.06.17, 18:44
Subject: **Taking one for the team**

Dear Julia

I too enjoyed our little tete a tete. We really must do this sort of thing more often. Morrison's café is wonderful, isn't it? They do a special meal deal there from 3 pm: any meal priced £4.50 or more includes one regular hot drink. I'm often there on weekend afternoons if you ever feel like joining me.

I will never tire of listening to your stories. I know you keep saying the world of television isn't half as glamorous as it appears, but when you talk about all the things you've done – the *Hello!* feature, filming in the Bahamas, kissing the gorgeous Gwilym Lee, it does seem impossibly exotic and a world away from my own life.

We rather skirted around the issue of Tom and Blue when we met, didn't we? But how perceptive you are to have picked up on my own qualms about the situation. It is, I agree, rather like an invasive species upsetting the fragile ecosystem of our little group. Their dalliance is very much the American grey squirrel in our English wood. Perhaps if they weren't so brazen about it, I might find it easier to stomach. The trouble is their constant touching, stroking and giggling is becoming a distraction, especially during the readings. It's hard enough to follow the tangled convolutions of Keith's plots at the best of times without also being forced to endure the sight of the Tomcat nuzzling his Bluesy Blue's neck.

And you're absolutely right, it won't play well in the documentary. You, after all, are the star of the show, and the last thing we want is for you to be upstaged by that lecherous pair while the cameras are rolling. Time is therefore of the essence. For the sake of the group and, more importantly, your fledgling career as a bestselling novelist, we must make sure that Tom and Blue are no longer an item by the time shooting commences.

There are times when one must make sacrifices for the sake of those one cares about. Clearly this is such a time. You might see it as a measure of my devotion to the group, and to you, dear Julia, that I am prepared, on this occasion, to step into the breach and 'take one for the team'. I shall wear make-up, maybe put on a frock. Please try not to snigger, dear, as I sidle up to Tom, laugh at his terrible jokes and generally try to unglue him from Blue. It shouldn't be a very difficult task. He's so shallow, so adolescent in his attitude to women, it shouldn't take much more than a flash of cleavage or a brush of my hand against his knee for Blue to go right out of his head. And let's not forget, he liked us long before he liked her!

As usual, Julia, you are so perceptive about me. It's true that I'm not entirely fulfilled in my singledom (though Tom, I promise you, is the very last person I'd ever be attracted to). It's funny, you know, fans of my blog are always so eager to try and interpret the real meaning of Freya's salad. None of them ever stop to think about the waiter and what he might represent!

But that is another story – part of the Everest that is the second half of my Sentence, which I don't want to think about right now. Suffice to say the subject of 'men and relationships' is a complex one, both for Freya and for me. I often wish it wasn't, but it is. Overall it's probably better for my sanity that I cohabit with a cat (though not a Tomcat, I hasten to add!).

Yes, do let's meet for another chat soon and an update on our battle plan. (I'm not sure they do soya latte at Morrison's. I can check.)

Alice xxx

From: **keith_sadwicke@techsolutions.co.uk**
To: Crawley Writers' Group
Sent: 17.06.17, 03:56
Subject: **Goffs Park Sheepnanigans**

'*Blimëe!*" as Bäm the Uttęrly Bööz̀led of Misty Fyde Moor declares in Vol 6, '*Wòt-the-fūkk-wázzåt??*'

Still, thanks, Pete, for 'hosting'...! What can I say? It started weird and just got weirder. That clearing in the woods you sent us to was hard to find! It was like trying to navigate the Forest of Fangorn in Middle-earth! Unlike the Hobbits, I had GPS, or else I may never have found you guys. To be fair, you found me when I yelled out in pain after walking into a tree. I couldn't complain, though, when I saw the snacks laid out on the picnic blanket: every flavour of yogurt, Edam, lychees, you name it. Delish! It was only later that we realised the significance of the food: it was everything you'd shown us in that Skype tour of your fridge, Pete mate. Everything except... well, that became clear later on.

Jon, your story about the bear king was brilliant, as usual. It was so sad how he got killed by his own wolfpack bodyguard, especially when everyone blamed that poor little squirrel for his death, just because the squirrel was in a tree overlooking the bear king's parade and may have lobbed a nut on his head. Everyone droned on about the parallels with the Kennedy assassination. I'm sorry, people, it was set in a forest! And since when was Lyndon B. Johnson in any shape or form a raccoon?

Alice, you gave us your usual 20-minute spiel on your battles with The Sentence. I don't want to be unkind but I can't help feeling that this time might have been better used by the active writers in the group. It didn't help that you kept looking over at Tom, as if wanting to make sure he was listening. Not that you needed to worry. Tomboy was, as usual, totally distracted by Blue. The cat has got his cream all right!

I wasn't distracted, though, Alice – you had my total attention. In fact I couldn't help noticing that you were looking (how can I put this sensitively in the #metoo world?) pretty frigging hot in that dress! Well, there wasn't too much of it, was there? And I did wonder, as the night got chillier, if you needed a bit of warming up.

Anyway, as I was listening and watching, I suddenly had this idea that maybe I could have a crack. At your Sentence, I mean. I reckon I could knock it into shape in a couple of minutes for a reasonable fee, and maybe even follow up with a page or four as a bonus for no extra charge. I've got some ideas. Here's one for free, just as a taster: maybe Frieda can kick the waiter in the nads for trying to steal her olives? What do you say? Why don't you let me have a look at it, Alice? It would get you out of your rut and you'd be doing us all a favour.

After Alice, there was Blue – once Tom had removed his mouth from hers for long enough to let her speak. Lots of fruit and veg this time, wasn't there, Blue? We definitely got our five a day! All that stuff about the aubergine with its shiny girth peering into the depths of the cantaloupe. You had Tom rolling about, and drew some blushes from the ladies. Not really my taste, though, tbh. I'm more of a meat man myself.

But you didn't get to finish, did you, and no one else got to do theirs either, because right in the middle of it all came PeterPeterPeter's piece of resistance. Fuck me! Was that supposed to happen then, Pete? Or did it come early, when Alice suddenly got up in the middle of Blue's poem and began wandering about, and then tripped on a wooden peg attached to a rope...

Down it came, the dead sheep, descending on the picnic like a blood-soaked gatecrasher to our party. Everyone jumped at least ten feet. There were screams. OK, I screamed. But there was a reason for that. My nerves are completely shot right now, what with this stalker business. I am totally on the edge these days, and your ovine surprise nearly tipped me over it!

You recorded it all, Pete, all our reactions, didn't you, you demonic imp? We should have predicted it because the sheep's brain from your fridge was the only thing that wasn't there when we arrived. But the rest of the sheep was, suspended in the trees above us all that time, waiting for its big moment. So what motivated this? Art, was it? Or revenge for the muting of your Skype vid? We deserve to know.

Keith

From: **aliceknowles@mewriter.com**
To: Crawley Writers' Group
Sent: 17.06.17, 10:47
Subject: **Shocked!**

I am in shock, as perhaps we all are, after the business with the sheep.

The effect on Keith must have been especially horrific, for how else can one explain his extraordinarily inaccurate memories of the evening?

For one thing, as I'm sure everyone else can attest, I was not in any way under-dressed. While thanking Keith for his elegant compliments on my appearance, I can assure him I was very well covered and did not require any 'warming up' as he puts it.

Secondly, I most emphatically did not go 'wandering about' during Blue's poem. I remained seated on the ground throughout. Whatever it was that caused the sheep to fall, it had nothing to do with me!

As for your offer to help me with my Sentence, Mr Sadwicke, shall we just say, when it comes to WRITING, you have your methods and I have mine, and leave it at that.

Alice

From: **blueyblu@blueyonder.com**

To: Crawley Writers' Group

Sent: 17.06.17, 13:01

Subject: **No more outdoor!**

Dear all

Sorry I ran after the sheep dropped onto the picnic spread but I was totally freaked. I'm surprisingly OK now but as a vegan I felt my space had been horribly violated. Also the stink was revolting.

Keith, I'm sure Peter wouldn't have done anything so disgusting.

I saw some teenage boys hanging around drinking and smoking and looking up to no good when I was looking for the meeting site and I bet it was them. I was sure I heard rustling and giggling in the thicket when we were reading.

Alice, please ignore Keith, your dress was lovely – it's nice to see you trying for a 'younger look'. The high heels probably weren't the best choice – in all that mud and after slightly more to drink than usual they were probably the reason you fell onto Tom.

Twice.

Please no more outdoor meetings!

Blue

From: **disclosure_now47@aol.com**

To: Crawley Writers' Group

Sent: 17.06.17, 15:06

Subject: **Do not adjust your mind**

Blue, I agree, not even Pete could do that…

Did no else notice the faint purplish flash before the sheep materialised?

It's clear what happened – animal mutilations are associated with UFO activity, it's well attested to by credible witnesses in the USA. The creatures are probably experimented on aboard the alien craft and then the remains teleported back to earth after DNA has been extracted. THAT'S what we experienced.

Also, when I was making my way back to the car I briefly saw a smallish, furry humanoid amongst the trees, doubtless a junior version of the so-called Bigfoot or Sasquatch. I didn't point it out to Keith because he already seemed distressed enough.

I've done some online research and the Tilgate Forest/Pease Pottage area has 'previous':

2014: a group of teenagers claimed they had seen 'fairies' in a clearing.

2006: a couple arrested in the woods said they had seen mysterious lights and were investigating. As part of a cover-up they were charged with 'dogging'.

1995: observation by an ambulance driver of a 'floating, shimmering sphere' in the area.

1967: a woman walking a dog reports seeing a puma.

I'm sure further digging will reveal more. We are obviously dealing with a 'window area' for strange phenomena, probably an inter-dimensional rift.

I've declared a UFO Event code RED and have scrambled fellow members of the World Anomaly Network, Crawley: we will be investigating the site thoroughly.

If any of you have any other 'odd' experiences, do let me know. I don't want to worry anyone but exposure to UFO phenomena may lead to further encounters.

IF YOU THINK YOU MAY HAVE BEEN ABDUCTED, PLEASE CONTACT ME ASAP.

Jon

From: **tom@tomcat.com**

To: blueyblu@blueyonder.com

Sent: 17.06.17, 17:59

Subject: **Home safe (Marmite redux??)**

Hey Bluest Blue (dreaming of you)

I'm so sorry I lost you in the woods after that bizarre sheep night. Blooming Peter and his artistic experiments, eh?

Julia and Alice and me were traipsing round for ages trying to find you in the dark. And Julia. I was so glad when you texted to let me know you were home safe.

Maybe I could pop round tonight or tomorrow and make sure you're OK? Perhaps a spot of Marmite on, ah, toast??!

Your Tomcat xxx

From: **tom@tomcat.com**

To: aliceknowles@mewriter.com

Sent: 17.06.17, 20:34

Subject: **Into the woods (or among the trees…)**

Hi Alice

I do hope you managed to get the mud out of those glamorous stockings you were wearing – what a pain to have such a lovely chic tenue ruined by having to traipse through a dark boggy wood in the middle of the night like that! Typical bloody Peter, eh? (If it was Peter, that is. It wouldn't surprise me if the whole sheep thing was a stunt dreamt up by Keith and Jon just to drop Peter in it. Jon has never liked Peter, and Keith is quite a one for the old amateur dramatics, if you cast your mind back to the group before. And I'm sure I heard some blokeish giggling coming from somewhere close by as we were struggling through the thickets…)

I so enjoyed our hot chocolate afterwards at the Goffs Park Hotel bar (and what a shame Julia had to rush off for that Skype call with her life coach in Waikiki. How the other half live, eh?). I really relished our chat about writer's block and the eternal struggle with form. You may write the least of us in terms of brute wordcount, but I often feel that you are the most artistic and dedicated of us all. (And I speak, remember, as someone who has read Blue's entire *Electrocuted Angel in the Headlights of My Dead Lover's Eye Sockets* sonnet sequence.)

It was no bother whatsoever to walk you the three miles to Three Bridges and see you home safely. The nightcap was most welcome too. You were wonderful company and, if you'll permit the impertinence, I find it extraordinary that a lovely lady such as yourself hasn't been snapped up. Not that you need a man or anything!

As I strolled back the three miles to mine (I live just by Goffs Park if you remember), I was in quite a dreamy mood, and barely noticed the downpour. As I always think: whatever we lose, like a you or a me, it's always ourselves that we find in the woods, n'est-ce pas?

Here's hoping we can do it again soon

Tom

PS Good luck with that preposition btw! I can see that 'from the olives' has its merits, it's direct and intuitive; but I also think 'among' brings a lovely dying fall, as in 'among the olives'. It adds a touch of subtle mystery and elegance which suddenly seems very you...

From: **JuliaGeeGee@gmail.com**

To: Crawley Writers' Group

Sent: 17.06.17, 21:06

Subject: **Something I need to tell you all**

Hi all

First off – and something perhaps we don't say often enough – a massive thank you to Peter yet again for such an inventive hosting idea. It was wet and dark and a bit scary – but was it not wonderfully stirring?!

And no, of course, I don't think for a moment that Peter had anything to do with that disgusting sheep thing.

But was it a sheep, though? It actually looked to me more like a possum or a sloth? Or a badger? Which took me back to the early days of my acting career, when I was cast as 'killing-spree victim #5' in a straight-to-video (but actually rather underrated) slasher movie called *The Beast in Me*.

All the murders involved pretty young things being bludgeoned with stuffed mammals in a variety of gruesomely inventive ways. Which took me back to Bob, chief make-up artist, effects coordinator and head of lighting on that low-budget pic. Bob's effects were wonderfully realistic – sights, sounds and, alas, smells were all so convincing that when it came to screaming for one's life not much faking was required. This animal stunt smacks very strongly of Bob's finest work.

Now why would Bob be coming to Goffs Park Woods of all places, you ask? Well, I suppose I should divulge that we had a brief flirtation on set (this was in my pre-hubster days, I hasten to add!). It was a bit of fun but ultimately Bob wasn't for me; Bob, alas, has never quite got over me and continues to 'stalk' me via Facebook messages and Christmas cards. I've never encouraged him in any way, but it looks as though my lack of response has driven his frenzied passion for me to bloody new heights. I did happen to mention on my socials that we'd be meeting in a local park, and Bob must have put two and two together.

Sorry to disappoint Keith, but I think you can sleep safe tonight! The object of obsession is me; but I shall stay strong and, with all your support, I will get through this. Bob is fundamentally harmless, I believe, though his feelings naturally go very deep.

Hold your loved ones a little closer tonight, my darlings.

Julia x

From: **peterpeterpeterpeter@gmail.com**

To: Crawley Writers' Group

Sent: 17.06.17, 21:32

Subject: **<no subject>**

And that is all from me at this time.

Peter, writer

From: **aliceknowles@mewriter.com**

To: JuliaGeeGee@gmail.com

Sent: 17.06.17, 22:08

Subject: **Oh dear...**

Hello Julia dear

I thought I'd drop you a line to update you on developments. Needless to say, my attempt to lure Monsieur Le Chat from his current fixation with Blue did not proceed quite as planned. Although, despite Sheep-gate, all is not lost on that front, thanks to our hastily improvised swoop, Operation Goffs Park Hotel. (Well done, by the way, for playing your part so well!) Actually, things might have succeeded a little too well and got completely out of hand. More on that later.

Back to last night: my plan to sidle over and distract him during his girlfriend's poetry recital was derailed when that horrid thing of blood and matted wool came crashing down. I thought at first it was some sort of fleshly metaphor for my writer's block, this deadness I carry around inside me that I dismissively call my mouse but is actually much more like a giant rotting carcass.

But it wasn't only the sheep that made me sit down again so fast. Was it just me or did you also see an odd sort of movement just after it fell? It may have been the wine or the shock, or possibly the shadows – it was quite dark by then – but I'm sure I saw something small and hairy skittering away from us into the forest. As I said, maybe it was nothing – but one thing's for certain, despite what Keith says, it wasn't me who tripped the rope or whatever it was keeping that sheep suspended. Perhaps it was your stalker. Was Bob a small man by any chance? What is it about some men and their obsessive targeting of women??

Which brings me rather neatly back to Tom…

After you left us at the hotel (and thank you for faking that urgent Skype call), we continued to chat and he was actually rather sweet about my struggles with The Sentence. He even offered some half-decent advice that I may feed into my next Strategy Session (these are the fortnightly deliberations I told you about when I try to think about The Sentence holistically rather than in its constituent parts).

I don't know if he spiked my hot chocolate, but as he talked these warm feelings started to develop inside me, and I found myself thinking he's actually quite attractive (I know he is quite handsome, objectively speaking, but previously I'd been unable to see beyond those huge character flaws that disfigure him like facial warts). It was all going wrong. This was supposed to be Project Distract Him From Blue, not Project Fall For The Stupid Man Yourself, Stupid...

At some point he suggested walking me back home, which was quite ridiculous and I told him so, but he kept insisting. On the way, he told me how much he loves my blog and what an artist I am and so on, and I don't know what came over me but when we got to my house I invited him in for a nightcap. I don't even think I'd have minded if he'd made a move on me that evening. (He didn't, as it happens.) As for Tiggy, she was a complete slut with him, draping herself wantonly across his lap. But Tom was a gentleman throughout – very kind, very courteous, and he didn't outstay his welcome. After he left, it started to rain, and I nearly ran out after him. I'm not sure why or what I would have said. What a fool!

So I woke up this morning with a headache that lasted until lunchtime, and a bad case of infatuation that I'm sorry to say is still with me. Not even the email he sent me earlier, which was full of his usual crassness, could break me out of it. I can hear you now, Julia, telling me to stop being an idiot. Actually, you'd probably say something much gentler than that, because you're so kind. But who on earth was I kidding, playing the *femme fatale*? That's not me! I could never be that cool.

So here we are, my dear. Actually I don't know where 'here' is. Tom is still with Blue, as far as I know. And I'm here, alone, and I don't know what to do. I can only hope that the feeling, like my hangover, will fade.

Right now, I'm supposed to be writing my blog but I can only think about him. I've tried writing out a list of his flaws: his promiscuity and opportunism with women, his Trump-size ego, his constant need to brag about his literary achievements. He has erotic prints on his wall for God's sake, and a black leather jacket that screams midlife crisis. But it makes no difference. All I can think about are those deep brown eyes staring meaningfully into mine. Help!

Seriously, Julia, how should I respond?

Alice x

From: **keith_sadwicke@techsolutions.co.uk**

To: Crawley Writers' Group

Sent: 22.06.17, 02:14

Subject: **Sheepish**

Hail, comrades in ink. How goes it? Have we all recovered from the Night of the Dead Sheep? And who was responsible? Was it Peter the Bleater? Or Jon's Ewe-F-Os? Or Julia's sheepeshal effects stalker? I guess only time wool tell...

Speaking of stalkers, though, my one struck again last night. You remember how cold it got? Well, my kitchen window got steamed up and I found this message scrawled in the condensation: *Kill Bink And You Will Get Hurt!* It gave me quite a turn, especially when I remembered that condensation collects on the *inside* of windows! The message was signed by some outfit calling themselves the Bink Freedom Fighters, which I reckon must be a militant breakaway faction of the Save Bink Society, who only ever threatened my laptop. These BFF maniacs are actually threatening physical harm. Did Bob go that far, Julia? I doubt it. When it comes to stalking, my guys are pros.

I was scared, I don't mind telling you. I started racking my brains trying to think of how they could possibly have got hold of the Bink death storyline. Like I said, the only possible witness was the Scarlet Witch's dog. I started trying to picture the dog, wondering if maybe I'd underestimated it. But then I realised, she never had a dog – at least I can't remember seeing one at her house. Do you remember, Jon? You were probably too spaced out to notice. But it did lead me to wonder: who did I share a bed with that night??

All of which brings me to the subject of the next group, which I am due to host. How do you feel, people, about the prospect of coming here, considering that there may be one or more violent brutes lurking in the vicinity, waiting to strike? True, all their anger seems directed at yours truly, so far anyway – although they might see you guys as collaborators, especially if you are seen to encourage me in any way to kill off my character. I have no idea how these fanatics' minds work, but it's probably best to be ready for anything.

Thoughts, please.

Keith

From: **JuliaGeeGee@gmail.com**

To: Crawley Writers' Group

Sent: 22.06.17, 19:16

Subject: **Deep breath, everyone!**

Hi Keith

Thanks ever so much for agreeing to host.

It's very sweet of you to worry for our safety. But we are all adults, are we not, and I'm sure we can look after ourselves. After all, what are we really dealing with here? Some sort of grown-up nerd stuck in adolescence, who's squeezed themselves into a fluffy space-alien costume or the like?? Not, fortunately for you, a cinematic FX genius with a sexual obsession of such burning intensity that passion can drive him to acts of the darkest despair. (That burden I shoulder alone. I found an African violet in my lobby from an unknown sender only this morning. One shudders.)

Moving on to more agreeable things, it will be lovely to see you all chez Keith. I'll bring some wine and some more of my home-made cheese straws (special request from Alice). Any other requests for drinks or nibbles?

Hope you all get some wonderful writing done between now and then. Looking forward to a really productive session, one where we can really focus on *the work*, free of distractions like imaginary stalkers or excessive canoodling.

See you on the 6th!

Love to all

Julia xx

PS The plant turns out to have been from my neighbour, Moira, as a thank you for cat-sitting. But still.

From: **JuliaGeeGee@gmail.com**

To: aliceknowles@mewriter.com

Sent: 23.06.17, 19.02

Subject: **Almost there...**

Alice darling!

You have performed your role to a T! Isn't it embarrassing how easy it is to sway the hearts and minds of men by flashing a little leg in their direction?

I thought you might have overdone it a tad by suddenly dressing in such a fashionably feminine way but of course I overestimate the foolish Tomcat. You were wonderfully distracting, and it was clear he just didn't know where to look. Such fun!

By the time I left the hotel, I could see that he was angling for a way to get you alone. Don't worry about falling in love with him, darling – I think your feelings are just a side-effect of the intensity you've brought to the seductress role. You know, I really think you might in another life have been quite an accomplished actress! Too late in the day for you now, of course, but still.

I think our plan is progressing wonderfully, but we need to stay focused and see it through. I fancy that Blue likes her men intense and obsessive (a bit like Bob actually) and I fancy that she'll soon spot it if Tom's attention levels start to waver (because he's thinking about you, you scarlet hussy!). So we can expect some sort of response as she tries to win him back, and need to be ready for that. Suggest you continue the seductive line, get Tom really confused and Blue really riled, ideally force the break-up. Obviously don't take things any further than you feel comfortable with, though if you do fancy him anyway, then... *result!* (As our dear friend Keith might say.)

Thanks so much for your help with this, darling. I was talking to the doc people yesterday and mentioned you. They thought it might be fun if we cut to you every few minutes as you try and squeeze out another word of that nefarious Sentence! Sort of a metaphor for the artistic endeavour! The fine line between eccentricity and excellence, all that. Wonderful stuff – and you at the heart of it!

Coffee soon?

Julia xx

PS Which of these book cover mock-ups do you prefer (see attached)?

5.

CROSSOVER POTENTIAL

From: **peterpeterpeterpeter@gmail.com**

To: Crawley Writers' Group

Sent: 24.06.17, 12:12

Subject: **<no subject>**

Dear all

I wish to inform you that I have begun work on a Mills & Boon novelette.

My intention is for us all to present the first chapter at our next meeting.

The rules for the content and presentation style are very strict – I have attached the guidelines, and would ask you all to help me comply with them to the letter.

The working title for my work is *Love Between the Lines*. You'll be assigned your parts in due course.

And that is all from me at this time.

Peter, writer.

From: **blueyblu@blueyonder.com**

To: tom@tomcat.com

Sent: 24.06.17, 23:54

Subject: **Getting in... touch?**

Darling Tomcat

Haven't heard or seen you for a couple of days, you OK babe?

Sorry I didn't fancy the marmite thing again – you know my 'rules of engagement' as you called them (it makes me laugh when I think of it). I know I am a bit slow but I think it should only take two or three months to get to a more y'know fully 'physical' expression of the special thing we have.

You have awakened something in me and I'm dizzy with confusion. You probably didn't notice but at the last meeting Alice was all dolled up and – it's hard for me to write this – I found myself strangely attracted to her! I think I've been open about my sexuality but I am really confused. I was a bit catty towards Alice because of my conflicted feelings but I just want to say that I would never do anything to spoil our relationship. I hope you don't think ill of me, it's just a 'pash' as we called it at my girls' school.

Please call me, my lovely tommy tomcat.

your true Blue xxx

From: **disclosure_now47@aol.com**

To: Crawley Writers' Group

Sent: 25.06.17, 03:16

Subject: **Your round...**

Hi everybody,

I'm still on enforced leave so I'm around during the day if anyone fancies a lunchtime pint.

The 'powers that be' are putting the pressure on; it's doubtless due to my involvement with the UFO disclosure movement (gathering momentum all the time!) but they have dressed it up as a problem with 'irregularities' in my processing of payment claims at the Board.

I've never made any secret of my friendship with the CEO of one of the larger dental groups in the Home Counties area and there is no question that I've processed their invoices with anything other than the utmost probity.

They're making a lot of fuss about alleged 'gifts' from the group but the holiday in Goa was a personal gift from the director. As was the car.

On the up side I'm in regular contact with my old band members and I've had a bit of time to go through some of our old tapes. Happy memories!

Anyway, I'm in the Wetherspoon's in the high street most days about 12.

Jon

From: **blueyblu@blueyonder.com**

To: aliceknowles@mewriter.com

Sent: 27.06.17, 09.47

Subject: **Out of the blue... Blue!**

Hi Alice

Would you like to meet up for a drink or something to eat?

luv

Blue

From: **aliceknowles@mewriter.com**

To: blueyblu@blueyonder.com

Sent: 30.06.17, 17:54

Subject: **Why not!**

Hello Blue

Sorry for the delay in replying to your kind offer. I'm feeling a little fragile and confused at the moment, and terribly busy with The Sentence, possibly as a displacement activity for my life, which is more than mildly stressful right now.

Today I've been playing around with the second main verb, describing the waiter's approach to/appearance at the table (to take away Freya's salad). What do you think about these possibilities: 'arrived', 'presented himself', 'turned up', 'rolled up', 'fetched up', 'ended up', 'materialised'? The waiter, by the way, is 28, of Swiss-Zimbabwean descent, an amateur ornithologist and son of an unsuccessful sock importer with a dysmorphic antipathy towards his left foot and dreams of breaking into competitive falconry. He only makes this one, brief, appearance in the novel, but I felt it was important to sketch him a backstory to better understand his most likely approach to the table ('limped up'?).

I'm tempted to ask, Blue, what prompted your invitation, but I won't, and please don't tell me unless you want to. How are you and Tom? Is it all going blissfully? I don't mean to pry, and I'm not, I'm really not. Couples deserve their privacy. You seemed very happy together, perfectly matched I thought, and I'm so happy for you, assuming appearances don't deceive and you are, indeed, blissful? If not, that's your business, not mine, and I shall not pry, because that's not my style. But if you want to talk about things, feel free. I'm all ears, and also a shoulder (to cry on, if you need one – only if you need one).

Perhaps, after all, it would do me good to get out. The waiter can wait! You choose the venue, Blue. I'm free most nights next week, except Thursday (writing group at Keith's of course!).

Alice

From: **aliceknowles@mewriter.com**

To: JuliaGeeGee@gmail.com

Sent: 30.06.17, 18:34

Subject: **Now what??**

Thank you, Julia, for your kind remarks about my 'performance'. If only it were just that and I could discard the character I played that night as easily as you do after one of your acting roles.

The strangest thing has happened: Blue has emailed to ask if I fancied a bite to eat and a drink. What's she playing at? Has she cottoned onto our plan? Is she trying to spook me, or perhaps get some sense of my intentions? She seems so sweet on the surface, if a little intense, but I suspect there's quite a lot of guile within that poetic heart of hers.

I played a straight bat (as my cricket-obsessed dad used to say) and told her I'd be happy to meet up, without giving any hint that I was suspicious of her motives.

As for Tom, I know you told me to continue the seductress line, but I'm finding it really hard – I'm just not as adept at 'playing a role' as you are, Julia, and I find it almost impossible to see where the part ends and the heart begins, if you know what I mean. In fact there's a huge overlap right now. So I've done the cowardly thing and not replied to him – hoping, I guess, that the whole thing will blow over and my life can return to normal.

I've retreated to the sanctuary of my Sentence, where I feel a lot safer. I realise the danger of this strategy – that my silence is only going to make Tom keener, but I can't think what else to do. If I write to him, I may just be too honest or end up hating myself or I don't know what. Please forgive my cowardice but it's far easier right now to take shelter under the metaphorical lettuce leaves of Freya's salad.

If only you could have taken on this role, Julia. You'd have been so much better at it than I. But don't worry, I know that would have been impossible – you're married, too much scope for misunderstanding, etc.

By the way, thanks so much for getting me a significant role in the documentary. I feel honoured, and also terrified. I hope the prospect of cameras filming me doesn't bring on another onset of the mouse. I've been feeling incredibly productive of late.

In terms of the covers you sent, I prefer the one with the glamorous woman casting off that Greek actor mask more than the one with the faces emerging out of the flowers. Blown away, though, with envy and admiration to see your name on such brilliantly designed jackets. Are you totally happy with the new title, btw?

Alice x

From: **tom@tomcat.com**
To: blueyblu@blueyonder.com
Sent: 30.06.17, 21:23
Subject: **Love in the third person**

Hey Bluesy Blue

Sorry I couldn't make the other night. Things have been manic at work – our social activities coordinator has broken a leg playing football, and I ended up having to take 30 Italian teenagers to a pub quiz…

'Meester, why is beer warm?'
'Meester, what is joker?'
'Meester, why no serve espresso?'
'Meester, what is imperfect tense of *vomit*?'
…You get the idea.

You know I just love being with you, however/whenever. Let's just let this thing unfold, I say, take us wherever it takes us. And if you want to bring Alice in on this, I'll do my very best to get on board, babe. It's obviously not the sort of thing I've ever thought about before – never even crossed my mind, ever! – but if that's the way you/we three want to play it, I'll do my best to make it work.

love you

Tomcat xxx

PS Is Alice up for it?

From: **JuliaGeeGee@gmail.com**
To: aliceknowles@mewriter.com
Sent: 01.07.17, 11:06
Subject: **The plot thickens!**

Oh Alice darling – you are so clever!

Don't you see what's happened – you've only gone and turned Blue's head too! She's so bi-dextrous or whatever it is she'll fancy anyone!

So now you can take your pick! Or have them both! Anything you like – so long as they break up (and you promise not to start snogging anyone in the documentary…).

Julia xx

PS I know what you mean about the book title. *Bare Naked Ambition* is a bit in-your-face for what is essentially a deeply felt and exquisitely crafted contemporary coming-of-age psychodrama. *The Casting Couch* was a bit more subtle. But then, as my agent says, 'We have to face up to the fact that you've got that erotic It-factor, darling.' All I can do is bow to the experts!

PPS At least I think that's what's happened. The only other possibility I suppose is that Blue senses you're moving in on Tom and wants to scare you off. Might be wise to bring a small blade or something – go 'tooled up', as darling Keith would say. She's so unpredictable there's no knowing if she'll try to stab you or snog you!!

PPPS In any case do let me know how it goes – I'm on tenterhooks...!!

From: **aliceknowles@mewriter.com**
To: blueyblu@blueyonder.com
Sent: 02.07.17, 19:38
Subject: **Cake and crushes**

Dear Blue

It was so lovely to meet up this afternoon at the wonderful Veggie-Might Café. The vegan chocolate cake was yummy. I had no idea you could replace egg with silken tofu! And it was so much fun to gossip about the other members of the group. I totally agree with you about Jon by the way! You're so cool and funny and I'm sorry I spilled my tea when you suddenly reached into your pocket. I don't know what I expected you to take out – but how cute to discover that you bring your own 'special spoon' to the café. I wasn't nervous, really! Or if I was, it's only because I'm at such a critical stage in my Sentence. What a good idea, by the way, that I should try acting it out. I may just give that a go.

It was a lovely conversation, so full of unexpected twists and turns. How on earth did we get onto crushes on other women? As I said, the only one I've ever had was on my French teacher Mlle Aubin when I was 14. Nothing like as impressive as your record in that department! Thanks, by the way, for being so nice about my dress the other night. I always assume ulterior motives when men say those sorts of things, but from a woman I know it's genuine. Saying that, the heels were definitely a mistake, and I know you're sick of hearing me say it, but they are the *only* reason why I fell on Tom – both times.

Alice x

From: **peterpeterpeterpeter@gmail.com**

To: Crawley Writers' Group

Sent: 03.07.17, 12:12

Subject: **<no subject>**

Hello group

Here are your roles, as promised.

Please turn up for Keith's group dressed in character. I will circulate a script for us to work through on the day, and pin mics.

And that is all from me at this time.

Peter, writer.

Julia = Kev

Kev is a geeky sci-fi hack whose professed dream in life is to turn his leaden yet unfortunately prolific prose into hard cash. Actually, his real dream is to have a girlfriend, or to impress his dad (two things which he has never yet achieved).

Jon = Gilly

Gilly is an unreconstructed Lady who Lunches, who – through a series of undeserved old-boy contacts – has managed to parlay her modest acting career into a much-hyped debut novel. Her secret fear is that her husband is so nice to her he must be hiding a terrible if banally predictable secret.

Keith = Alexa

Alexa is desperate to be a real writer, but in several years of trying is still on her first sentence. There is a profound sense of blockage at the core of her being which, to her great shame, does not come from any profound psychic wound. It's more just a case of her not being able to pull her finger out.

Tom = Jimmy

Jimmy is a conspiracy theorist, real-ale obsessive and prog rock bore, who enjoyed a brief moment of niche fame in the 1970s and has never really got over it. His desire to prove that we are all being watched by dark forces masks a profound despair that there is in fact nothing out there, and that – since the death of his young friend, in which he may have been implicated – nothing really matters.

Blue = Tone

Tone is a fading small-town lothario with a successful career he despises and a desperate need to predate on any vaguely pliable woman who comes within his cheesily undiscriminating orbit. His extraordinary radar for symptoms of female desperation contrasts sharply with his blindness to his own secret self-loathing at a life given over so wholly to inauthenticity and bad faith.

Alice = Piers

Piers is a profound artist of great complexity and vision. The cross he bears is to be cruelly misunderstood in his own time, and only the distant dream of a thoughtfully adoring reappraisal by posterity enables him to continue with his exquisitely painful excavations of the terrors of being alive.

Peter = Aquamarine

Aquamarine is a latter-day suburban Plath, writing highly derivative and mawkishly intense poems of self-lacerating heartbreak from the depths of her suburban bedroom. Her secret fear is that deep down she would rather be hoovering.

From: **keith_sadwicke@techsolutions.co.uk**
To: Crawley Writers' Group
Sent: 08.07.17, 02:12
Subject: **Eyes right for mega-jellies!**

I like a challenge. So kudos to Pete for laying out the gauntlet. Acting is in my blood, as you well know. I'm not one of those method types like Daniel-Day Lucas who spends six years preparing for a role, but I do take myself seriously. So when I was assigned the role of Alexa I thought, what do we know about this person? The first thing we notice is that Alexa is a lady, so most probably she has breasts. After a few hours of patient preparation, I managed to fashion my chest area into something attractively feminine and I felt ready to begin exploring her character. I dug deep. I tried, as they say in the acting manuals, to 'reveal the inner Alexa'... and I came up empty. What sort of person is this, I thought. She's about as useless as Fütyle the Flòb, Frōōtless Frôth-drìbble of Flöōbling Forest. So apologies, friends, if my performance was less than scintillating. But I think the fault lay with the writer. Sorry, Pete, but she's just not realistic or well rounded, except – I think we can all agree – in the breast department.

As for the rest of you, well, a bit of a parson's egg, wasn't it? Let's just say that some made more of an effort than others. Best acting prize has to go to Julia, who was a complete pro, as you'd expect. Saying that, what a peach of a role Pete handed her! I mean, what a lovely bloke! If he'd been real, I just know Kev and I would be best mates!

Golden Raspberry, sad to say, has to go to Jon. Sorry, mate, I know you're up against it right now with all the dark forces ranged against you from the Serious Fraud Office to the CIA. Still, not sure if your 'lady who lunches' character would sport a faded black KED T-shirt and three-day stubble, or reek of Old Speckled Hen.

Special mention to Blue. Not bad at all, though you weren't really masculine enough to fill Tone's leather jacket (borrowed, I'm guessing, from Tom), not the way I managed to fill Alexa's bra, for example. And chatting to Piers the poncy artist for most of the evening (when he wasn't being bored by conspiracy theorist Jimmy) didn't seem true to your womanising character, especially with a hottie like Alexa sitting right beside you!

All told, a decent evening I thought, expertly hosted (though I say so myself!). Thanks for the cheese straws, Julia. And sorry, everyone, for the weird howling outside, which forced me to close the windows on such a warm evening.

Keith

From: **JuliaGeeGee@gmail.com**
To: Crawley Writers' Group
Sent: 08.07.17, 10:52
Subject: **What a night!!**

Hello everyone!

I just wanted to say what a splendiferous evening we had yesterday – thanks so much to Keith for hosting, and sorry for those howls (ongoing stalker pains, I'd rather not discuss). And thank you so much to Peter for masterminding such a truly memorable evening!

Full marks to everyone for doing their best to get into character. Keith – those breasts were extraordinary! Not like any I've ever seen on a real woman, mind, but an engineering feat nevertheless. Some did better than others, if I'm going to be honest, as we professionals must be. But at least everyone had a go (well, almost everyone, Jon – and you had such a fascinating and complex role to get your teeth into too!).

I found Alice's performance as Piers especially captivating – and I could well understand why Tone/Blue wanted to spend so much time with you, darling! Even conferring furtively in the loo at one point! Piers was so fascinating he practically seduced Tone!! Talk about method acting! Poor old Jimmy/Tom kept knocking on the door, trying to join in for a smoke, but didn't seem to be getting much of a look-in. The look of dismay and exclusion on Jimmy's face was true pathos, darling Tom – wonderfully drawn characterisation. I could hardly have done it better myself. (Well, a bit better, obviously.)

Some of you have been kind enough to remark on my own performance. It's a while since I played a man (I was a much-admired Viola in a school production of *Twelfth Night*) but it's amazing how the thespian muse provides when one is open to the moment. Thank you, darlings, it was a thrill and a privilege to bring Kev to life and bore the pants off everyone with such geeky, mercenary vim.

What with the sheep's head and the recent romances and the play-acting and so on, it's great that we're getting all the high jinks out of the way before the televised group at my house, which has now been scheduled for September 14! (So in about three groups' time. The new swimming pool should just about be ready by then too.) And guess what? In a TV first, the producers want to broadcast our writing group live as part of Channel 4's *Work in Progress* series!!! So we'll all be live and on the telly, darlings! Nearer the time it'd be useful, I think, to have a little chat about how we can best present ourselves as the serious and conscientious artists that we are, all in our different ways, striving to be. (Rather than coming across as oddball fantasists or deluded misfits, say.) But for now, let's enjoy the news!! You're welcome!

Au revoir, mes amis – until the next group!
Jx

From: **aliceknowles@mewriter.com**
To: Crawley Writers' Group
Sent: 08.07.17, 11:54
Subject: **Out of my comfort zone (and rather enjoying it!!)**

Thank you, Peter, for involving us all in your evening of experimental theatre. Rarely if ever have I strayed so far from my comfort zone, yet I have to admit I enjoyed myself, and learned something too! The first thing to say is that I've never acted before, and I literally had no idea what I was doing, so I'm stunned by Julia's kind remarks about my 'performance'. If it had any merit, I can only think it was because I recognised something of myself in Piers, 'the artist of great complexity and vision doomed to be misunderstood by his contemporaries'. I may also have been 'helped' by the wine that Tom/Jimmy so generously kept plying me with.

Blue whispered to me at one point that there was something searingly honest and deeply heroic about my struggle, and that my sacrifice of words for truth made me a more authentic artist than anyone in the group. It was honestly the most beautiful thing anyone has ever said to me, yet it left me hopelessly confused. Was she saying this as Blue or as Tone? And was she saying it to me or Piers? I was so moved and perplexed I started to cry.

I retreated to the loo, trailed by Blue proffering apologies and by Tom proffering more wine. I'm sorry, Keith, if I knocked one of your magnificent breasts askew as I ran out. I wasn't myself – in every sense. And sorry to everyone for hogging the bathroom for such a long time – especially to Tom, who kept knocking and rattling the door handle. I hope you managed to find relief for your bladder (or whatever was troubling you) elsewhere. I just couldn't show myself, I'm sorry. I only allowed Blue in because I hoped she might explain what she'd meant. She never did, and I didn't dare ask. I'm not asking now either. But she was, nevertheless, a comfort with her aromatic cigarettes and her heartfelt ode to the toilet brush. It made me laugh. I think we were both pretty wasted by then.

In the end I found it all strangely liberating. By donning another identity I was able to gain some perspective on my own, including certain negative habits of thought and feeling. Blue showed me that I don't need to be defined by how others think of me. I am what I am, and if I only ever write a single sentence in my life, that's something to be proud of. At least I might get read!

She showed me something else too, a hidden side of me I didn't know existed until that night. But that's something that must remain between me and Blue.

Alice

From: **blueyblu@blueyonder.com**

To: Crawley Writers' Group

Sent: 08.07.17, 17:12

Subject: Re: **Out of my comfort zone (and rather enjoying it!!)**

OMG what a great evening!

I must say I was dreading it but since joining the group I've been on a journey – I've discovered SO much about myself and found a new resolve to become who I truly AM! So thank you Peter for your brilliant role-playing idea! How did you ever come up with such a crazy bunch of characters?

I'm pretty comfortable with fluid identities but even I was surprised at how completely I got into the role of Tone. A leather jacket and distressed jeans really made me feel confident and, dare I say it, raunchy!! So apologies to Keith for constantly squeezing his 'attributes' and repeatedly asking 'how about it, darling?' It wasn't me – it was Tone talking! Apologies as well for slopping beer everywhere and dropping fag ash on the carpet. And the swearing.

But dear dear Alice, the things we said, the time we shared in Keith's frankly disgusting loo was ME, not Tone, communing with YOU, not Piers. (Unless you prefer me as Tone lol!)

Blue x

From: **disclosure_now47@aol.com**
To: Crawley Writers' Group
Sent: 10.07.17, 03:52
Subject: **Sorry**

Sorry, just sorry.

As has been pointed out several times I didn't really rise to the occasion at the last meeting. In my defence I have to say I have been having a hard time of it recently and I've maybe been drinking a little too much.

Pete, I thought this was another of your wind-up psychodramas but, probably much to your disappointment, everyone else seemed to really get into their roles and had a good time with it.

I really feel for you, Alice, as I'm sure we all do. On the positive side, if you can survive that long in Keith's malodorous bog you can get through anything: 'what does not kill us makes us stronger'!

Anyway, I *am* trying to get my head together.

Today I gave the morning trip to the pub a miss and drove out to the country. Back in the day, after a night of laying down some tripped-out sonic vibes, I'd watch the sun coming up. Everyone would be sleeping it off in their vans and tents but I'd look over the fields, at the standing stones, whatever… and it was Albion, you know? The real England, an England of crazy eccentrics and madmen and visionaries and I'd see the ley lines stretching away in glittering lines of energy, I'd watch hares boxing and badgers making their way about and catch glimpses of the elves from the corner of my eye. I thought the silver dazzle of the saucers would manifest at any time, bringing the Wise Ones, philosopher kings who would bring a reign of benign rule. Universal love. Creativity. Peace.

Today I found a Curated Nature Experience with a signposted walk. A dumped fridge. A photocopied sheet pinned to a noticeboard saying 'Multiculturalism = White Genocide'. Ffs.

Nowadays it seems it's just bad orgone energy and Greys and government cover-ups.

I've got my disciplinary hearing next week. Wish me luck.

Jon

From: **MPranesh@gmail.com**
To: Crawley Writers' Group
Sent: 11.07.17, 21:37
Subject: **I would have been there**

Hello everyone

I was planning to come this week. Really! but in the end I just couldn't. I'm in a bit of a bad state at the moment – angry about everything! – and I don't think any of you would like me very much if you met me.

Please don't drop me tho. I'll feel better soon I know it. Keep me on the email list because I feel like I'm part of the group and I do like reading about what's going on. I promise to try and make the next meeting, if I can just sort my head out.

Mavin Der

PS Isn't it a bummer when your heroes let you down.

To: **aliceknowles@mewriter.com; blueyblu@blueyonder.com**

From: tom@tomcat.com

Sent: 12.07.17; 09:16

Subject: **Dîner à trois?**

Hi both

Just wondered if you fancied a meet-up for a chat on all things literary and poetical ahead of the next group (which will be at mine btw, on August… three)?

Obviously the last group was a real success and threw up lots of interesting creative challenges and opportunities. It'd be great to hear your perspectives on all that. I was trying to talk to you both more at the group, actually, but think you both got a bit distracted.

With my TEFL advanced composition students – and in my own fiction recently – I find I've been reflecting a lot on the magic of three – that mysterious and yet infallible principle which holds that a trio of events or clauses or wishes or characters or anything really is somehow more aesthetically captivating than two or four elements, or any other arrangement. Life, love and liberty. The Holy Trinity. The three-act structure. Omnne trium perfectum, and all that jazz.

Did you know that Churchill actually offered the British people his 'blood, toil, sweat and tears' – but people only remember ‘blood, sweat and tears’ – a noble tricolon? Things do just seem to go better in threes.

Anyway, I thought perhaps the three of us might meet at the pub – The Three Stags does a nice selection of wines now – or if you prefer I’d be very happy to host? The new Cookshop that’s opened in Langley Green is supposed to be very nice. I could sort us something tasty for starter, main and afters. There – another perfectly delicious trio!

See you soon

Tom x

From: **JuliaGeeGee@gmail.com**
To: aliceknowles@mewriter.com
Sent: 12.07.17, 13:19
Subject: **Well played, darling!**

Alice darling – such fine work! You have completely wedged yourself between our embarrassing lovers! It looks to be all over – or all over the place, at any rate, which is half the battle.

But what were you doing with Blue all that time in the loo? Is she still weeping over T-Cat, or were you sharing a sneaky doobie? (No need to hide these things from me, darling – I’ve been to drama school you know!)

I did enjoy Peter's role-play night – fair play to him, he does have some good ideas. And of course if it was all calculated to show up what a killjoy his arch-enemy Jon is, well it worked a treat, didn't it? Let's just pray that he (and the rest of them) can stay relatively sane on September 14th!!

Getting very excited about the doc now, especially as I have just signed with Fitzrovia Books and the US is already sniffing round film rights... My only worry is getting everything shipshape ahead of filming, especially as we'll only be back from our Ayahuasca Visioning retreat in Peru three days before... as well as seeing that the pool is done in time, I'm going to have to get the whole upper garden terrace completely relandscaped and replanted, I can see it now!

Anyway, let's meet for a coffee and a catch-up soon ABM.

Jxx

From: **aliceknowles@mewriter.com**

To: JuliaGeeGee@gmail.com

Sent: 13.07.17, 18:45

Subject: **Oh who am I? (And what is ABM??)**

Julia, thank you for this.

Yes, I've certainly put the cat among the pigeons with regard to Tom and Blue. The trouble is right now I'm feeling rather like a pigeon being fought over by two cats!

I feel very conflicted about Tom. I know exactly what he wants, and in my last email to the group I was deliberately playing the innocent. Playing him along, you might say – only that sounds too cruel. I'm attracted to him, no question. But he's so ardent and needy and it's actually quite stressful. I just need some space to think and breathe, and get my head straight.

As for Blue, she's lovely, and so perceptive! She's been through a lot, a refugee from suburbia, as she calls herself, with a fragile yet uncrushable spirit. She told me that, for her, life has never been a one-way street, but a meadow to roam through. Boundaries are never fixed, always blurred. I hope I'm not giving too much away when I say that her performance as Tone wasn't entirely an act. As for what we got up to in there, that must remain between me, Blue and Keith's toilet brush (by the way absolutely the cleanest, least used thing in that bathroom!). All I will say is that sexuality is a very elastic concept. You may go through life thinking you're one thing, but that doesn't mean that now and again you can't be another!

And yet, despite all that, I feel almost as much pressure from Blue as from Tom, but coming from a different direction. I sense she wants me to be more like her, or, as she puts it, to be 'the real me'. Only I don't know, in the end, if that's what I want. A drunken hour in Keith's loo is one thing, but to live like that all the time, with no boundaries? I fear the real me might be closer to what Peter said about 'Aquamarine': deep down I'd rather be hoovering.

Sorry, Julia dear. I know that neither of us intended any of this when we started out. I suppose, in a way though, we got what we wanted, in that the lovebirds will no longer be distractingly twittering around each other during the documentary. The fact that they'll both now be twittering around me is a result of sorts. Isn't it?

Congratulations on signing with Fitzrovia and fingers crossed about a film deal. I can really see Damian Lewis playing Fenton Ainsworthy!

By the by, what's ABM?
Alice

From: **JuliaGeeGee@gmail.com**

To: aliceknowles@mewriter.com

Sent: 13.07.17; 18:48

Subject: **Re: Oh who am I? (And what is ABM??)**

Anywhere but Morrison's!!

xxx

From: **aliceknowles@mewriter.com**

To: blueyblu@blueyonder.com; tom@tomcat.com

Sent: 16.07.17, 22:10

Subject: **Three's company!**

Hello Tom

Yes, I'm sorry we didn't get more time to chat at the last group.

It's very interesting to hear your views on the number three. Actually, it's a number with a lot of negative connotations for me. I was an only child, often caught in the crossfire of my parents' rows. And I had these two friends at school, or I thought they were my friends until I realised they liked each other much more than they liked me. So, for me, being the third in any triangle has always been a little bit toxic.

Having said that, of course I'd be happy to meet up with you and Blue at The Three Stags. I can do any night but Thursday (I'm taking Tiggy to the vet that afternoon for her urinary tract condition and I know she'll be anxious if I go out that evening).

Speak soon.

Alice

From: **keith_sadwicke@techsolutions.co.uk**

To: Crawley Writers' Group

Sent: 04.08.17, 05:53

Subject: **Free the Balcombe Road 1!**

Cool evening at Tom's last night, wasn't it, folks? So nice to reacquaint ourselves with the leather sofa, low lighting, background jazz and smutty art photos on the walls (though disappointed that you haven't yet added a snap of your current squeeze to the collection, sir. Give it time, right? Hint, hint!). And thanks, everyone, for letting me read three chapters this time instead of the usual two, as we approach the climax of Vol 7. You're all getting so much better at processing my speed-reading, which is now approaching 220 words per minute. I got no complaints, except from Blue when a fleck of spit went in her eye – an unfortunate side-effect of faster mouth movements, I'm afraid! I glanced up at one point and was well pleased to see you all listening in rapt concentration. Jon even had his eyes closed, which is definitely the best way to picture the arid, icy plains of Greensky. I noticed Tom and Blue were both staring at Alice, obviously trying to picture Bink Hallia, who it's true she vaguely resembles, if you imagine Bink as a pale anxious woman living in Crawley.

Speaking of Bink, I have to decide very soon what I'm going to do with her, as her final scene is coming in the next chapter.

Do I kill her off as I originally planned, or do I bow to the demands of the Bink Liberation Front and let her somehow survive the Kaldron of Fyre?? The BLF are, by the way, the latest and (so far) most militant of the groups to threaten me. They're the self-declared armed wing of the Bink Freedom Fighters, who are themselves an extremist faction of the Save Bink Society (ah, how I miss those moderate, easy-going terrorists of the SBS!). The BLF it seems will stop at nothing to get their way – even threatening to put Aragorn's severed head in my bed if I don't accede to their wishes.

I'm really tempted to back down. Anything for an easy life, right? But then I think of Salmon Rushdie. He went through hell and he never gave in! It comes down to your principles in the end, and how much you're prepared to sacrifice for them. Salmon would understand: if I want to kill a character, it should be *my* choice. And if I need a safe house to lie low in once the chapter's written, I know I can count on you guys to step up, right? Because you believe in free speech as much as I do, being writers, and you would never want me to give in to terrorism. I could even get some 'Je Suis Keith' badges made so you can all show your solidarity. What do you think?

Speaking of badges, I've still got boxes of Xȩn"dährin merch cluttering up my spare room from Comic Fantasy Con, which I'm prepared to sell to you for just 80% of the asking price. I'm probably about to become huge due to the imminent release of Vol 7, plus all this Bink notoriety, so this could be your chance to pick up some bargains. Not that you would, but just think what this stuff'll be worth on eBay once all the Bink stuff hits the news. It could even help with the publicity for your new novel, Julia – the fact that you're associated with me I mean. Something to think about, yeah?

Keith

From: **keith_sadwicke@techsolutions.co.uk**

To: Crawley Writers' Group

Sent: 05.08.17, 02:11

Subject: **Update to yesterday's message…**

Just to keep you guys in the picture, I'm currently involved in negotiations via encrypted text messages with a representative of the moderate Save Bink Society calling him or herself Arden Vim. S/he suggests that I might want to consider injuring rather than killing Bink, and we're discussing what that injury might consist of and how serious. Trouble is, SBS can't guarantee that any deal will be respected by the more extreme BFF, let alone the fanatics of the BLF who probably wouldn't countenance so much as a Chinese burn to the blessed Bink, so all this may come to nothing. Still, it's a glimmer of hope, right?

Keith

From: **disclosure_now47@aol.com**

To: Crawley Writers' Group

Sent: 05.08.17, 11:34

Subject: **Great news!**

Hi dudes,

Good meeting I thought – I was still slightly out of sorts again but very enjoyable.

Blue and Alice, it was great to see you both relaxed and having such a good time. Keith mentioned Blue and Tom both staring at Alice but it seemed to me that you two ladies had bonded over some shared private joke. Not sure why any mention of 'three' is quite so funny and your hilarity when Blue pulled out a jar of Marmite was totally perplexing. Poor old Tom, no offence but you looked a bit 'piggy in the middle', mate!

Keith, you were right – I had my eyes closed the better to envision the cinematic scope of your epic work. Great stuff, mate!

Blue's effusion was as challenging as ever; the image of 'the kitten of hope' sailing a fatberg down the 'sewer of life' was certainly startling. To be frank, I felt slightly nauseous for several hours after but it certainly lived with me.

Even Pete's contribution, a reading from an IKEA assembly booklet, read in a dull monotone, with random growls and shouts was... nah, it was bollox!

Anyway, I have some news. As I told you at the meeting, I'd just had my disciplinary hearing and was awaiting their judgement. Well, the jury is in and I have been found innocent of any impropriety!

Luckily, one of the three members of the disciplinary board had previously bought some 'pharmaceutical supplies' from me a while back to help take the edge off a team-building weekend in the Brecon Beacons. I reminded him of the very strict policy on drugs of the Dental Estimates Board and he obviously played a blinder advocating on my behalf.

Not only was I, rightly, found not guilty but we came to an agreement on a fairly substantial redundancy package. Free at last!

It gets better!

After several meetings and a couple of informal jams we are getting the band back together! That's right – The King of Elfland's Daughter rises again, like a phoenix from the ashes! With my redundancy money we can get on the road again and this time nothing can stop us!

Jon

From: **tom@tomcat.com**

To: blueyblu@blueyonder.com

Sent: 06.08.17, 01:58

Subject: **How you doing?**

Hey Bluesy Blue

How you doing?

Long time no speak?

I've called you a few times (OK, quite a few times) but no joy. And I popped around the other night (OK, nights) but you never seem to hear me knock (though I thought I saw your light??).

Not being paranoid or anything but... are you trying to avoid me, babe??

It's cool if you are. I mean, if you want to cool things for a bit. Just be nice to know where I stand. But all is well. We never made any bourgeois pledges or anything. I really don't mind, unless of course you're still up for stuff (or for stuff one day) then obviously that'd be really cool too. But only if you fancy it. No sweat otherwise at all. All is well.

Take it easy.

Speak soon (or maybe not – whatevers, babe)

Tomcat xx

From: **JuliaGeeGee@gmail.com**

To: Crawley Writers' Group

Sent: 06.08.17, 12:50

Subject: **The countdown begins!**

Hi all

A lovely evening I thought.

Peter – IKEA! So original. And did you have to assemble that monologue all by yourself? Arf arf!!

Sorry – couldn't resist! Perhaps I'll attack the comic novel for my follow-up!!

Julia x

PS Don't forget, darlings – September 14 for group at mine (televised! yikes!)

PPS Tom – do hope all is well. You seemed a bit out of sorts at the group, and no wonder – such a shame your piece didn't make the shortlist of the Sharpthorne Guild of Flash Writers annual contest! £75 is not to be sneezed at! But don't give up, darling – I mean, look at me! Plucked from obscurity to feature in the *Evening Standard*'s annual Ten Writers to Watch in 2018 feature! (Allegedly…) I mean – just look at me!

From: **tom@tomcat.com**

To: aliceknowles@mewriter.com

Sent: 06.08.17, 13:13

Subject: **Fancy a bowl of the good stuff?**

Hi Alice

Hope this email finds you well and The Sentence is progressing spiffingly!

I know we talked about meeting up the other week but somehow we never managed to firm up the details?

I was wondering if you might fancy a catch-up some time over the weekend instead, perhaps? You mentioned you had a thing about home-made pasta, and I just happen to have taken the day off and spent the last eight hours making fettucine from scratch! No big deal – just something I like to do from time to time. But obvs if you fancy a bowl of the real mccoy, it'd be lovely to see you. I could do Friday night or Saturday, but if they're no good I could manage Thursday or Sunday (or Wednesday).

I'd ask Blue to join us but haven't seen much of her recently tbh – am guessing she's deep in the throes of composing her new ottava rima cut-up novella-in-flash – working title 'Nunchuck Aureole'.

Tom

PS Interesting group, didn't you think? Peter's piece actually made me laugh for once (not sure if it was supposed to). Keith's saga is actually growing on me too – pretty sure Jon slept through the whole thing, though.

PPS Or Tuesday or Monday night I could do.

From: **aliceknowles@mewriter.com**
To: Crawley Writers' Group
Sent: 06.08.17, 14:38
Subject: **THANK YOU ALL!!**

Fellow WRITERS

Can I just say, once again, thank you, all of you, for being there with me through all the trials and tribulations of my Sentence. There have been a few ups and many more downs, false dawns, lights at the end of tunnels that fade to yet more darkness. So I hesitate to say this, not wishing to offer yet another hostage to Fortune (who must have a small village of my hostages by now – I hope she's treating them well!), but I do feel I am finally nearing the end.

This morning I have been hard at work on the very last part of The Sentence, the verb or phrasal verb that describes the waiter's future action, i.e. the action that Freya fears he will perform upon her salad when he arrives at her table. She is anticipating a negative, destructive kind of action, one that should serve to foreshadow her fears about her future more generally. I just need to find a way of visualising it, of playing it out in my head before committing it to paper.

But all this is a discussion for the next group. Suffice to say, I'm nearly there, folks! These days, when I read over what I've written thus far, I no longer feel the urge to vomit or slash my wrists or worse: delete the whole thing and start again. I feel sort of, you know, OK about it, sort of calm.

You all played your part in this, and it will be you, dear friends, who will be the first to witness the fruit of my labours (all 35 words of it!) when it's done. That day will soon be upon us.

Love

Alice

From: **aliceknowles@mewriter.com**

To: tom@tomcat.com

Sent: 06.08.17, 15:43

Subject: **A small favour to ask...**

Dear Tom

That's so kind of you. Yes, let's meet up. I can do Wednesday if that works for you? The fettucine sounds amazing – thank you for remembering my secret passion! Would you mind if we have a starter, too? I'm thinking salad. Specifically a Greek salad: half a red onion, thinly sliced, two large ripe tomatoes, half a cucumber, 100g reduced fat feta cheese, drained and cut into cubes, 50g black olives pitted and drained (v important!), oregano, olive oil and lemon juice. I can deliver the ingredients earlier in the day, if you wouldn't mind preparing it?

Also, would you mind dressing up for the occasion? I know how much you love the leather jacket/jeans combo, but could you maybe try something a little different for our evening: white shirt, black trousers (close-fitting if possible), bowtie, an apron around your waist, and perhaps apply a little gel to your hair? In other words, I want you to dress like a waiter. If this makes you uncomfortable, please say, but could you also try to imagine that your flat is an exclusive restaurant, and when I arrive, greet me as a guest and show me to the table? I know, you're thinking crazy lady, what's she up to? But it would mean so much to me if you'd do this! Oh, and would you also mind walking with a very slight limp?

Finally, and I hope this isn't too much to ask, but could you attempt a different way of speaking, by which I mean adopt an accent? I'm thinking something that sounds a little Swiss (either French or German would do) and at other times Zimbabwean (think South African). Best of all (and I know this might be tricky) would be if you could actually combine the two accents. Thank you so much, Tom. You're such a friend!

By the way, as you saw in my last email to the group, I'm making super progress on The Sentence! Are you proud of me?

À bientôt

Alice

From: **tom@tomcat.com**

To: aliceknowles@mewriter.com

Sent: 06.08.17, 17:42

Subject: **Wednesday it is (and can I take your order, ma'am?)**

Hi Alice

Lovely to hear from you!

I'm guessing you need me to help enact The Sentence – am I right? How wonderful and how clever of you! I shall be delighted to oblige in a little creative role-play! I always say that you can have anything you want in life if you dress for it. Clothes mean nothing until someone lives in them, after all.

Shall we say 8 pm at mine for an aperitif? I shall of course be suitably attired and our starter shall be ready and waiting! (But not, of course, wilting...) An excellent choice too – the hues of a natural fresh garden salad are so splendid, no painter could possibly improve on them.

Tomcat x

PS What will you be wearing? Fashion is like eating – we don't have always to stick to the same menu, and sometimes life is best lived à la carte...

From: **disclosure_now47@aol.com**
To: keith_sadwicke@techsolutions.co.uk
Sent: 06.08.17, 23:54
Subject: **Another time perhaps?**

Hi Keith

I got your messages suggesting that my band work on a series of concept albums based on your work. It's incredible that you've already written three albums' worth of lyrics in a couple of days – how do you work so fast?

Of course, I'd be *totally* on board for this and I'm sure it would, as you say, create a unique 'marketing syzygy' but I have the other guys in the band to reckon with. So, for the moment, we're going to be completing songs that we were working on before the break-up. To be honest I'm not sure the lads would be up to learning lyrics in your various invented languages!

Maybe some day, mate...

As you know I've been seeing the guys for a while now but they never seemed that keen on re-forming the band; it was a happy coincidence that they all decided to finally commit just as I got my mitts on a fair old wedge of dosh. I really feel things are on the up.

Maybe a beer soon? But not too much – gotta get gig fit!

yours aye

Jon

From: **blueyblu@blueyonder.com**
To: tom@tomcat.com
Sent: 07.08.17, 19:07
Subject: **Feng shuiing my life**

Hi Tom

Sorry I have been a bit reclusive, it's really bad manners not answering your calls etc. it's just that I've been in a right tizz thinking loads of stuff through.

I've been having a big clear out of the house which is literally like a metaphor for my life now. Don't worry it's not a bad thing, I'm not in a bad place just thoughtful and feeling actually really quite confident which is not me at all, lol.

All my old clutter, the skulls and stuff, have gone in the bin and I'm repainting the walls in brighter colours (it's a bugger painting over black!) and got some house plants in. The place seems fresh and new and I really like it!

Anyway I realise I haven't said anything about US. I really need to think a bit more about what's going on with me now. I'll get back to you soon...

Blue

From: **blueyblu@blueyonder.com**

To: tom@tomcat.com

Sent: 07.08.17, 19:08

Subject: **<no subject>**

Fuck it! Can you come over on Wednesday?

Bring a bottle of tequila and we'll have a bacon butty and get pissed.

No promises...

B

From: **tom@tomcat.com**

To: blueyblu@blueyonder.com

Sent: 07.08.17, 23:11

Subject: **See you at 4**

Hey Bluey-Blue

Is that really you? You sounded quite different in your last email...

Yes – let's meet on Wednesday. I can be at yours for just after 4, for when you get back from the charity shop.

Hope you don't mind, but I've promised to help out a mate who's short of servers for this charity dinner silent auction gala quiz thing he's running later that night, so I'll be dressed accordingly. Will probably need to get away about 7 if that's OK.

See you Wed

T

From: **peterpeterpeterpeter@gmail.com**
To: Crawley Writers' Group
Sent: 08.08.17, 12:12
Subject: **<no subject>**

Hello group

I appreciate Julia's joke about my IKEA monologue, the entire artistic purpose of which was to collect if possible a full set of such IKEA jokes as an exploration of the inevitable process of embourgeousification that will always attend the operations of a well-meaning hive mind. I'm delighted to say that with Julia's contribution I now have them all, to wit (and here I use the word 'wit' loosely):

Tom: 'Nice one, Peter, did you put that together yourself?'

Julia: 'Did you have to assemble that monologue by yourself?'

Keith: 'You can pay people to build these things for you now, you know. Nice little business idea, that.'

Alice: 'Sometimes I see my opening line as a flat-pack unit with one vital screw missing.'

Blue: 'The Allen key represents the tender indifference of the universe, is that right?'

Jon: 'Did you build that all yourself? Was it worth it?'

Thank you for your input. I shall make these into an auto-destructive audio collage.

In case anyone failed to notice, the text I read was actually not a straightforward set of IKEA assembly instructions but actually an IKEAlipogram of my own devising, in which the letter 'e' has been removed from the original, as in this sample:

Original version

The recommended height for the top level of your sink is 33½-35⅜". Because there are different heights of sink, in the assembly instructions you will find a minimum and maximum recommended height for the holes you need to drill for the cabinet. Below, are 2 examples of height measurements for different types of cabinets. Note that these measurements are intended as a recommendation only. These measurements can be changed according to your personal height preference. Once you have established the height of your drilling points, you can concentrate on the width between them. These measurements are given in the assembly guide of your cabinet. Use a level to ensure your measurements will result in an even line. You should mark the intersecting points (height + width) with a cross (+) to give you a precise drilling point.

IKEAlipogrammatic version

How high to put your sink's more high flat part? 33½-35⅜" is most good. As sinks vary in how high sinks go, our instructions for building posit most good minimums and maximums for the point at which you should drill into your wall so as to support this bathroom wall cupboard. Look down for a pair of illustrations of varying sorts of bathroom wall cupboard. Understand that our counts of how high or what width or how long to go should go down in your mind as but notionally optimal from us. Such counts can go up or down as you wish. Upon confirming for you the tallness of your drilling points, you can focus on the width that is the span connecting said points. You can find such counts in your bathroom wall cupboard's building instructions. With a spirit tool you can supply a flat, straight axis. You should mark the points that cross (how high and what width) with a cross (+) so as to turn out a drilling point of good accuracy.

A few of you thought the text I was reading was merely a bad IKEA translation, rather than a daring experiment in form – but then I suppose the difference is hard to see... for those who find it hard to see that the re-versioning makes possible some bold re-seeing of the world itself.

And that bombshell is all from me at this time.

Peter, writer.

From: **keith_sadwicke@techsolutions.co.uk**

To: Crawley Writers' Group

Sent: 08.08.17, 12:37

Subject: **Oops**

Nice one, Peter. Very clever. Sorry I didn't get it first time round. But nice to see someone else besides me getting inventive with language. However, I couldn't help noticing that there are in fact more than a few 'e's in your supposedly 'e'-less version of the IKEA instructions. Here's a tip when inventing a new language, mate: obey the rules you set out for yourself!

Keith

From: peterpeterpeterpeter@gmail.com

To: Crawley Writers' Group

Sent: 08.08.17, 12:52

Subject: **<no subject>**

My email server appears to have sent the wrong version. The email client may have been corrupted by all those messages Keith keeps sending with odd symbols in.

It should of course have read as follows:

IKEAlipogrammatic version

How high to put your sink's maximally high flat part? 33½-35⅝" is most good. As sinks vary in how high sinks go, our instructions for building posit most good minimums and maximums for that point at which you should drill into your wall so as to support this bathroom wall cupboard. Look down for a pair of illustrations of varying sorts of bathroom wall cupboard. Know that our counts of how high or what width or how long to go should go down in your mind as but notionally optimal from us. Such counts can go up or down as you wish. Upon confirming for you high limits of your drilling points, you can focus on that width that is that span linking said points. You can find such counts in your bathroom wall cupboard's building instructions. With a spirit tool you can mark a flat, straight axis. You should mark such points as cross (how high and what width) with a cross (+) so as to turn out a drilling point of good accuracy.

***Peter, writer*.**

From: **disclosure_now47@aol.com**
To: tom@tomcat.com
Sent: 08.08.17, 15:28
Subject: **Beers?**

Hi Tom,

If you're around lunchtime tomorrow (Wednesday) I'm meeting Keith at 12.30 for a plate of grease and a couple of jars. You're more than welcome. Usual venue.

Fair warning: Keith wants to share some new 'merch' – so brace yourself for some badly produced tat featuring the Barf Wranglers of N'arg or whatever.

On a more positive note, the barmaid with the lazy eye and big gazonkas was asking after you and I happen to know that she's on the day shift at the moment...

atb
Jon

From: **tom@tomcat.com**

To: blueyblu@blueyonder.com

Sent: 09.08.17, 15:34

Subject: **Along in one shake of a thingie's thing**

Hey Bluesy Blooooooo

Lookinfg forwra to seeing yopoooooooooo

sorry runnig a bit late – Jon bumped into me in pub and he seemed a bit lowly and loneley so I treated him to an ale

why do they call it a lazy eye by the wy? it's quite endearinfg really

see you as soon as I can xx

From: **tom@tomcat.com**

To: aliceknowles@mewriter.com; blueyblu@blueyonder.com

Sent: 10.08.17, 11:01

Subject: Sorry

Dear Blue, Dear Alice

Sorry Sorry Sorry Sorry Sorry Sorry Sorry Sorry Sorry Sorry Sorry Sorry Sorry Sorry Sorry Sorry Sorry Sorry

Sorry Sorry Sorry Sorry Sorry Sorry Sorry Sorry Sorry
Sorry Sorry Sorry Sorry Sorry Sorry Sorry Sorry Sorry
Sorry Sorry Sorry Sorry Sorry Sorry Sorry Sorry Sorry
Sorry Sorry Sorry Sorry Sorry Sorry Sorry Sorry Sorry
Sorry Sorry Sorry Sorry Sorry Sorry Sorry Sorry Sorry
Sorry Sorry Sorry Sorry Sorry Sorry Sorry Sorry Sorry
Sorry Sorry Sorry Sorry Sorry Sorry Sorry Sorry Sorry
Sorry Sorry Sorry Sorry Sorry Sorry Sorry Sorry Sorry
Sorry Sorry Sorry Sorry Sorry Sorry Sorry Sorry Sorry
Sorry Sorry Sorry Sorry Sorry Sorry Sorry Sorry Sorry
Sorry Sorry Sorry Sorry Sorry Sorry Sorry Sorry Sorry
Sorry Sorry Sorry Sorry Sorry Sorry Sorry Sorry Sorry
Sorry Sorry Sorry Sorry Sorry Sorry Sorry Sorry Sorry
Sorry Sorry Sorry Sorry Sorry Sorry Sorry Sorry Sorry
Sorry Sorry Sorry Sorry Sorry Sorry Sorry Sorry Sorry
Sorry Sorry Sorry Sorry Sorry Sorry Sorry Sorry Sorry

Tom

From: **tom@tomcat.com**
To: aliceknowles@mewriter.com
Sent: 10.08.17, 11:07
Subject: **<no subject>**

PS I still have your fascinator.

From: **blueyblu@blueyonder.com**

To: tom@tomcat.com

Sent: 11.08.17, 16:56

Subject: **Bog off!**

Tom

I guess you want to know why I threw the cauliflower at you; you looked so perplexed as you withdrew under a hail of root vegetables that I'm sure you have no idea and *that* lack of insight is part of your problem.

Firstly, you turned up late and half cut. The fact you stank of a perfume that smelled like a floral scented chemical weapon and had a scarlet lipstick kiss on your cheek made it worse. Claiming that Jon was having a gender identity crisis and was in drag at the pub and that he was responsible was pitiful – did you really think that I wouldn't check that out?

I don't know why I let you stay but, my bad, I did, watching you plough your way through a bottle of Pinot Grigio and listen to your unsubtle passes.

Things went from bad to worse when my weekly Fruit and Veg box arrived. An avalanche of puerile innuendos ('Fantastic melons!' and 'That's a nice pear!' etc.) followed.

The bottom of the barrel was scraped when I came back from the loo to find you putting a novelty Curry'n'Chips flavoured condom (presumably from a pub vending machine) onto a cucumber and giggling like a schoolboy.

That's when I saw red and started throwing fruit and veg at you.

The thing is, I had decided before you came I would take the plunge and ACTUALLY HAVE SEX with you. Luckily I saw you as the man-baby you really are before that happened.

I suspect that will cause you more grief than me – I have realised I am better than that and will be fine on my own.

In short: bog off!

Blue

From: **disclosure_now47@aol.com**

To: tom@tomcat.com

Sent: 11.08.17, 23:12

Subject: **Nice one**

T

Good sesh at the pub the other day!

Amy the barmaid, she of the generous frontage, gave me her phone number to pass on to you. She scrawled it on a beer mat but unfortunately it got a bit wet and the ink ran so it's a bit of a blur. Unreadable frankly. Sorry.

As I'm sure Amy told you, she's going back to Pudsey to look after her aged mother. She was certainly emotional – all the regulars got a hug and a kiss but she seemed very keen on you! Sure you could track her down somehow.

see you soon
Jon

PS I got a curious email from Blue asking if I was experimenting with cross-dressing!? I put that rumour to rest; no disrespect to anyone else but it's not for me!

From: **aliceknowles@mewriter.com**
To: tom@tomcat.com
Sent: 12.08.17, 14:25
Subject: **Badly let down**

I don't understand you, Tom. Really I don't.

First of all, you show up late, leaving me waiting outside your door for 25 minutes. And it's raining. I am in my short black dress, black tights, silver heels. I painted my nails to match my blush pink coat and my fascinator, all of which are now getting wet. I'm about to storm away when you finally arrive, showering me with slurred apologies, your collar askew, speaking like Igor from *Frankenstein*. We go in and you show me to 'my table', walking as if dragging a lead weight with your right foot. You hurriedly clear it of your PlayStation console and empty pizza boxes. It's clear by now, you have not prepared for this. There is plenty of fettucine, of course. Your pasta-making machine is still gummed up with it. But no salad! *No metter*, you say. *No mitter!* Your accent is wandering drunkenly all over Central Europe and the Balkans. *Vee ken improvize!* you say as you toss cubes of Tesco 'salad cheese' onto a bed of iceberg ripped from a bag. No tomatoes, no cucumber, no – and this is the real killer – no olives! The one ingredient I said was most important. *Peekled onions?* you offer with a sheepish grin. I think that's when I start to cry. You limp over to hug me, like Quasimodo, still dragging that stupid lead weight. I can smell the beer on your breath, and something else. A certain perfume I recognise! I fight you off. We get into a tangle. I stab you in the bottom with my fascinator, then run off.

Oh Tom! You've let me down badly. I wish I'd never asked you to help me with this. In fact right now I'd be quite happy never to see you again. But we're both part of Julia's group, and that's bigger and more important than either of us. So let's try and put all this behind us, and maybe not communicate any more outside of the group or group emails. Instead let's put all our energies into supporting Julia for her big day.

Please don't bother replying. I won't read it anyway.

Alice

PS Hope you weren't too badly hurt – in the nether regions, I mean.

6.

HEADING OUT FOR THE STARS

From: **keith_sadwicke@techsolutions.co.uk**

To: Crawley Writers' Group

Sent: 18.08.17, 05:02

Subject: **Nice one, mate!**

Hey Jon

Great hosting, mate. Nice to see the inside of your pad at long last. And sorry for raising that blackout blind – I didn't realise you like to keep it closed for 'security'. Thing is, I'm sure I'm being followed by this doglike animal, and I heard some barking in your back garden. Sorry also for tripping on that guitar lead and knocking over your amp, but you've got to admit the place was a teeny bit cluttered. You seemed in a pretty dark place, Jon, and not just because of the blackout blinds. I couldn't help noticing all the beer cans. You muttered something about old wounds being reopened with Harry Warde. I can't believe he never understood that the sky creatures are real! Still, I hope you patch things up in time for your reunion gig.

Julia, you mentioned you had a book tour lined up by your American publisher. Well, I did a reading once at Waterstones in The Martletts. Actually it was just outside Waterstones, because the stuck-up manager said he didn't want any self-published authors. So I set up my stall in the arcade, and read a bit of Vol 1 and eventually got quite a crowd. But then came the book signing. Let me tell you something, Julia: people are stingy. They always want a discount. Well, don't give them one! Fair enough, write their name above your signature, but when they start asking you to sign it to their children and their parents and their pets, just remind them that you're a professional writer and you charge by the word. That'll soon shut them up!

Blue, glad you're back mining that gloomy theme with your poetry. Something about finding your soulmate in a mirror but then the mirror shatters, and you're left holding a shard of mirror glass. Then a dead crow plummets out of the sky into a black pond, which turns red with blood. Totally flew over my head. But it sounded great. Really gloomy and negative. Loved it!

Tom, you were quieter than usual. Nice to see you attempting a bit of poetry. But you're not yet in your girlfriend's league. Something about a sore arse cheek and finding a Brussels sprout in your hair. Could have been funny, but you sounded so glum about it. Come to think of it, everyone was a bit subdued. When I asked Alice about her Sentence, she just muttered to me that the waiter was a prat.

But my favourite piece of the night had to be Peter's silent poem. Best thing you've ever done, Pete, though I thought three mins was a bit long. You could have got it down to two by not speaking a bit faster!

Keith

From: **MPranesh@gmail.com**

To: Crawley Writers' Group

Sent: 18.08.17, 08:04

Subject: **Sorry**

Hello everyone

Sorry, I couldn't make it. I've got a bit of a sore throat.

Ma Vinder

From: **keith_sadwicke@techsolutions.co.uk**

To: JuliaGeeGee@gmail.com

Sent: 19.08.17, 02:12

Subject: **Optimising crossover commercial potentialities... (more cash yeah?)**

Hey Julia

As the group's two most commercially successful authors, I thought it would be a good idea for us to have a chat ahead of the documentary, just to establish what my role's going to be. Am I going to be interviewed, or will I just be doing a reading? If you could put me in touch with the programme's producer, I'd like to discuss my fees.

I'm sure that if we can work something out, it could be to our mutual benefit, as we both have quite distinct readerships – you with your metropolitan liberal luvvies, me with my army of geeks and cosplay enthusiasts – which could potentially double the audience if the TV people do their marketing right. And no doubt there is some crossover potential, with some of your fans liking my stuff and vice versa. For example, according to Google Analytics, 33% of visitors to my site are ladies, and ladies like your stuff, right?

Keith

From: **peterpeterpeterpeter@gmail.com**
To: Crawley Writers' Group
Sent: 19.08.17, 12:12
Subject: **<no subject>**

I am reassured, almost gratified, to see that my efforts at the last group have – as always – gone misunderstood and unappreciated.

There is a certain pleasure in the plodding consistency of the philistine response when confronted with true creative innovation.

I was of course performing the first and last movements of John Cage's *4'33"* (missing out the middle section, which for me has always seemed rather overblown and derivative).

Contrary to public misconception, the piece isn't just '4 and a half minutes of silence' but is rather a silent Zen prayer that is the sum of the ambient noises made by its performers and listeners, and so a completely new work each time – in this case a symphony of Keith's mucoid coughs, Tom's quiet but profound sobbing, Julia's stifled sighs, Alice and Blue's tense whispers, and Jon's real-ale belches.

Note that many of these noises were not caused by, or even directed at, my performance. But in a wonderfully selfless way, they actually *became* the performance itself. (Don't worry if you missed some of these subtleties. I have it all recorded, so we can enjoy a playback one night – perhaps at Julia's?)

And so, yet again, my work is all about *all of you* – just like your own self-congratulatory efforts are *all about you* too! People think of my work as weird, but perhaps what's really weird for you people is the thought that *art can be about something other than ME!!* (i.e. YOU).

Yes, I alone have managed to transcend the narcissistic limitations of the 'damned egotistical self' (Woolf), to produce work that lives beyond the wet embrace of the subjective and looks at the world afresh from a truly interjective, even objective, perspective. And who knows? Perhaps one day I will at last be recognised for the extraordinary achievement that I have wrought. Perhaps one day people will at last see that I am a genius.

But I wonder.

Peter, writer.

PS Jon – Setting basic hygiene issues aside – which took some doing – I couldn't help noticing that the fuse 'box' in your 'flat' is not compliant with current electrical regs. As it is of wood construction, it needs to be replaced with an amendment 3 consumer unit providing RCD protection and circuits with miniature circuit breakers. Also gas and water supply must be earthed, and existing circuits tested and any faults rectified.

From: **JuliaGeeGee@gmail.com**
To: keith_sadwicke@techsolutions.co.uk
Sent: 20.08.17, 17:15
Subject: **What a fine idea!**

Dear, dear Keith

Thank you so much for your email regarding your role in the documentary.

Of course I personally think the idea of commercial cross-promotion makes massive sense, I really do. And I guess it's quite conceivable that one of the readers of my delicately calibrated and yet quietly erotic coming-of-age drama might also have a sort of guilty pleasure in the speculative department. I mean, who knows what floats people's boats these days? You've only got to read the papers.

So yes, if it was up to me, I'd say let's collaborate and cross-promote away! Alas, the dreaded powers that be – my agent, publisher and the programme producers – are all much more rigid and old-fashioned about these things and believe in a strict division of church and state, or art and pulp as it were.

But it will be great to give your words an airing in the doc, n'est-ce pas?

Julia x

From: **tom@tomcat.com**

To: Crawley Writers' Group

Sent: 22.08.17, 02:57

Subject: **A sorry state(ment)**

The wolf of oblivion sits howling at my gate
It rains all day in the hovel of my mind
My heart lies splintered, my soul awaits its fate
What would I not give for a life-rewind!
One is Blue (as indeed am I)

The other has me Alice-banned
I wooed them both, I led them on
Betrayed them with my outstretched hand
He dare not hope for phone to ring
This feckless traitor of female goodwill
Tum-tumpty-tumpty-tum tum-ting
...Of my empty words you've had your fill
I rack my brains, I search my heart
For a way to make reparation
But this I know, a truth hard earned:
Love knows not its depth 'til the hour of separation

Tom Hilden

PS As I get comfortable with midlife, I see more poetry in my future.

From: **JuliaGeeGee@gmail.com**
To: aliceknowles@mewriter.com
Sent: 23.08.17, 15:17
Subject: **Now look!**

Alice

See Keith's message (attached). The gods spare us! Or rather – and pardon my French, darling – fuckez-moi.

No sooner do we neutralise Tom and Blue than the geek-man rears his greedy little head.

I know you're probably in need of a rest after all your recent adventures, darling, but do you think you could possibly work your magic one last time?

You're such a natural, darling! Show Keith a little attention – and a bit of leg, why not – and we'll have him eating out of your hand and whimpering about getting you back to his dungeon in no time... with all thoughts of self-promotion quite forgotten!

Will you do this for me, darling? I'd be forever in your debt...

Another coffee soon ABM??

Jxx

PS Did you see Tom's awful poem? What a loon! You had a close shave there, darling... whatever made you encourage him in the first place?

From: **JuliaGeeGee@gmail.com**

To: MPranesh@gmail.com

Sent: 23.08.17, 15:30

Subject: **Hello darling!**

Dear Mavinder

Don't know if you're coming to the next group and/or if you'll be at mine on September 14 – the televised one?

Sorry to be a pain, but it just occurred to me that we've never actually heard any of your writing or seen what you look like? So, just for the purposes of continuity and overall conceptual fit etc., the programme-makers have sort of asked me to ask you to send over a sample of your work, and maybe a photo or two? Just want to make sure you don't have two heads/ don't write really weird stuff (got that covered!)/aren't so beautiful you'll outshine me!! Joking, darling! You'll get used to my humour soon enough. But please send the pics and words ASAP and don't worry about cc-ing anyone else AT ALL.

So can't wait to meet you vv soon, darling!

Julia x

PS Keith is really keen to meet you. He's such a card – and he's so intrigued by you! Do please give him lots of attention if you meet...

To: **keith_sadwicke@techsolutions.co.uk**

From: aliceknowles@mewriter.com

Sent: 25.08.17, 19:16

Subject: **I need you!**

Dear Keith

I feel that I may have been a little hasty, not to say rude, in my rebuffing of your kind offer a few weeks ago to help me with my Sentence. For that I can only apologise. Having thought about it some more, I'd actually appreciate some help/feedback, if you can spare the time. As you know, I'll be hosting the next group (warning: Blue will be providing the snacks, so you might want to get a McDonald's in, or something of that ilk, beforehand!). If you can get here perhaps half an hour early, we could go over The Sentence together? I feel it's very close now. But it's still lacking something, some 'edge', that might help to really 'sell it' as an opening sentence to all those strangers out there who I hope to turn into my readers. And I sense that you of everyone in the group, with your commercial eye and your immense experience in the field of popular genre fiction writing, might be the one to identify what that missing element is. Will you help me, Keith? I can even open a bottle of wine (or a can of lager, if you prefer) to oil the creative wheels so to speak.

Alice

From: **aliceknowles@mewriter.com**

To: JuliaGeeGee@gmail.com

Sent: 25.08.17, 20:01

Subject: **All in hand, darling...**

Dear Julia

How utterly extraordinary! Was there ever a commercial opportunity that our Mr Sadwicke hasn't found some way of trying to exploit? He'd sell his own mother for another 10,000 downloads, I shouldn't be surprised! He just doesn't get it, does he? This is *your* show, and *your* moment to shine. We're just the supporting cast, and I, of course, will support you in any way I can. As you know I found the whole Tom episode emotionally exhausting and quite dispiriting. He let me down badly and it still hurts. I also feel, perversely, quite sorry for him, especially after reading (and re-reading) that terrible poem of his. He's in a bad place – we both are – and I regret the whole episode.

Keith, however, is an entirely different kettle of fish and chips. For one thing, there is zero chance of me ever falling for him. Also, he's really overstepped the mark here, and it would be a pleasure to put him back in his dungeon for you. In fact I've already set the wheels in motion. If all goes to plan, by the time of the next group he'll have forgotten all about trying to upstage you in your documentary and will have eyes only for me.

Warning: that dress (the one I wore on the night of the dead sheep) may have to make a reappearance – it seems to have a strange effect on him!

Alice xxx

From: **disclosure_now47@aol.com**

To: keith_sadwicke@techsolutions.co.uk

Sent: 27.08.17, 03:13

Subject: **Let's do this**

Hi mate,

It's fair to say that I have been in a pretty dark place recently but I'm heading out for the stars... and soon. Can't say too much now but DISCLOSURE is coming!

You're right that Harry Warde is a constant source of friction. He never had any spiritual insight but always had an eye out for the main chance and pop-pap success. That said, despite the bust-ups, we knocked out some good stuff back in the day and we can do it again. He's the irritating grain of sand in the oyster of my creativity!

To be frank, I've got him over a barrel now – he always held out against re-forming the band because he was doing well in production but he blew it by 'accidentally' walking into the changing rooms of an all-girl band he was working with once too often. He always was a sex-mad cokehead, though more Benny Hill than Harvey Weinstein to be fair.

Anyway, now I'm holding the purse strings I can steer us in the right direction – suffice to say, all will be revealed at the filming of the documentary! It's gonna be COSMIC!

And talking of the documentary, I think I may have been a bit premature in dismissing your idea of us joining forces in order to promote ourselves.

I was wondering – and this is strictly between us – that maybe you could round up some of your fantasy con cosplay chums and get them to 'invade' Julia's place towards the end of the broadcast, wearing promo stuff for both the band and your books. It would create a fantastic surprise party atmosphere, make great TV and generally everyone will be happy! What do you think?

yrs

Jon

From: **blueyblu@blueyonder.com**
To: aliceknowles@mewriter.com
Sent: 27.08.17, 23:21
Subject: **What can we do (stress! #confusion)**

Hi Lovely

Gosh what a lot we two have been through together! I feel closer and closer to you, a sisterhood of shared adversity – you with your Sentence and me with just about everything else. We must huddle together like frightened abandoned ducklings waiting in a pond for another shopping trolley or bicycle frame to be hurled at them by the drunk shouty man that is... LIFE!!! Or maybe not.

But I worry that maybe we have been too unkind to poor Tom?? His poem is the cry of a lost soul. Should we do anything? Let me know your thoughts, dear Alice.

your Blue xxx

PS I am cooking up a lot of treats for the next meeting – you can do so much with tofu, don't you think? Also my signature dish: sticky peanut cauliflower bites. Make sure we check that no one's allergic. bx

---

From: **peterpeterpeterpeter@gmail.com**
To: Crawley Writers' Group
Sent: 28.08.17, 12:12
Subject: **<no subject>**

All

The last line of Tom's morosely self-regarding 'poem' struck me as interesting (and this was in itself interesting, as the rest of the poem had very much not). The line was: 'Love knows not its depth 'til the hour of separation'.

It sounded familiar, and I quickly realised why – it's actually adapted from a line in *The Prophet* of Khalil Gibran. It occurred to me that I have had this sense of *déjà lu* before in reading Tom's emails and listening to his work, and I thought it would be an interesting artistic project to try to sketch a fuller picture of the acts of *hommage* that appear throughout his *oeuvre*. To assist me I contacted Alice and Blue, who were only too happy to cooperate with my project at this time. They shared with me all their personal emails from Tom, which gave me quite a decent corpus to work with.

For those who are obsessive completists when it comes to collecting my work, the full findings of my research are presented in the attached spreadsheet, which compares original and borrowed versions and gives full source details. I also sketch some tentative thoughts about the relationship between incidences of textual theft and the writer's frame of mind. The attached graph gives the detail, but the overwhelming conclusion is that love (by which I mean the promise, however distant, of sex) appears in Tom's case to massively over-stimulate the plagiarism gland.

Date and recipient	Borrowing	Source
Group, 22.08.17	Love knows not its depth 'til the hour of separation	Adapted from Kahlil Gibran, *The Prophet*
	As I get comfortable with midlife, I see more poetry in my future	Brad Feld, blog post, 'Midlife and the great unknown'
Alice, 06.08.17	I always say that you can have anything you want in life if you dress for it.	Attributed to Edith Head, Hollywood costume designer

	Clothes mean nothing until someone lives in them…	Marc Jacobs, fashion designer
	… the hues of a natural fresh garden salad are so splendid, no painter could possibly improve on them.	Found on Pinterest here, sourced to Friends Eat blog, author unknown
	Fashion is like eating – we don't have always to stick to the same menu…	Adapted from a quote attributed to Kenzo Tanada, designer
Alice, 17.06.17	… the eternal struggle with form.	Possibly Virginia Woolf, research ongoing
	… whatever we lose, like a you or a me, it's always ourselves that we find in the woods, n'est-ce pas?	A clear steal from 'maggie and milly and molly and may' by ee cummings: For whatever we lose(like a you or a me) it's always ourselves we find in the sea
Blue, 12.05.17	Blue is the colour and poetry is your game!	Football song associated with Chelsea FC, recorded 1972: Blue is the colour and football is the game…
	Everything has changed and yet I have never been more myself.	Iain Thomas: Everything has changed and yet, I am more me than I've ever been.
	Without you, life itself were a mistake.	Friedrich Nietzsche, *Twilight of the Idols*: Without music life would be a mistake
	The curve of your eyes does the tour of my heart.	Title and first line of a poem by Paul Eluard in his collection, *Capitale de la douleur*: La courbe de tes yeux fait le tour de mon coeur
	Not even the rain has such small hands as yours!	Almost identical to final line of the poem 'somewhere i have never travelled,gladly beyond' by ee cummings

	You have the mind of a mermaid – shall I dare swim in its depths??!!	Clearly adapted from these words by J. Iron Word: She is a mermaid, but approach her with caution. Her mind swims at a depth most would drown in
	Not all that wander are lost, and yet now I find that I am found.	Not all those who wander are lost – said by Frodo in J.R.R. Tolkein's *The Fellowship of the Ring*
	If I had a flower for every time I thought of you…	Attributed to Tennyson, and widely quoted online; source is disputed, research ongoing: If I had a flower for every time I thought of you… I could walk through my garden forever.
	I'm told they do lovely vegetable sambars, rasams and kootus, which are of course three common stew-like dishes typical of southern Indian cuisine, a style less seen in British restaurants but distinguished by its drier dishes, loose-textured curries and griddle-cooked snacks.	Adapted from Wikipedia entry on Southern Indian cuisine
	I sometimes feel there is nothing more artistic than to, uh, like someone vv much.	Adapted from letter of Vincent Van Gogh to his brother Theo, 18.09.1888: …the more I think about it the more I feel that there's nothing more genuinely artistic than to love people
	So… shall we meet at midnight tonight… in the forest of my dreams?	Attributed to Christy Ann Martine: Meet me at midnight in the forest of my dreams
	Please, please, just go on being constantly, consistently, continually, adorably, you.	The phrase constantly, consistently, continually you is an oft-repeated internet meme. Research ongoing
	And that is all from me at this time. Tom, lover	Shameless borrowings of the email sign-off of Peter, writer

Group, 05.05.17	Closeness has nothing to do with physical distance, after all.	The phrase closeness has nothing to do with distance is an oft-repeated internet meme. Research ongoing
Group, 04.05.17	I always think that if everyone is moving forward together, then success can only take care of itself.	Attributed to Henry Ford: If every-one is moving forward together, then success takes care of itself
Blue, 24.04.17	Sometimes I think that even cowards can endure tough stuff; but only the really brave can endure suspense!!	Slight adaptation of a phrase attributed to Mignon McLaughlin
Blue, 23.04.17	I didn't mean any of this, but then you made it so easy…	The phrase I didn't mean to fall in love, but you made it so easy… is an oft-repeated internet meme. Research ongoing
Group, 22.04.17	I always think that women and cats should do as they please, and men and dogs had better just get used to the idea…	Robert A. Heinlein: Women and cats will do as they please, and men and dogs should relax and get used to the idea
Email from Julia, 22.04.17	@Tom, I marvelled anew at your inventiveness – I love the idea of a short story that turns out to be narrated by a cat!	A clear echo of a short story by Jeffrey Archer, 'Just Good Friends' – which was itself the subject of a plagiarism claim
Blue, 12.04.17	Remember that when you create, it's your job to have mind-blowing, irresponsible, condomless sex with what-ever idea it is you're writing about!!	Lady Gaga: When you make music or write or create, it's really your job to have mind-blowing, irresponsible, con-domless sex with whatever idea it is you're writing about at the time.
Group, 27.03.17	the road to hell is paved with adverbs	Stephen King, *On Writing*
Julia, 29.01.17	Alone we can only do so much, after all; but together we can do SO MUCH!	Attributed to Helen Keller: Alone we can do so little; together we can do so much.

Email from Julia, 26.01.17	…clearings in the story forest…	Possibly an echo of a line from the poem 'Clearing' by Martha Postlewaite: create a clearing in the dense forest of your life…
	…your own story about the cyclist who doesn't know he's dead	A clear reference to the plot of *The Third Policeman* by Flann O'Brien, a novel in which the narrator turns out to have been dead all along, also populated by two policemen obsessed with bicycles
Alice, 25.01.17	Perhaps we could sit down at our typewriters and, as it were, bleed together?	Attributed to Hemingway but disputed; research ongoing: There is nothing to writing. You simply sit down at the typewriter, open your veins, and bleed.
Group, 19.01.17	You don't get harmony when everyone's singing the same note, after all…	Attributed to Doug Floyd
Group, 01.01.17	The suspense is terrible – I do hope it will last!	*The Importance of being Earnest*, Oscar Wilde: This suspense is terrible. I hope it will last
	…is the text not at its most delightfully suggestive when it shows a flash of meaning/ cleavage?	A clear echo of the ideas in *Le Plaisir du Texte* by Roland Barthes. Cf. Is not the most erotic portion of a body where the garment gapes?
Group, 19.12.16	I write therefore I am.	Widely available as a meme on the internet; see also 'I am, therefore I write' – title of an article by Jonathan Coe, *The Guardian*, 2004
	It's about trying to say something so well it's been said once and for all, then failing, then trying to fail better next time.	Clear echo of the widely meme-ified – and quite grotesquely misunderstood – line from Samuel Beckett's *Worstword Ho!*: Ever tried. Ever failed. No matter. Try again. Fail again. Fail better.

	Intolerably ill-put, of course. But still.	Spoken by Quentin in *Dead Babies*, Martin Amis: It occurs to me that one's mannerisms, one's behavioural tics, are neither quite innate nor quite fortuitous. We project them as mechanisms of defence and appeal, of withdrawal and capitulation; they are means of stylizing our attitude to others and to the world. Forgive me — intolerably ill-put.

I wonder what fellow members will feel as they survey this catalogue of creative copycatting, this taxonomy of textual tea-leafery, this litany of literary light-fingeredness? Should we applaud the audacity and scope of the borrowings, or should we feel insulted at the lazy googling, the assumption that a tired meme will be enough to dazzle and delude the poor befuddled rest of us?

Then again, some of you may be wondering why I would choose to highlight this behaviour – I, whose artistic projects are so often preoccupied with the transcription of the lived. And are we not bound anyway to repeat ourselves and others in everything we do? Surely we are living too late in history to hope for any true originality? To say 'I love you' is to utter a quotation, after all, as someone has doubtless already said.

I myself am sanguine. As a detached observer-artist, I merely present the facts. But plagiarism can provoke many reactions – such as scorn, dismay, disgust, consternation, a sense of betrayal, violent rage – each of which is not without interest to the recorder of the real/*real*. I will leave you all to pick your own reaction, as you try to deny the terrifying truth that you are all yourselves living but poor replicas of the lives you truly wish for.

Peter, writer.

From: **aliceknowles@mewriter.com**
To: Crawley Writers' Group
Sent: 29.08.17, 23:02
Subject: **Very sorry**

Hi all

It is with deep regret that I must cancel this week's meeting at mine. This morning I found some gunk in the corner of Tiggy's eye and I fear it may be the return of the dreaded conjunctivitis. Consequently neither she nor I will be in a fit emotional state for hosting duties. Sometimes I think that Tiggy might be our group's spiritual weathervane, and when she's down it's because she senses a deep and troubling malaise in all of us. She must have picked up that we're in something of a sorry place at the moment, and perhaps some of us, or one of us, have more reason to be sorry than most. Sincere apologies for this, Blue. I know how hard you've been working on your kale chips and tofu frittatas, but because of Tiggy and other things, it may be for the best that we don't meet this week.

Alice

From: **JuliaGeeGee@gmail.com**

To: Crawley Writers' Group

Sent: 01.09.17, 13:45

Subject: **All shall be well, friends!**

Hi all

Alice – so sorry to hear about Tiggy. Do hope the gunk goes away quickly.

Your email is quite good timing in a way, actually, as others of you have contacted me privately about recent events, and it does seem that a period of reflection is in order for all, and indeed for some perhaps more than others.

I do also, however, think it's important to remember that we are all humans, and furthermore we are all part of the great sister/brotherhood of writers, a noble clan of fictional adventurers who stand shoulder to shoulder in an unending war against the mediocrities of the shallow bourgeois world around us, and that we need to offer each other support even in the darkest times – even, indeed, when some of our number seem to have lost their way and our first thought is perhaps to condemn rather than to forgive them. To err is human, of course, but to forgive is… divinely artistic.

And so I suggest a brief pause while we gather ourselves for the filmed group at my place on September 14. Don't forget to wear your best (i.e. most appropriate) outfits and bring your best (original) words! And please don't be weird!! (only joking…)

Julia xx

PS Advance sales of my hardback are up 10% week on week, so this week hasn't been a complete disaster.

From: **tom@tomcat.com**
To: Crawley Writers' Group
Sent: 01.09.17, 19:58
Subject: **Re: All shall be well, friends!**

Hi Julia

Sorry – can't make that one

Tom

7.

TRANSCRIPT OF *BLEEDING TYPEWRITERS* DOCUMENTARY, FIRST BROADCAST ON CHANNEL 4, 23.03.18

Continuity announcer: And now on Channel 4 it's time for another in our *Work in Progress* series, in which we document the working methods of creative people at first hand. This week, we get an exclusive invitation into the home of debut novelist Julia Greengage, as she hosts the latest meeting of her writers' group. Welcome to the world of the Crawley Writers' Group – viewers are warned that the following programme contains scenes that are frankly quite weird. This is *Bleeding Typewriters* . . .

Narrator: Julia Greengage, 49, is a rising star on the UK literary scene. Her debut novel, *Bare Naked Ambition*, has already sold 15,000 in hardback, and there are rumours of interest in the film rights from not one, but two, Hollywood studios. But the former *Midsomer Murders* star says her writing only really took off when she started a writers' group here in her home town of Crawley.

Julia (pre-recorded piece, to camera): Oh! I was burning with the urge to write for so long! But somehow I just couldn't put pen to paper, couldn't manage to see an idea through to completion. And then it was my hubby – he's travelling in Venezuela on business at the moment, alas –

who said: Why don't you start a group? And so I began gathering this group of dear, creative souls around me . . . and that's when I started to *fly*!!!

Narrator: The group has been running in Crawley for about nine months now. Today's meeting will be their first since Julia's book was published.

Julia (pre-recorded piece, to camera): Thrilled! They're *thrilled* for me, the darlings! We all support each other. I mean, it's just the most wonderfully creative, nurturing . . . **vibe.** And we're like a family – we all bring something different. I suppose I'm a bit like their muse and their mother . . . They're so dear to me. I mean, they're like *my children* . . . [voice breaks] Sorry, guys, can we cut there? Was that too much? Too little? Did you get my exposed knee as I crossed my legs? No worries. I'll do it again, with a bit more blub and flesh.

Narrator: Tonight's group will prove to be an eventful night. A night full of banter . . .

Cut to Jon, arriving:

Jon: Jeezuz, Julia! Look at that pool! Is your hubby in organised crime or something??

Narrator: A night of tension . . .

Cut to Peter, arguing with Julia:

Julia: Peter, please leave the sound guy alone so he can get on with his job.

Peter: He is here to record proceedings, Julia. But every recording is a lie. And that is why we must record the recorders!!!

Narrator: A night of creative breakthroughs . . .

Cut to Alice in mid-group, looking up entranced:

Alice: I get it at last, Jon! What you're saying is that we all have to give voice to the mischievous squirrel-warrior that's buried deep inside each and every one of us!

Jon: No. Not really.

Alice: That's *so* inspiring.

Jon: Yeah, no. That's not it at all.

Alice: Wow! And there was me thinking it was all about UFOs and counter-surveillance or something!

Jon: Er, well yeah, it is.

Alice: Wow!

Narrator: A night of unexpected romance . . .

Cut to Keith talking to Alice:

Keith: Have you done something different with your hair?

Alice (fondling her hair suggestively): Have I?

Keith: New perfume or something?

Alice: Ooh, Keith, I don't know. Maybe my dress?

Keith: Oh yeah, that's it. Top cleavage.

Narrator: A night of personality clashes . . .

Cut to Keith, shouting at unseen figure:

Keith: Look, I invented her! She's mine! And if I want to kill her, I will!

Narrator: And a night of extraordinary personal revelations . . .

Cut to Blue, sitting tearfully by the pool, confiding in someone unseen:

Blue: Sometimes I just want to stop writing about suicide and go for a stroll round the garden centre, you know?

Cut to Peter, face illuminated:

Peter: I've got something to play you all . . . [groans]

Narrator: But right now, it's 7.45 pm, and Julia is putting the finishing touches to the set-up of her newly remodelled garden and poolside area. A man known only as 'Peter, writer' is the first to arrive – no one knows his original surname. Exactly on time, as always, Peter is a self-styled 'conceptual provocateur with an interest in the regressive agonies of the transcribing mortal'. He is without doubt the group's most experimental writer. Idiosyncratic, audacious and difficult to summarise, his work challenges assumptions and stimulates fierce debate.

Peter (pre-interview, to camera): Who am I? Who are you? What is the difference between me and you? How do you see me, and how is this *seeing* of me *by you* . . . to be seen by me? What is this? [gestures to space in front of him] Do they hear what I hear? [points at screen] How does the act of observation intrude on the observed? [sits back] These are the sorts of questions that interest me. I am *a writer*; I am, therefore I write. But my true medium is reality, I suppose. [points at someone, presumably sound man, off-camera:] I see you're using the Rode NTG8? Personally I'd favour the WS6 sock over the dead-cat with that, but let's see how you get on. I've got quite a few recordings I must show you later . . .

Cut to Peter's arrival:

Julia: Good evening, Peter!

Peter: Good evening, Julia. Here are the four bottles of Shloer we agreed, two white grape and elderflower, one white grape and apple, and one white grape, raspberry and cranberry.

Julia: Oh! Thanks very much, Peter. Do you notice anything? [gestures to brand-new fully re-landscaped and replanted garden, decked out with blazing copper fire torches, colour-changing movement-sensitive remote-controlled deck lights, and a graceful display of achingly tasteful festoon lighting over the poolside table alcove where an elegant, quietly expensive rustic oak table has been expertly set for the group alongside an illuminated and brand-new heated kidney-shaped infinity swimming pool. Newly opened bottles of bubbly stand smoking in silver ice buckets.]

Peter: [pauses] I notice . . . a slight tension in the interpersonal vibrational field between us? Perhaps I am experiencing mild arousal stimuli as a biochemical reaction to your perfume? [pauses; briefly looks down at his groin] Unless you are menstruating? [pauses] No, I see what it is now. You've switched your brand of alcohol sanitiser gel.

Julia [subtly arching one eyebrow for the camera's benefit]: Oh yes I have, Peter. Sorry, darling. But you might find some of the old stuff over by the artisanal *cheminée* . . .

Peter: Which one?

Narrator: Next to arrive are Keith and Alice.

Cut to Keith and Alice's arrival:

Keith: So you're still writing that blog for writers about how to write? What a headfuck. *Love* it. There must be loads of merch angles in that.

Alice: Well, yes. I suppose so. But I suppose for me it's more about uncovering the subtle process of . . .

Keith: Let's meet round yours again and I'll draw up a quick business plan for you. Multi-channel retargeting, social selling, pay-per-click, simple e-commerce functionality, all that. We'll have you monetising the fuck out of all that in no time, with my report. It won't take me five minutes to bang one out.

Alice [weakly]: Oh. [pauses] Thanks.

Cut to Julia (pre-recorded piece, to camera):

Julia: Keith and Alice . . . are two of my favourite babies! [giggles] Apart from all the others of course! Mummy can't have favourites, can she? It's funny, they seem to be spending a lot of time together recently, not sure what that's about . . . [winks to camera] And yet in so many ways they're chalk and cheese as writers . . .

Narrator: Keith Sadwicke, an IT consultant with a local firm, has been working on *Dragons of Xęn"räh*, his epic speculative sci-fi sequence, for three years. He prides himself on his prolific output, and has already written seven volumes, plus several spin-offs, stand-alone adventures, a full-length feature film script and five albums' worth of song lyrics. He self-publishes online, and though not yet a household name, he has a few extremely passionate fans.

Cut to Keith (pre-recorded piece, to camera):

Keith: Yo, the fans are crazy, yeah? I've got a few now, they don't want me to kill Bink off. She's one of my main characters, a sort of intergalactic Amazonian warlady. You wouldn't believe the threats I get, the noises at night. But the thing is, as the author, you are the owner of your creations and you ultimately control their fate. Some fans may not want to hear this but there's probably nowhere left I can take Bink in terms of her character and story arc. Plus I've got a hot new idea for a sort of hard-soft, Bangsian, nanopunk space opera. It's gonna have super-catchy choons and at least a dozen royalty/licensing streams. Now obviously I can't get into all that if I've still got the fiendishly seductive Bink flexing her rock-hard obliques at me and toying with my inner artiste . . .

Cut to Alice (pre-recorded piece, to camera):

Alice: For me, it's all about the process. What is writing? What does it mean to be . . . a *writer*? How do we write . . . *right*?

Narrator: Alice Knowles works as a payroll clerk at a college of further education. Where her friend Keith can produce several thousand words a day, Alice has been sculpting the same opening sentence for over nine months.

To the group, it's known only as . . . The Sentence.

Cut to Alice (pre-recorded piece, to camera):

Question from off-camera: Have you finished any pieces yourself?

Alice [playing with her hair awkwardly]: Well, yes and no. [pauses] I mean, there's my blog.

Question from off-camera: What about fiction?

Alice: Well . . . there's my Sentence. [pauses] It's sort of ready – NO, I didn't say that!

Question from off-camera: Will we hear it tonight?

Alice [looking flustered at her feet]: Oh I don't know about that. It's really at a very raw stage. [suddenly brightens] But I do think that the adverb in the concluding relative clause is really close to something that I'd want to seriously consider as almost fully satisfactory at first draft stage . . .

Narrator: Julia's last expected guests for tonight's writing group are Jon and Blue. Blue is a poet who volunteers in a charity shop, while Jon – once the vocalist with '70s prog rock band The King of Elfland's Daughter – writes 'deceptively simple fables with a message for those with eyes to hear'.

Cut to Blue (pre-recorded piece, to camera):

Blue [looking very uncomfortable and anguished, head down the whole time]: I just write from my soul, you know? [extinguishes rollie with shaking hand, wipes stray painted strands from heavily mascaraed eye] If I feel hurt somewhere in me, I push towards that. I press on the bruise. The pen is my blade and I plunge it back into the wound so that I can really *live what I feel* and [pauses; looks up tearful] sorry can we stop there, this is just so intense. [head in hands, quietly sobbing]

Cut to Jon (pre-recorded piece, to camera):

Jon [looking rather sleepy]: I don't over-think this stuff too much, you know? I mean, look at Christ, look at the parables. He just got up there and made his shit up, and in the end loads of people dug it. He didn't worry about PR or foreign rights or shite like that. [pauses] Not that I'm a God-botherer or anything. [swigs from a can] I guess . . . *music* is my religion. That's where it's all circling back for me. Back to the good mothership *Albion* . . . [chortles to himself, takes another swig]

Narrator: The writers find their places around the table and have one last look at their pieces. In a moment it will be time for the first brave performer to take the stage. But there's an elephant in the garden . . .

Julia: OK, darlings, everyone got some bubbles that wants some? Are we just about ready?

Peter: Where is Tom?

Blue: Can't you guess?

Peter: If I could guess I would not have needed to ask. And in any case, guessing implies the absence of any expectation of certainty . . .

Jon: Fuck me.

Narrator: Tom is one of two other members of the group. But he's not expected to turn up tonight, as he's under a bit of a cloud. The group has recently discovered that many of Tom's writings were plagiarised from a variety of sources. And there seem to be other issues too.

Cut to Alice (pre-recorded piece, to camera):

Alice: Well, it's awkward. I mean, I shouldn't have stuck it in his . . . not there. But then again, he has behaved very badly. I mean, I very nearly opened up my . . . And Blue. Such a lovely, gentle, beautiful soul. She nearly did too, you know. And for Blue to throw a cauliflower at your head, you've got to have done something pretty unforgivable, believe you me . . . [pauses; looks thoughtful] Maybe there could be cauliflower florets in the crudités – next to the olives?

Cut to live, group setting:

Julia: OK, darlings, who'd like to kick us off?

Alice: Not me, darling. I think I might just observe tonight.

Julia: Oh no, darling, come on. What about your Sentence? No?

Alice: I just don't know if I can. Yet.

Julia: Jon?

Jon [consulting his laptop and checking for signal/messages, and looking round at bushes]: Have I got the wifi-code right? Think we should just wait a bit till we do my piece, yeah?

Julia: Oh, er, OK, darling. [strange rustling sounds off-camera]

Keith [looking around uneasily]: What was that?

Peter: Probably a paparazzo. They're no doubt tracking your every move, Julia.

Jon [singing raspily]: *I see the moon and the moon sees me, the moon sees somebody I wanna see.* [cackles mirthlessly] Don't say I didn't warn you all.

Julia: OK, then. Shall I kick us off?

Alice: Ooh yes please! Show us how it's done, darling!

Julia [starting to read]:

> He was an attractive man, the dark curls at the nape of his neck accentuating the taut subtle power of his frame. But he was also, as she well knew, a man who could have any starlet he wanted.

'Well?' he said, gesturing for her to join him on the canapé.

'Well,' she replied smartly, sitting opposite him instead.

'I think you know why we're here,' he purred.

'I think we both know why *you* think we're here,' she shot back.

Julia [suddenly looks up annoyed, then spots a camera and quickly rearranges her features into an expression of charm]: Sorry, Keith, darling, is something the matter?

Keith [who's been waving his arms around and gurning wildly]: Nothing, Julia, love! Just making sure I'm getting my profile and book cover in shot, you know? The fans need to see me in action, yeah?

Alice [picking up on a pointed look from Julia]: Keith, darling, you'll get your shot in a sec. [puts hand on his knee] Let's sit tight and enjoy Julia's piece.

Keith [pecker obviously up]: Ooo-er missus! Don't mind if I do!

Cut away as Julia starts reading to an aerial shot of the

group. Julia declaims dramatically, Keith and Alice are hunched awkwardly together, Peter sits up ramrod straight, Blue has her head in her hands, Jon is virtually prone.

Narrator: Julia's piece, as always, meets with a rapturous reception. And next up is Blue . . .

Blue [nervously, as clapping dies down]: This is a piece about the way cotton wool makes me feel. It's a very personal thing, and I've never felt able to talk about it before, but this group has given me the strength to confront some of my innermost demons – the demons that secretly live inside my demons . . .

Cocoon of stealth, envelope of asphyxiation
I crawl through your white womb, I tremble at your pervasion.
Nurse dabs at my cuts with this alien foam.
My cuticles cringe and I plunge unknonaaaaaa-aaaaaaaaa-aagh!!!!!!!

[piercing unearthly scream]

Peter: Is that part of the performance? Bravo!

Alice: You just threw a big wad of cotton wool at her head! How could you?

Peter: It was just a metaphor, wasn't it?

[more shuffling noises in the undergrowth]

Keith [looking around wildly]: What was that?

Julia: Now come on, darlings, can we keep this together, please?

Alice: Did you get that cotton wool from my bag, Peter?

Peter: Well, it was open. I didn't have to rummage. That much.

Blue: That is *such* a violation.

[ad break]

Narrator: Tensions in aspiring novelist Julia Greengage's writers' group seem to be mounting. Blue is traumatised because she has had to touch cotton wool, the thing she fears most in the world. Alice is furious with Peter for upsetting Blue and rummaging in her handbag. Keith is disturbed by noises coming from the poinsettia. And Julia is struggling to keep the show on the road . . .

Julia: OK, darlings. Let's hold it together now, please.

[stage-hisses to Alice] Do something!

Alice [with sudden inspiration]: I think maybe Keith would like to go next.

Julia [brightening]: Actually, yes, that's a wonderful idea. Let's hear your contribution, Keith . . .

Keith: No, no no! Come on, I want to hear this lovely lady's Sentence. [oozing over Alice] Come on, babe, I'll hold your hand . . .

Alice [recoiling from Keith]: It's all right, thank you, Keith. I think I can manage.

Group [variously]: Go, Alice! Yey! Here it comes! Sssh, everyone – it's The Sentence!!

Narrator: Alice's Sentence is the culmination of over nine months of reflection, planning and ruthless self-editing. No one in the group has ever heard more than three words from it: 'waiter' and 'olives' and 'salvage'. (There was an adverb at one point, but Alice later retracted it.) To say that this moment is a crucial milestone in Alice's writing career is a huge understatement.

Alice [nervously clears throat]: Thanks, everyone. Well, you all know what this means to me, and what it's taken to get here. I warn you, I've changed it a bit since the last draft. A lot actually. Not that you'd know because none of you have heard it yet. [laughs nervously] But these last few days have been a revelation. I really like it now. Really really! I think this is what I was striving for all along . . . So here goes . . .

[utter silence; camera closes in on Alice's face as she reads:]

> As Freya sat in the restaurant contemplating the remains of her salad and listening to the soft limping footsteps approaching her table, she decided that what she liked most in life was eating olives and the waiter.

Group [cheers and shouts]: Hurray! Nice one! Go, Alice! Yay! You did it, girl!

Julia [dabbing at her eye with a tissue]: Oh, darling! Come here! [they embrace] I'm so proud of you.

Keith [eyeing up the two embracing women]: Oh yes.

Blue: Let's hear it again!!! [everyone cheers and claps in agreement]

[utter silence; camera closes in on Alice's face as – with a calm smile this time, and no need of a script – she declaims:]

> As Freya sat in the restaurant contemplating the remains of her salad and listening to the soft limping footsteps approaching her table, she decided that what she liked most in life was eating olives and the waiter.

[more cheers and applause. Gradually silence resumes.]

Peter [picking up script and examining sentence]: Is it just me . . .

Jon: Don't go there, mate.

Peter: Or . . .

Jon: *Do. Not. Do. It.*

Peter [ignoring him]: Or does it sound as if . . . *Freya wants to eat the waiter*???

[close-up on Alice's face: shock, dismay, tears, horror, rage pass rapidly across her features as the realisation sinks in]

Alice [to Peter]: Go fuck yourself!! [she picks up a bottle and heads towards the pool, starts swigging aggressively]

Keith [to film crew, producing a small point-of-sale unit loaded with branded mousemats, key rings and USB sticks]: I'm up next, yeah? Which is my best side, do you think? And can you see the merch OK if I stand like this?

Julia [looks at Keith despairingly, runs after Alice]: Jesus Christ, *Alice* – you had one fucking job! Could you not keep your little fucking geek-man on a lead? All you had to do was put your hand on his cock or something.

[Alice, ignoring Julia, carries on sobbing by the pool.]

Producer, with clipboard and headset: Is everything all right, Julia love?

Julia: Oh yes, sweetie. All in hand. Just a minor glitch. [she gestures helplessly at the showboating Keith and the inconsolable Alice, who is sitting on a chair by the pool necking a bottle of prosecco] It's just what comes of working with . . . *fucking civilians*. [goes over and places tentative hand on Alice's shoulder] Alice, are you ready to get back to work, darling?

Alice: Did you like my Sentence, Julia?

Julia [insincerely]: What, darling? Yeah, sure. It was really special. Now can we get back to filming. Maybe try not to ruin my entire life, lovely??

Keith [cheesily, coming over to Alice]: Fancy a hug, babe?

Alice [odd look on her face]: Oh yes, Julia *dear.* I'm ready. [Alice swings wildly at Julia, catches her on the side of the shoulder; Julia loses balance and falls into the pool; Alice looks at the astonished figure treading water] You don't give a fig about anyone but yourself, do you?

Jon: Yeah, man. Rock 'n' roll.

[ad break]

Narrator: The evening is not going to plan for up-and-coming novelist Julia Greengage and her Crawley Writers' Group. Alice has got upset at Peter's less-than-ecstatic reaction to her Sentence, which had taken her over nine months to craft. Julia didn't seem to care, so Alice tried to punch her and Julia fell into her own brand-new pool. But for Julia, like any experienced actor, the show must go on. After a quick break in filming, she reappears with a whole new outfit, make-up and hair, and the group is ready to go again.

Next up, it's Keith. And the section he is about to read is a very big moment in Keith's *Dragons of Xęn"räh* epic, as the rest of the group are about to discover.

Keith [narrating very fast]:

> And so Lord Idris drew the Sword of Slashispike from the Stone of Rocqhard and plunged it into Bink's side. 'I die! I die!' cried Bink, clutching one slender hand to a perfectly formed mammary lobule and looking incredulously at the blood that was now streaming down one sleekly curved inner thigh . . .

Jon: Good Lord. He's only gone and done it.

Alice: Done what?

Peter: Bink. He's killed her.

[An almighty shriek rises in the bushes and all at once a huge spinning furball emerges from behind a hydrangea and throws itself at Keith, knocking him to the ground. As the group stare in shock, hands emerge from the furball and tighten round Keith's neck. Keith's head bangs up and down dangerously on the floor, until . . .]

Tom: Noooooooooooooooo! [Another figure, clad in a leather jacket, shoots out of the newly planted hibiscus bank, grabs the furball from behind, and starts to pull it off Keith. Locked in a fierce fighting embrace, the three end up rolling into the pool.]

Keith [surfacing]: Tom! Am I glad to see you, mate.

Tom: You too, Keith.

[A third head emerges from the pool, removing a furry mask. It is . . .]

Keith and Jon [together]: Riva!!

Mavinder: Mavinder actually.

Everyone: Mavinder!!!

Julia [recovering first and extending a hand]: Darling, how lovely to meet you at last!

Mavinder: You kill that space goddess off, Keith, and I'll fucking kill you. [starts speaking at Keith in fast incomprehensible tongue]

Alice: What on earth is that?

Keith [admiringly]: Fluent Xȩn"dährin!!

[ad break]

Narrator: Julia Greengage's writers' group has been a night of surprises. The latest people to take a dip in her brand-new pool are Tom, Keith and his fur-suited attacker, who turns out to be his #1 fan and stalker Mavinder.

Mavinder has actually been part of the group since the beginning, sending regular emails but never actually showing up to a meeting before. But Jon and Keith now realise that they know her from a boozy trip to Comic Fantasy Con. It turns out that Mavinder has been tracking Keith obsessively for months, initially because of her love for his work. But when she sensed that Keith was thinking of killing off her heroine Bink, she felt compelled to act.

Cut to live group setting:

Mavinder: I *am* Bink.

Keith: Err, are you? I mean, I invented her.

Mavinder: Yeah, but I *live* in her. To kill her is to kill me.

Keith: Eh?

Peter: Mavinder raises an interesting question. Who owns the work?

Julia [briskly]: What a fascinating debate!! Who's next to read?

Peter [ignoring her]: I mean, once the work has been published, does the author retain any special rights over what happens to it?

Keith: Er, well if by rights you're talking commercial, subsidiary, electronic, translation, etc. etc., yeah they're all mine, mate.

Mavinder: But that's just it. To you Bink is just a *property*. But she *lives* in me. And you will not kill her!

Tom: 'Some of you may die, but that is a sacrifice I am willing to make.'

Alice: Are you doing it again?

Tom: Sorry. Can't seem to help it. I do love *Shrek*.

Mavinder: We can't help being ourselves. As myself is . . . Bink.

Keith [rubbing his neck]: Two things, Mav.

Mavinder: What's that?

Keith: One, you've got unfeasibly strong wrists.

Mavinder: Like Bink.

Keith: Yeah. And two: you're the only person who's more obsessed with me and my work . . . than I am!

Mavinder: Guilty as charged.

Tom: 'Madame Bink, c'est moi!'

All: Shut it!

[ad break]

Narrator: It's been an eventful evening for the Crawley Writers' Group, although perhaps not in the way Julia had anticipated. She's been punched in the face and she's fallen in her brand-new pool. Tom and Keith have also taken an unexpected dip, along with Mavinder, Keith's stalker, who is furious about him killing off her favourite character. But surely now things will start to calm down, especially as the next person to read, Jon, appears to be smoking something very relaxing . . .

Jon: OK. So me up now yeah? [whistles over his shoulder] Boys!

[Four men, all bearded, receding hairlines, rather paunchy and the worse for wear, appear from behind a newly planted bougainvillea. They are sweatily heaving instruments, amps and other equipment.]

Peter: Who else have you got secreted in your vegetation, Julia??

Narrator: Unknown to everyone else, Jon has prepared a special surprise for his writer friends. He's chosen to perform his piece with the help of his old band, The King of Elfland's Daughter. This documentary will be their first live musical performance in 23 years, which may explain why they've taken a few herbal remedies to help take the edge off their nerves . . .

Keith [still in the pool with Mavinder]: Oh my days! The King of Elfland's Daughter are back!

Jon: Just give us a few ticks. Is it just me or is the outside inside? Here, Pete, hand these round, me old mate. Blow your socks off. Help you appreciate the music. [Unidentified substances are distributed.]

Peter: Interesting.

Narrator: In the pause while Jon and his bandmates set up, Alice, Blue and Tom have been chatting by the poolside. It seems that both women are in a forgiving mood.

Blue: You can't really help it, can you, Tom? I don't think you mean any harm. You're just a bit of a crap bloke.

Tom: I am a crap bloke.

Alice: You're harmless really.

Tom: I *am* harmless really.

Blue and Alice: Stop quoting us.

Tom: Oh God! Sorry I—

Blue: Joke. [Alice giggles.]

Tom: There's something about you two as well.

Blue: How do you mean?

Tom [to Blue]: Well, you've stopped wearing all that Goth stuff.

Blue: I know. I've chucked out about a litre of black eyeliner.

Tom: Er, that's good. Is it?

Alice: She's moving up in the world, Tom. You're looking at the new area manager for Cat Hospice UK, with responsibility for five shops across the whole South-East.

Tom: Wow! Go you. The thing I always say about cats is . . .

Alice: Are you about to quote someone, Tom?

Tom: Oh fucking hell. It's like an illness. [pause] And what about you, Alice? How does the world look post-Sentence? [Alice stares mournfully at the pool.] Actually, Alice, can I say something original?

Alice: I don't know. Can you?

Tom: Something that will probably make you hate me all over again.

Alice: At this point, I don't really care.

Tom: I think you're a fine writer, I really do. I've read your blog, I've seen other bits you've done.

Alice: But? I take it there's a but?

Tom: . . . *But* I don't think The Sentence is your best work. [he ducks involuntarily as he says this]

Alice: Tom, you absolute fucking . . .

Blue: Wait!

Alice: Wait. [she thinks for a long moment] Actually, Tom, you're absolutely right. It's a shite sentence.

Blue: It's as clunky as fuck. [the three of them start giggling helplessly]

Alice: I really fancy snogging you right now, Blue.

Tom: Er, don't mind me.

Blue: What's stopping you?

Alice: Oh come on, we both know it's just not me. I'm more of a crap-bloke girl.

Tom: I mean, I really don't mind.

Blue: Yeah. I guess we all have to stop trying to be what we're not at some point. I mean, I'm 47 for fuck's sake and I'm still writing poems about cotton wool. [the three of them start giggling helplessly again]

Tom: Did you partake of that substance Jon was giving out?

Blue: No!

Alice and Tom: Yes! [more helpless giggling]

[Suddenly the air is rent with violent feedback noises and distorted mic plosives.]

Jon: One-two. One-two. Oh yes. Ladies and gentlemen, it's good to be back. I don't know why you're all hovering like that or why you're all purple, but I love you all.

Ready, boys? One, nine, three, FOUR!!!

[As Jon bursts into song, there is a massive power surge, the festoon lights explode, and a piece of falling cheminée knocks Jon to the ground. Total and sudden darkness.]

Jon: It's the mothership!! It's the bloody mothership! Albion, take me home! I fly to thee my country!!

[ad break]

Narrator: The evening has descended into total chaos for the Crawley Writers' Group. Alice is off somewhere getting drunk with Tom and Blue, Julia is frantically trying to locate the producer, Jon and his bandmates are hallucinating under a monkey puzzle tree, and some odd sucking noises suggest that Keith and Mavinder are getting better acquainted in the pool. Only Peter is unaccounted for. Peter, who no one has remembered has yet to give his performance.

[A megaphone beeps.]

Peter [speaking into the megaphone, an upturned torch beam oddly illuminating his face]: Good evening, ladies and gentlemen. For the final piece this evening, I'd like to play a recorded compilation I've made of you all. Things about you all I have captured in, er, unguarded moments.

All: Oh fuck off, Peter!! [boos, hisses, catcalls from around the garden] Fucking weirdo! Bloody spy! Peeping Tom! Surveillance troll!

Policeman [speaking into a megaphone of his own]: This is the police! The house is surrounded! Please come out with your hands up! Drop all weapons and do not attempt to evade arrest!

[Suddenly sobered up by the arrival of the police (except Jon and his band, who are led away smiling blissfully), the group are escorted from the garden by a series of beeping officers in high-viz jackets.

To an audience of absence and silence, Peter's recording finally kicks in. The audio plays a series of member soundbites from different group meetings:]

Tom: I really love the way you write from your heart, Blue . . .

Julia: Gosh, Keith! My pulse is racing!

Keith: Jon, mate, I fucking love your stories.

Alice: Tom, you have a wonderful way with words. So witty!

Blue: Alice, why don't you just put The Sentence behind you! You're enough being you!

Jon: Peter, you're a fucking berk.

Peter: Thank you, Julia.

[The tape runs in silence for several seconds. In the background, receding police sirens. There is a click, and the end of an old recording begins.]

Peter: I am a genius. I am a fucking genius. I am a genius. I am a fucking genius. I am a genius. I am a fucking genius. I am a genius. I am a fucking genius. I am a genius. I am a fucking genius. I am a genius. I am a fucking genius. I am a genius. I am a fucking genius. I am a genius. I am a fucking genius. I am a genius. I am a fucking genius. I am a genius. I am a fucking genius . . . [repeats on an endless loop]

[ends]

POSTFACE (Do not read)

The ostensible origins of the Crawley Writers' Group date to December 2016, when one Julia Greengage – a failed actress sitting in a gilded cage in Langley Green – gathered around her a group of rightly unpublished men and women unified only by crass insecurity, muted narcissism and the faint ache of literary ambition.

Together they planned to share their writing in the hopes of developing as artists in an atmosphere of constructive feedback and mutual encouragement. So far, so bourgeois.

But I, artist-in-negative and conceptual deranger of the interjective space, also joined. I quickly saw that the group's activities presented an ideal canvas to explore my aesthetic preoccupations. What were/are those? you ask. What indeed? I reply.

As documented here, many rather tedious and predictable occurrences occurred over the course of the group's first nine months together. Some rather banal artistic success ensued too, as the result of a Channel 4 documentary which brought the group a level of exposure that was richly undeserved.

But the one truly great thing to emerge from this whole morass of mediocrity is the book you hold in your hands – a towering examination of the relationship between the real and 'the real' (and *the real*). It is the project of projects, the work of a genius, and the result of hours of tedious hacking.

Read it and seep.

Peter, writer.

Appendix 1

from **ENCYCLOPAEDIA PROGROCKIA**

The King of Elfland's Daughter (band, 1973–1982)

- Jon Armory-Wargrove – vocals, Mellotron, keyboards
- David Clements – drums, percussion
- Jason Pierpoint – cello, flute
- Richard Sinclair – bass
- Harry Warde – vocals, guitar

Discography:

- Apples of Avalon, 7" single, 1975
- *(Songs from) The Great Woods*, LP, 1976
- Sky Creatures, 7" single, 1977
- *Amoeba Station (parts i –iv)*, LP, 1978
- *Glimmers of the Crystal Mind*, LP, 1979
- Arcturus Kosmic Mechanism, 12" single, 1981

Fondly remembered, The King of Elfland's Daughter was an innovative band with a loyal live following whose career was tragically cut short by an accident just as they seemed on the verge of wider success.

KED was formed by Harry Warde and Jon Armory-Wargrove, who recruited the rest of the group from fellow day-boarders at their public school in Reading, excepting drummer David 'Dave' Clements, a 'town boy'.

They decided to pursue their music instead of going on to university and by dint of extensive gigging built a solid reputation in London and the Home Counties.

Their first single and debut album were competent if largely derivative efforts. Of *The Great Woods*, *Melody Maker* noted that it exemplified a 'certain pastoral Englishness, so cloyingly twee it makes Winnie the Pooh look like Charles Bronson', while adding that the epic 12-minute closing track, 'The Night Lands', showed a promise of things to come.

Armory-Wargrove was very much the ideas man of the band while Warde was the charismatic front man, and they allegedly had a difficult and stormy relationship. Whatever the truth, the band's second album delivered the goods as they found their own distinctive sound. A concept album, *Amoeba Station*, was based on Armory-Wargrove's theory that UFOs were actually creatures that lived in the sky. Even the prog-averse *NME* gave it positive notice, bracketing KED with King Crimson and Van Der Graaf Generator.

KED's third, *Glimmers of the Crystal Mind*, further consolidated their development, matching complex polyrhythms and contrapuntal lines with oblique lyrics that explored 'cosmic consciousness'.

'Arcturus Kosmic Mechanism', the band's swansong, promised a radical and promising new direction, adding elements of krautrock motorik and experimentation with synths to an already heady mix. The single gained rave reviews and prompted wide crossover interest. Success beckoned but then, returning from a gig in Aylesbury, the band's van left the road in the early hours of the morning. No one was seriously hurt apart from Jason Pierpoint, KED's genial classical musician. Jason was in a coma for two weeks before dying of his injuries.

The band couldn't weather the emotional fallout from the accident and they broke up shortly after. Warde went on to work as a producer and Armory-Wargrove apparently went on to be a trance DJ associated with the New Age traveller movement, playing at free festivals.

Appendix 2: Where Are They Now?

Following completion of this book, the editors caught up with the members of the group to find out what they've been up to since . . .

KEITH SADWICKE and MAVINDER PRANESH

Five years on, Keith Sadwicke is still banging out the words in his basement den. Having finished Volume 7 of *Dragons of Xęn"räh*, and believing he'd closed out the series with the death of Idris and the marriage of Odos and Bink – whom he decided not to kill – he had plans to move on to his exciting new nanopunk space opera project. However, pressure from his fans or, more particularly, one fan, his girlfriend Mavinder, forced him to continue with *Xęn"räh*, and he is now halfway through Volume 18. Odos died several volumes ago, and since then the books have featured just the one main character. Indeed, Keith regularly complains that the series could quite accurately be renamed *The Bink Hallia Adventures*. Yet he dares not deviate from the current format in case he upsets his fan(s), who have, in the past, demonstrated violent tendencies.

Keith still aggressively pursues all possible revenue streams for the *Xęn"räh* franchise, from peddling merch to selling ad space for his YouTube channel. In fact, he admits to enjoying the commercial side of the business even more than the creative aspect these days (especially now that it's become the Bink Hallia show), and is currently researching a new form of AI writing software that he hopes will be able to handle text output going forward. His plan is to upload the entire (so far) 4.7-million-word Xęn"räh canon into his computer, to teach it the Keith Sadwicke prose style, or at least produce a decent enough simulation to satisfy the fans.

Mavinder is a forceful and somewhat fearsome presence in Keith's life. She has had to stop going to Comic Fantasy Con, having received a lifetime ban following a biting incident in 2021. But she remains by his side at all his other public appearances, whether it's hawking merch at Crawley Market on a Saturday, or at a pop-up book reading outside Waterstones in The Martletts. She is a ball of energy on such occasions, acting as Keith's minder and PR person, arguing with Waterstones management and the police who want to move him on, and cajoling shy or reluctant fans to come up and buy a signed copy.

Mavinder is active on social media, relentlessly tweeting her thoughts about Bink, offering Bink beauty and fighting tips, and weapon reviews. She's also the founder member and chief moderator of the *Xęn"räh* Fan Forum and its offshoot, the Bink Hallia Appreciation Society, and threatens to rip a new one in anyone who repeats the charge that most of the site's visitors are perverts, borderline psychopaths and former fans of *Buffy the Vampire Slayer*.

APPENDIX 2

TOM HILDEN

Tom remains Director of Studies at Pease Pottage International School of English Studies. He continues to write fiction and poems, though he is better-known these days as compiler-in-chief of the *New Oxford Dictionary of 21st Century Memes*. He asked us to mention that he is still single.

JONATHAN AMORY-WARGROVE

'Hi, my name's Jon and I'm an alcoholic. I haven't had a drink for, let's see, nearly three years now.

'I was at the Crawley group but as this is my first meeting with you guys, I'll tell you a bit about myself.

'I've just moved to Alfriston; I've always loved the Sussex Downs and it's great being so close to the Long Man. I love long walks, following the ley lines. Not sure if I believe all that stuff but the countryside is beautiful.

'I started habitual substance abuse at an early age but five years ago I had a psychotic episode brought on by drink and drugs. It was all very public – probably still on YouTube if anyone's interested – and I fell apart bigtime.

'I'd like to thank my good friend Harry Warde for getting me through that dark period. We've known each other since school and have always had a rocky relationship. But he stuck by me when it counted.

'Sorry . . . something in my eye. Give me a minute . . .

'So, me and Harry had been in a band and there was a lot of unresolved stuff from those years. I could never bring myself to admit that I might have been responsible for . . . what happened.

'Anyway, Harry was there waiting for me when I was released after a few months in a psychiatric secure ward. I didn't have a job, lived in a sty of a place and still had a head full of crazy ideas. Gradually I pulled out of it with his help and the help of a couple of other dear friends. Keith, Blue. It was a bloody long hard slog.

'Sorry, I'm going to blub again. Deep breath. I really am a silly old man.

'We set up a company and with his contacts started making a modest living doing radio and TV soundtracks. I'm semi-retired now but we still make music together – it means so much to me, I can't tell you.

'So, that's me. Music and long walks.

'Oh, and I do a bit of writing, short stories and poetry. In fact I'm thinking of forming a writers' group.'

JULIA GREENGAGE

Julia Greengage's novel, *Bare Naked Ambition*, has been made into a bestselling film, in which she also secured a co-starring role. She has also, of course, become a household name as the domineering countess in the post-*Downton* drama, *A Family at War*. In between filming, she is at work on her next book, *A Wild Rose Among Thorns*, which tells 'the story of a beautiful, talented artist who sacrifices her own chances of fame and fortune by bringing together a commune of misfits and no-hopers and teaching them valuable lessons about life through the medium of creative writing'.

Six months after the airing of the *Bleeding Typewriters* documentary, Julia's husband was tried and found guilty in absentia on charges related to organised crime, money laundering and armed robbery. He has yet to return from his native Venezuela, which does not have an extradition treaty with the UK, and is rumoured to be studying for the Catholic priesthood in Caracas. Julia says that her husband is the victim of a malicious conspiracy, and poo-poos recent reports that she has been stepping out with Jeremy Irons.

PRISCILLA FOSTER ('BLUE')

From the *Crawley and Horley Gazette and Advertiser* – Online Edition:

'Talking Business' with Barney Green

This week I chat with local entrepreneur Priscilla Foster, CEO of Beet Box, a direct-to-your-door vegan delivery service. In less than four years Priscilla has built up a thriving business, supplying top quality produce to health-conscious eaters as far afield as Redhill, Horsham and Haywards Heath from her company HQ in Oakwood Trade Park.

I meet Priscilla at the Veggie-Might Café, which she has recently acquired. Casually but stylishly dressed in cargo pants, an animal print

T-shirt and topped with a beanie, she joins me, a bundle of nervous energy, to share a Spinach and Cinnamon Smoothie and TALK BUSINESS.

So, Priscilla . . .

Call me Blue, everyone does!

Blue, yours is a tale of relatively late success; how did you get started?

Well, I'm 53 now, so yeah, a bit of a late starter. To be honest, when I was younger I spent too much time in gloomy bedsits writing bad poetry (laughs). I worked in a charity shop for ages and eventually became an area manager. Much to my surprise I found I had a knack for management.

What is the secret of good management in your experience?

Oh gosh! Just listening and responding openly and honestly. Empathy, in a word!

And after working in the charity sector?

I had been area manager for a year or so and then something totally unexpected happened. I'd been looking after a neighbour for quite a few years. She had no family and I just looked out for her, shopping and making the odd meal – just being there, you know? Sadly, she passed on and I discovered that she had left me something in her will.

Not a lot, but more money than I was used to having. I became determined to do something worthwhile with this unexpected bequest, for myself and in her memory. Being a vegan has always been important to me and I had often thought that a local delivery service would be a great idea. Not some overpriced hipster thing but cheap and cheerful. I ummed and ahhed for a while and then took the plunge. So thank you, Rose!

So how did you come to grow your business?

It's all been a bit of a whirl. It seems like only yesterday I was getting up at the crack of dawn to buy wholesale produce and coming home to make up boxes on my kitchen table and then going straight out again to deliver them. It was word of mouth I guess, and with the continuing growth in the vegan lifestyle it just took on a life of its own. First I hired a full-time driver, then more people to put together our boxes – and so it just grew and grew!

What does the future hold for you and Beet Boxes?

I'd like to open some more cafés and extend our delivery catchment area. I already have a profit-sharing scheme for employees and I'd like to move towards being a full cooperative. It's difficult because we're also looking at franchising to other parts of the country, so I don't know how that would work. I'm also thinking about a range of vegan clothing, cosmetics and so on.

Lastly, is there some secret to your success?

I . . . well, I don't think so. Just luck and stuff happening and . . . I find it all a bit of a happy mess in retrospect. I tend to live on my nerves a lot and I think I've just learned to live with that and channel it into something I really, really care about.

#PET^ER< WRITER~

I|I

You|uoY

Dog|goD

ALICE KNOWLES

Five years on, Alice has found happiness – not because she became a successful author, but in spite of it.

Following the TV documentary, she was mercilessly mocked and lampooned on social media as an archetypal pretentious writer without the talent to justify her extremely low output. But this caricature was already out of date: ironically, Alice's epiphany by the pool during the course of the documentary had unblocked her, and she was thereafter able to novelise at will. So when she was approached by a literary agent suggesting a book version of her blog, 'How to be a WRITER', to cash in on her notoriety, Alice submitted instead a 60,000-word manuscript for a well-crafted cosy mystery. By the time she'd published her third Pandora Prendergast novel, she was earning enough to give up her day job as a payroll clerk and become a full-time author.

Despite this, she continued to feel a profound emptiness at her core. She was plagued by dreams about an unfinished salad with olives, and a waiter limping slowly towards her. It dawned on her that she didn't actually care that much about being a writer, now she was one. It had never been about that: it had always been about The Sentence.

One day, out of the blue, she received a letter from Yannis, a restaurant manager in Naxos. He was a big fan of her books, and had wanted to write to her just in case she was the same Alice Knowles he'd met all those years ago when he was working as a waiter. She was a customer and he'd shown her to an outside table beneath a parasol. It had been a quiet day, and they had chatted for more than an hour. He felt they'd made a real connection. But then he got called away to another table, leaving her to finish her salad. He remembered her remarking how much she liked that salad, especially the olives. Yannis was on his way back to join her, and she had half turned towards him, so she didn't see the car mount the pavement and smash into her table. With great sadness and some guilt, he had watched her being taken away in an ambulance.

Receiving this letter came as a profound shock to Alice. She now remembered the accident that had taken place in her mid-twenties, and waking up in Crawley Hospital with some broken bones and no memory of what had happened to her. She had pieced together quite a lot of it with the help of friends and family, but had never, until now, known the exact circumstances of the accident. The Sentence, she realised, must have been her brain trying to reconstruct that lost moment. She wrote a long letter to Yannis, and a few months later he boarded a flight to London Gatwick. They've been together ever since.

ABOUT THE EDITORS

Dan Brotzel is the author of *Hotel du Jack*, a collection of short stories, and *The Wolf in the Woods*, a novel, both published by Sandstone Press. More info at www.danbrotzel.com

Martin Jenkins is a freelance writer, researcher and editor. His publications include the novel *A New Science of Navigation* and a contribution to the Soul Bay Press short story anthology *13*.

Alex Woolf is an award-winning author of over two hundred books for children and adults, published by the likes of OUP, Ladybird, Hachette and Fiction Express.

ACKNOWLEDGEMENTS

We'd like to thank every single one of our supporters for taking a chance on this book and for bearing with us over the extensive timeline of its journey to publication. Your enthusiasm and encouragement kept us going on the long and winding crowdfunding road!

We'd like to pay special thanks to Brad Feld, whose extraordinary generosity gave us a vital boost at the very moment we needed it most. Thanks too to all the litmags and websites that were kind enough to spread the word about us.

Thank you to Martha and everyone at Unbound who has helped make this book a reality. Thanks to Hayley Shepherd for her brilliant editing. And a special thank you to Beth Lewis, who plucked this idea from the submission pile when it was still called 'Kitten on a Fatberg' (RIP) and decided to believe in it.

Unbound is the world's first crowdfunding publisher, established in 2011.

We believe that wonderful things can happen when you clear a path for people who share a passion. That's why we've built a platform that brings together readers and authors to crowdfund books they believe in – and give fresh ideas that don't fit the traditional mould the chance they deserve.

This book is in your hands because readers made it possible. Everyone who pledged their support is listed below. Join them by visiting unbound.com and supporting a book today.

Lynn Adamson
Rhona Allin
Paola Argiroffi
Christine Asbury
Claire Asherson Bartram
H Atmenmeer
Avid Reader
Steve Baldwin
Ed Balleny
Emily Bamford
Louise Barrett
Cath Barton
Hannah Belok
Paul & Cathy Belok
Robbie Belok
Clare Bennett

Julian Benton
Richard Berd
Jannette Berends
Kiera Black
Antony Bond
Paul Braddon
Anna Britnor Guest
Jenny Brophy
Eve Brotzel
Mick Brotzel
Jennifer Brown-Banks
Kelli Bryan
Erica Buist
Michael Campbell
Jacqui Castle
Samuel Catterall-Young
Belinda Chapple
Anne Cheesman
Karen Cheesman
Jamie Chipperfield
Mark Ciccone
Katrina Clarkson
Jason Cobley
Shalini Conn
Regina Connell
Grainne Connolly
Penny Cook
Carol Cooper
Rosie Corlett
Gareth Cotter-Stone
Philipa Coughlan
John Crawford
Melissa Cunningham
Ruth D'Alessandro
Nina D'Arcangela
Joshua Davis
Kelly Davis
Alison Deane
Wendy Dear
Angela Dierks
Samuel Dodson
Mark Drew
Sarah Dunkley
Jordan Ecarma
James Ellerton
Tom Ellett
Jessica Fellowes
Christopher Fielden
Adam n Helen Fielder
Jenny Fielder
Justin Fielder
Maria Fielder
Cindy Finkelstein
Liz Fish

Sarah Fisher
Suzy Fotheringham
Michele Foulger
Ian Francis
Andy Franks
Peter Gal
G.E. Gallas
Sarah Garnham
Andrew Gelling
Amber Gibbons
Peter J. Gibbons
Alan Gillespie
John Giovanacci
Allen Goldenson
Katie Goodall
Anne Goring
Emma Grae
Rachel Green
Jonathan Greensides
Cathy Griffiths
Phil Guest
Emma Hadfield-Hudson
Rebecca Hamilton
Donna Hardcastle
Alison Hardy
Andrea Harman
Maria Harrington
Liz and Michael Hartland
Petrina Hartland
Gabrielle Hase
Helen Hattersley
Maximilian Hawker
Katherine Heath
Louise Herbert
Bendy Hippy
Jeff Horne
Julie Howell
Miles Hudson
Pete Hufton
Janet Hughes
Chris Ingle
Oli Jacobs
David James
Gary Janks
Billie Jenkins
Daniel Jenkins
George Jenkins
Tom Jenkins
Ilona Jesnick
Louise Johnson
Emmy Maddy Johnston
Roger Jones
Kathryn Joy
Athina Kafetsiou

Matt Kendrick
Dan Kieran
Susan A King
Jacqueline Kingsley
Athina Kontos
Mit Lahiri
Rupert Lang
Christian Lapper
Adam Le Boutillier
Ruth Learner
Emilia Leese
Christy Lefteri
Jeremy Lloyd-Williams
Adam Lock
Tom MacKay
Russell Mackintosh
Gabi Maddocks
Tony Maddox and Julia Rees
Carina Martin
Jesús Martín Sánchez
Catherine Mason
David Mason
Janice McCombie
Barbara Joan Meier
Michael Miller
John Mitchinson
Ronald Mitchinson
Angela Monaghan
Daphne Moorey
Helen Moorey
Kristin Morgan-McCallum
Claire Moruzzi
Julia Mountain
Tony Murray
Carlo Navato
Ryan Neely
Bridgid Nzekwu
Diane Odling-Smee
Lindsay Pemberton
Jenny Pichierri
Bren Pointer
Helen Pointer
Marguerite Pointer
Robbie Pointer
Justin Pollard
Hester Poole
Dion Potter
Lawrence Pretty
Neil Pretty
Sobia Quazi
Christine Ractliff
Kate Reed
Caroline Reid

Tim Rhodes
Jake Richards
Max Richter
Jessica Riley
Josie Riley
Laura Riley
Liam Riley
Sam Riley
Sarah Riley
Nicola Rimmer
Mike Robbins
Andrew Roberts
Däna Roberts
Anthea Robertson
Sarah Robinson
Elizabeth Rowe
Clare Rushton
Bonnie J. Russell
Geraldine Ryan
Dan Salaman
Daniel Saunders
Shannon Savvas
Hilary Scurlock
Rebecca Seibel
Dick Selwood
Guy Sexty
Graham Sievers
Keith Sleight
Guy Smith
Ben Snowden
Lucinda Sporle
Graham Stanley
Ros Stern
Anne Summerfield
Claire Sutton
C M Taylor
Georgette Taylor
Lisa Thomas
Jemma Thompson
Mike Scott Thomson
Nikki Thornley
Catherine Thurtle
Sue Tickner
Jenny Tidman
Giles Todd
Neil Tookey
Gloria Travers
Richard Trinder
Alexis Trinh
Gabrielle Turner
Anna Tyrowicz
Patricia van den Akker
Christine Vassie
Peter Viner-Brown

Eleanor Walsh
Tom Ward
M. F. Webb
Keith Weller
David Willbe
Gary Williams
Louise Woodman
Steve Woodward
Emile Woolf
Matt Woolf
Michelle Worthington
Peter Young